THE LOST ANGELS

OTHER BOOKS BY MICHELE DOMÍNGUEZ GREENE

Martika's Magic

Keep Sweet

Cassidy Clarke

Hollywood Hit Men

Special Agent Emily Ray

My Name Is Emily Ray

Hayley Hope Is Gone

The Girl from Nowhere

THE LOST ANGELS

A THRILLER

MICHELE DOMÍNGUEZ GREENE

Published by Thomas & Mercer, Seattle

www.apub.com

EU product safety contact:
Amazon Media EU S. à r.l.
38, avenue John F. Kennedy, L-1855 Luxembourg
amazonpublishing-gpsr@amazon.com

ISBN-13: 9781662531682 (paperback)
ISBN-13: 9781662531675 (digital)

Cover design by Shasti O'Leary Soudant
Cover image: © ADLC / Getty

Printed in the United States of America

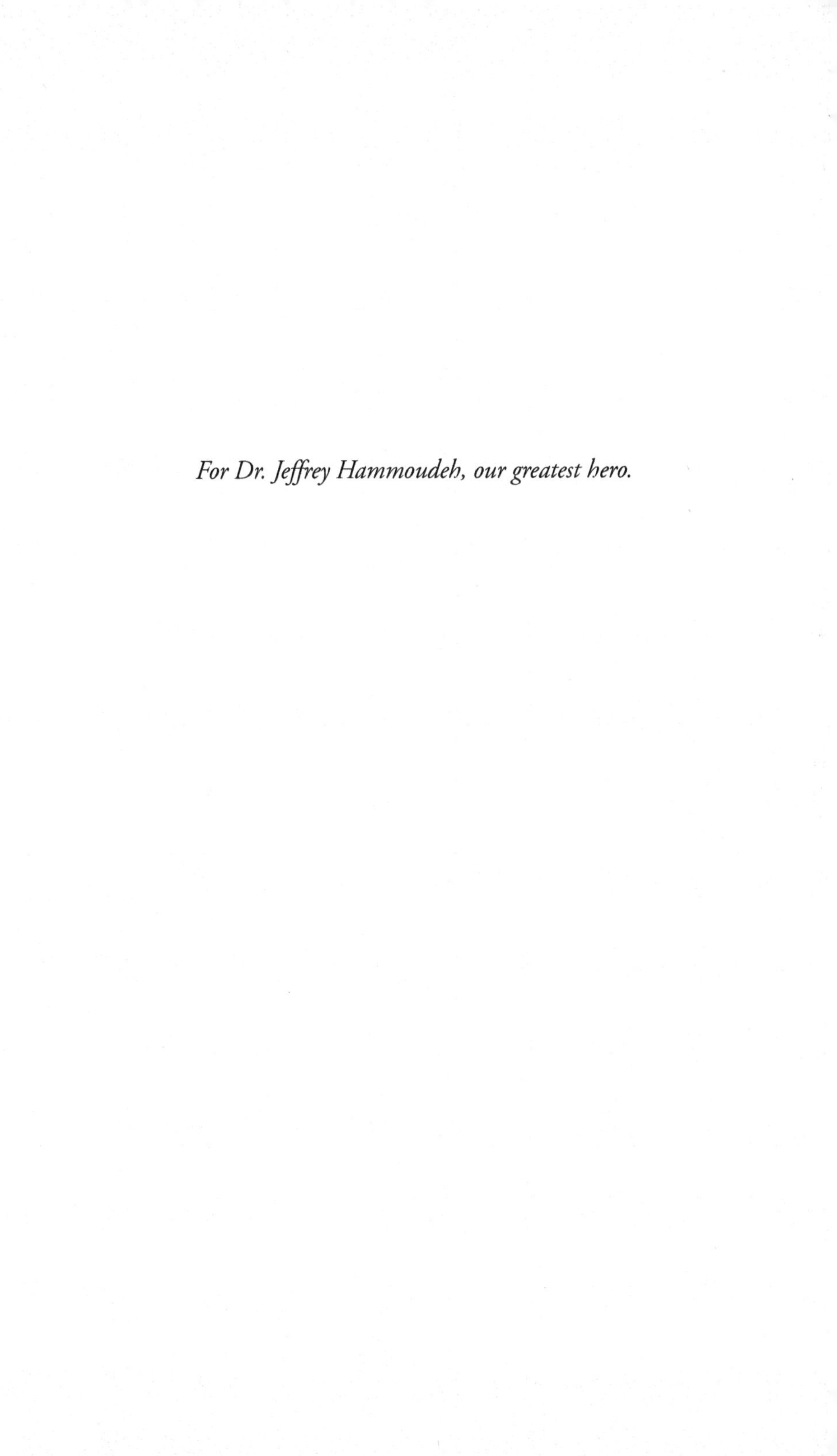

For Dr. Jeffrey Hammoudeh, our greatest hero.

CHAPTER ONE

Evie Peacock sat under the freeway overpass at Cahuenga and Franklin in East Hollywood. It was early evening, the traffic was heavy as usual, even in the relentless downpour of rain. She squinted her eyes at the passing cars; they looked like a painting by Monet, her favorite artist. A swirl of colors and movement: the red brake lights, the blue/green patina of a BMW, all washed with the iridescent shimmer of the rain.

She pulled her backpack deeper between her knees to avoid the water that streamed down toward the dry spot she had found to bed down for the evening. Most of her belongings were in the storage shed behind Cesar's Auto Repair, where they let her keep them in return for making coffee runs to the nearby Gelson's Market.

Tonight, she had just the necessities: a sleeping bag, water, pepper spray, and a discarded pillow she had found on trash day and washed at the laundromat. If she rolled them up tightly, they fit into her pack. She kept her money and wintergreen Mentos in a small belt bag around her waist with a pocketknife her dad gave her before he died. She checked her phone again. Still no message from Layla, her best friend.

A black-and-white police car drove up the Cahuenga Pass—connecting Hollywood to Studio City and Barham Boulevard—which traversed the heart of Burbank. Evie hunkered down to avoid being seen by the cops, but she figured that in this rain, they wouldn't hang a U-turn and climb up an embankment to roust her or worse.

At seventeen, she looked younger, with short-cropped brunette hair and freckles; if they ran her ID, she'd be put into CPS again and have to go through the whole sorry situation until she bolted and found her way back to the streets and Layla, Princess, Clyde, Pebble, and the other homeless teenagers who made up her friend group. She smiled, remembering the first time she referred to them as such and Layla said it sounded like they were suburban high schoolers in the spirit club.

She looked at her phone; the battery was running low, and she'd have to go out in the rain to Los Donuts, six blocks away, if she wanted to charge it. Layla should've called by now. Still, Evie was happy to be waiting for the call. It meant that things were going to return to the way they were before. For the past two years, she and Layla had been inseparable, each other's wingman in every situation.

But when Layla met a new boyfriend a few months earlier, he soon took up all her time and attention. Eventually, she went to go live with him out near Atwater. Evie had hoped maybe she could go, too, but it hadn't worked out. So, she stayed with Princess, Clyde, Pebble, and the others until Layla called her two days earlier and said she was coming back.

"It's a bad situation, Evie. I wasn't sure before, and that's why I didn't want you coming here, and I was right. I'll call you day after tomorrow, in the evening when I can get a ride. I've got some serious shit to show you, and we have to tell someone," she said, and Evie noted that she didn't have the same confidence she usually did, being the de facto leader of their group at nineteen years old. She'd sounded nervous, even scared. And Layla was never scared of anyone.

Layla was the one who knew the best spots to sleep where the cops wouldn't find you and the residents wouldn't report you. She knew which restaurants gave free food at the end of the night and which ones would run you off. She knew which places let you use their bathrooms and which ones were clean. Layla had been living on the street for two years when Evie met her. Evie had caught a thirty-seven-dollar flight from Oregon, paid for by her uncle Arthur, and taken a bus from the airport to Hollywood, the only California neighborhood she had heard of. And when she got off, there was Layla Waters, watching and waiting to protect naive young girls from the predators who frequented the area, looking for runaways.

Evie had almost been taken in by Aiden Howe, a fast-talking twenty-year-old who seemed like a godsend to runaway teens, offering them a place to stay before turning them out to work the streets for him. Layla had physically pushed him away from Evie before taking her in hand and leading her to the Clubhouse.

Now, Layla was coming back. To celebrate, Evie had gotten a bag of toasted pita bread and a small tub of hummus from the Carousel Restaurant, one of the places that gave free food from time to time. Her phone buzzed; it was a text from Princess with a photo of a license plate.

> I'm going with this guy, corner of western and santa monica check u later

Princess always sent a photo of the license plate of any guy who picked her up, just as Layla had advised her to. That way if she disappeared, they'd know who to look for. Evie had managed to survive thus far without resorting to sex work, but she was one of the very few who hadn't fallen into it to survive.

"Princess" was her street name; her real name was Charmaine Mendoza. A petite, waiflike Filipino, at seventeen she looked twelve and always wore a shiny tiara in her jet-black hair, cut with bangs to play up her resemblance to a schoolgirl anime character. Like any businesswoman, Princess knew her market and her buyers well. Evie texted her back.

> Waiting 4 a call from layla got hummus and pitas text me when u r done we can meet up im under cahuenga-franklin

Princess replied with a thumbs-up emoji.

Evie offered a silent prayer to a god she didn't believe in that Princess would come back safe and alive. It was a routine she always kept, a superstition at this point, like a major-league ball player wearing the same pair of unwashed lucky socks all through the World Series. She settled in to wait, trying hard to ignore the growing sense of unease that Layla hadn't called yet. It was hard to keep to a schedule on the street, with so many factors every day that spun out of control, but Layla was unusually organized about such things. She let everyone know where she was—they all had cell phones through the California LifeLine program, and Layla made sure they all used them to keep tabs on each other. A loud thunderclap shook the sky, and Evie's phone rang. It was Layla.

"Where are you?" Evie asked.

"Where're you?"

"Cahuenga and Franklin," Evie said.

"I'm behind the Home Depot on Sunset and Western, you know the one by the freeway?" Layla said.

"Are you okay? You sound off," Evie asked.

"I don't know, I feel really weird . . ." Her voice faded.

"I'll come to you. Stay there!" Evie said.

"I'm in the alleyway. I'm gonna sit down for a minute . . . I just got here, I had to run because he was—"

Evie heard the phone hitting the ground, and Layla fell silent.

Barely a mile away Layla Waters sat slumped against a wall in the dirty, narrow alley behind the Home Depot. Something was very wrong with her; her mind was like a speeding train in a tunnel filled with images, memories, fragments of thoughts she'd once had. She felt dizzy and nauseous. She remembered leaving the big house under the cover of night. She'd drunk a smoothie that Jeppe had given her as he gathered the group in the reading room. Before he noticed she wasn't there, she had run. Someone known to her gave her a ride—not a stranger. But who was he?

In her bag she had two flash drives in a plastic bag. She knew she had to guard them, but why? Who had dropped her here, in the pelting rain that hit her face like a thousand shards of glass? She saw that her pants were torn in the knee. She must've fallen. She called Evie, little Evie who always slept with one eye open. Had they spoken? She couldn't remember.

She panicked, realizing that Jeppe had drugged her, but she was too unsteady on her feet to stand up and get help. Like rising water in a flooding room, she felt herself going under, in a wave of self-reproach. How could she have trusted him at this point? Jeppe toyed with drugs like a child playing jacks in the schoolyard, always ready with a substance to maintain control of his lost angels.

Then headlights illuminated the dank alley, blazing beams of light that seemed to push everything aside, nowhere to hide. She heard footsteps and saw a face that was familiar. She smiled, not sure if that was the right response or not.

"Hey, you . . ."

Then everything went black.

Evie climbed down the embankment to the street, hurrying toward Sunset Boulevard. Her sneakers splashed through dirty puddles as she ran, soaking the ragged hem of her jeans. She held the phone close to her ear, listening for any sounds, but all she heard was the rain and another crash of thunder as the storm grew in intensity. She arrived at the bus stop heading east toward the Home Depot. The gutter was swirling with water that covered her shoes. She thought she heard Layla speak.

"Layla? Are you okay?" she yelled into the phone, which suddenly went dead.

Evie bounced up and down in her wet shoes, anxiety overtaking her. After another minute of terrifying silence, she dialed 911.

"A friend of mine is in the alley behind the Home Depot on Sunset, by the freeway. We were on the phone, she felt weird, now there's no response at all. Can you send an ambulance?"

"Do you know if she's under the influence of any drug or narcotic?" the dispatcher asked; her voice was flat and monotone.

"I'm not there, we were on the phone!"

"Why is she in the alley?"

"I don't know, she told me to meet her there."

"Did you go there to see why she stopped communicating?"

"No! I'm about a mile away, and it's pouring rain! I'm waiting for the bus," Evie said in exasperation. "Can you send someone over there right away?"

"Her name?"

Evie felt as if she would explode and shouted, "Layla Waters!"

"How old is your friend, and can you describe what she was wearing and what she looks like?" the dispatcher asked.

"She's nineteen, I don't know what she was wearing, but she's about five foot seven, long brown hair and green eyes. She has piercings in her lip and a tattoo of a snake on her left forearm," Evie said breathlessly as she saw an MTA bus approaching.

"And your name?"

Evie hesitated; she didn't want them to be able to track her down. She was just seven months away from eighteen, and she wasn't going back into the system.

"Cristina," she said, using the name of her uncle's wife.

"Last name?" the dispatcher asked with a complete lack of urgency.

"Gomez," she blurted out—the surname of her long-ago television idol, Selena Gomez.

"We need you to stay on the line until first responders arrive, okay, Ms. Gomez?"

The bus arrived. Evie climbed aboard and found an empty seat. The window was fogged over with condensation.

"No, my phone is about to die. Just get someone out there, okay?" she said, hanging up.

The bus was crowded and humid from the damp clothes and body heat of the passengers. It smelled of sweat, wet rubber, and marijuana. Evie fidgeted, unable to settle down, weighing if she should have traveled by foot instead, but the worsening storm would have made that a misery. Home Depot was not far; she'd get there in time to find Layla. After fifteen excruciating minutes in traffic, the bus pulled up, and Evie hurried off. She ran across the parking lot and found the entrance to the alley. It was empty.

Had the police come and gone already, taking Layla with them? She walked through the alley; the smell of rancid garbage and wet wood rose in her nostrils. There was no sign of Layla. The rain grew stronger, drenching her clothes and hair. She knelt and ran her cold fingers over the pebbles and busted concrete. Then she saw it.

A silver bracelet with a broken griffin clasp. It was dented, as if it had been yanked and crushed as it fell to the ground. Or caught on something. Layla never took it off. And Evie knew she would not have left it if she had walked out of the alley on her own, alive and awake.

Evie grabbed the bracelet, stuffing it into her pocket as she scanned the alley, willing Layla to appear. A deafening boom of thunder exploded in the sky, followed by a violent purple-white streak of lightning. She heard a siren, and then bright headlights swung across the parking lot, approaching the alley. Desperate to hide herself, Evie pulled an oversize appliance box over her and crouched beneath it, holding her breath.

She heard a car pull up, and the door opened, then footsteps in the alley. Through the small crack of space where the box top met the ground, she could see the bright flashlight beams sweeping the area.

"Dispatch said it was this alley, right?" a male officer asked.

"Yes, the caller said it was the alley behind Home Depot," a female voice replied. "Maybe it was a hooker and a john and something went south?"

"Yeah, or maybe a drug deal. Dispatch said it was a girl, nineteen, who might be under the influence of something. Shit, who would be out here in this downpour?"

"Well, there's nothing here and no sign of a struggle. Just a bunch of garbage. Let's check out the lot and maybe cruise through the Target parking structure next door," the female cop suggested.

Evie wanted to jump out and tell them how strange Layla sounded, that she had something important to show her. That she was coming back. But she was too scared to show herself.

She heard another vehicle arrive, and then the female cop shouted, "Nothing here. No need for an ambulance, thank you!"

Evie waited for them to leave. The box sagged from the weight of the heavy rain. She fought back tears of self-recrimination as the cardboard slowly collapsed in on her. The rain intensified, and a series of rivulets filled the alley. She stood up and ran to the empty parking lot, scanning the shadows and the traffic-clogged streets for something she couldn't even name.

The police were too late. She was too late. Layla was gone.

CHAPTER TWO

Cassidy Clarke closed her locker at the Hollywood station of the LAPD, ready for her first day returning to work after taking a stress leave in the aftermath of the Hollywood Hit Men arrests. Ron Whitty and Vithu Pham sat in jail, awaiting trial, and from time to time the DA's office wanted to speak to Cassidy about her interrogations of Whitty. She was prepared to testify at their trials, but she had avoided any public attention regarding her role in the case. Her patrol partner, Sean Riley, met her in the hallway as they headed to the bullpen.

"Ready to be back at work, Clarke?" he asked, cuffing her on the shoulder.

"More than ready," she replied, and it was true. After several weeks off to regroup, it was as if her nervous system had reset itself. Whitty and Vithu would go to trial, and with the evidence against them, they would be sentenced to life in prison. Her father, Bill, was on a better emotional and mental track, adjusting to retirement, even taking medication to help with his mood swings. He still carried the implacable sense of guilt over the death of his ex-girlfriend, Eden Balcomb, but he'd been cleared as a suspect when his DNA did not match the sample left by the killer on Eden's body.

But the whole experience still hung over both Cassidy and Bill. The terror she felt, thinking her father capable of murder, and his shocked disbelief that she suspected him had splintered something deep inside each of them. As she and Riley took their seats in the bullpen, Captain Landon Dykstra gave Cassidy an overexaggerated wink. Officer Diana

Montoya rolled her eyes at Cassidy. They'd grown closer since working together on the Eden Balcomb internal investigation, especially digging through Metro Officer Ethan Acevedo's trash bags for DNA evidence.

"I heard you and your lawyer boyfriend broke up, Clarke," Dykstra said.

Cassidy shot him an annoyed glance but said nothing.

Montoya grumbled, "Ignore him, he's like a gossipy old bitch."

"I intend to," Cassidy whispered, turning away from Dykstra without acknowledging him.

Watch Captain Steven Kriss entered. "Okay, everyone. We've got a hit-and-run yesterday near Odin and Cahuenga. You all have the license plate and the incident details in an emergency communication text message. The victim is in critical condition. It was a Caltrans worker, so one of our own city employees. Let's keep an extra eye out to catch this jerk. A string of residential burglaries in the area near Wilton and Franklin, all during daylight hours, as well as car break-ins. Suspects seen on video camera footage appear to be working in pairs, dressed in hoodies and sneakers. We have an exhibitionist flashing kids at Cheremoya Elementary and Le Conte Middle School. White, approximately five ten to six feet, thinning brown hair, usually wearing sweatpants and a baggy sweater." He paused and adjusted his tie before continuing. "And Metro Division officer Ethan Acevedo remains the primary suspect in the murder of Eden Balcomb, one of our volunteers at this station. He was last seen in Mexico, but he could return at any time. A lot of you know him, have worked with him. If you receive any information, you know what to do."

The officers shifted in their seats; everyone hated that a cop was implicated in such a brutal crime. Cassidy glanced around the room, taking in her coworkers—the same cops had also known that her father, Bill, was a suspect in the early days of the investigation. The Eden Balcomb murder was like a raw wound in the department, wrong in so many ways that challenged the LAPD identity as the good guys fighting the good fight. She saw Detective Judson Postiff arrive and linger as the patrol officers disassembled and headed out.

"Officer Clarke," Postiff said formally, but with a smile.

"Detective. How can I help you?" Cassidy asked. Since the Hollywood Hit Men case and Eden's murder, she and Postiff had become good friends, going out after work for the occasional beer.

"Sorry to be a bad news bear, but Ron Whitty is claiming his confession to you was coerced," he said. "His lawyer called last night. I didn't want to ruin your evening."

"Again? Haven't we been through this?" Cassidy sighed.

"He's just spinning his wheels. There was no coercion at all, but he thinks he can delay if he keeps making these false claims."

"Am I going to have to talk to Internal Affairs?" she asked.

"I don't think it'll come to that. This is the third time he's tried bullshit like this. It's all on video."

"I guess some guys just really hate getting caught," she said.

"He might be angling to get into a room with you again. You know he developed a kind of fixation on you. But don't worry, that's not happening. Just wanted to let you know in case you hear anything about it."

"Thanks for the heads-up. Hey, is Pete back yet?" she asked. His partner, Pete Barrera, had been her dad's partner for twenty years. He'd contracted his third case of COVID-19 shortly after the Hit Men case and missed weeks of work.

"Yes, he's coming back today. Any minute now, to be precise," Postiff said.

"Okay. Stay safe out there."

Half an hour later, Cassidy and Riley were cruising east on Hollywood Boulevard. The city had the just-mopped look that always followed a storm in Los Angeles, as if the built-up dust and debris had been washed off by a high-powered hose. The gutters were pooling with water, and everything looked clean and fresh. They turned toward the neighborhood experiencing residential burglaries and car break-ins. It was made up of older single-family homes sandwiched tightly between modern apartment buildings, giving the area a mismatched, transitional look. Soon the old Craftsman homes and the small, Tudor-style cottages would be gone, and the narrow streets would be completely overtaken by the big concrete boxes with their sad, narrow balconies barely big enough for a deck chair.

"How's your dad doing?" Riley asked.

"Pretty good. He had to give up boxing, so now he's coaching some of the kids in the youth classes. He's volunteering his time, and he seems to like doing it. He started playing pickleball at the gym."

"He's a true boomer!" Riley laughed.

"At least it's not golf."

"What's wrong with golf?"

Cassidy snorted. "Please. You walk slowly around a big grassy area for hours and hit a little ball with a metal stick. I don't know how a bunch of portly white guys managed to convince people that it is actually a sport!"

Riley grinned. "No one ever uses the word 'portly' anymore."

"It's a good word, it should be resurrected," she said firmly.

They had circled back and turned onto Gower Avenue, passing the local Unitarian church and the Kidz Clubhouse, a resource center for homeless teens and runaways. A middle-aged woman hanging a sign outside the Clubhouse waved them to a stop when she saw them driving by.

"Excuse me, officers!" she shouted. "Can I speak to you for a moment?"

Riley and Cassidy stepped out of the car, and the woman reached her hand out to introduce herself. Her curly hair was pulled back in a claw clip, and she wore no makeup or jewelry, outside of a pair of watermelon earrings.

"I'm Melinda Drake, the director of services here at the Kidz Clubhouse. I just wanted to see if there's been any update on the phone calls I've made?"

"We haven't heard anything about the phone calls, Ms. Drake. When did you place them and who did you speak to?" Riley asked.

Melinda drew her lips into a taut line and nodded her head dejectedly.

"Of course. It's the same old story, always is. These kids don't matter to anyone. I've only called about four or five times! Can we go inside to talk about this?"

They followed her into a large community room filled with long tables and folding chairs. The walls were decorated with brightly colored posters featuring positive affirmations.

YOU ARE WORTHY AND ENOUGH!
IT'S OKAY TO NOT BE OKAY!
TODAY IS THE DAY TO ASK FOR HELP!

Three scruffy teenagers sat eating plates of macaroni and cheese. When they saw Cassidy and Riley, they tensed. One boy slid his chair back, ready to bolt.

"Don't worry, Clyde. They're just here to talk to me. No one's come for any of you," Melinda assured him.

Clyde went back to eating but remained cautious. Seeing the wariness and fear in the boy's eyes, Cassidy wondered how effective the happy slogans were, weighed against the reality of his life—if he appreciated that it was okay to not be okay. A small office was connected to the main room; Melinda guided them inside. Her face looked as if it were frozen in a permanent mask of anxiety. She took a seat at her desk across from them.

"I've called the police several times in the past ten days. We serve this local community of homeless and runaway teenagers. We have several kids, regulars who come every week for services, who've just disappeared, as if they evaporated. None of the others have seen them out and about. They didn't tell anyone that they were leaving. I'm worried that there may be something going on," she said cautiously.

"Are they underage? Isn't this an issue for CPS?" Riley asked.

Melinda looked at him with a sad smile, as if he had just asked if the moon were made of cheese.

"They're minors, yes. But they ran away from other cities and states, they have no legal address or family here in LA. And most of them have been put into care and have run away from that as well. No one wants to think about it, but over eighteen thousand kids in LA County have been abused by their foster families. And those are just the ones that we know about."

"So, you provide support services without calling in CPS?" Cassidy asked.

"Yes, that's the only way some of them will keep coming. I've learned the hard way, believe me. I've been running the Clubhouse for twelve years. But this is something different, the way these kids have just vanished."

"Trafficking is a big problem, I imagine," Riley said.

Melinda nodded. "Oh yeah. They wait for the kids getting off the buses here in Hollywood, and they know exactly who to target. There's one young guy named Aiden Howe, he's a low-level pimp who gets the kids to work for him. He could be involved, but I haven't seen much of him lately, which is kind of suspicious. He's usually around. Once we get kids established here, we're used to seeing them regularly, we have a connection to them. Here are their names, the ones who've just stopped showing up."

She handed Cassidy a sheet of paper printed with a series of names and photos.

Zephyr Star, Kyle Christiansen, Anya Atwell, Autumn Lindo, Zeno Kaspar.

Melinda continued, "The kids on the list were the ones who came by all the time. They talked to us; they counted on us. I've called the police several times, and I was told that someone would come by to take a report, but no one has showed up. That's why I flagged you down."

"Do you remember who you spoke to at the Hollywood station?" Cassidy asked.

"Yes, I wrote it down. His name is Captain Dykstra."

Riley and Cassidy exchanged a look, then he asked, "Could you show us around?"

As Melinda gave them a tour of the Clubhouse, Cassidy stared at the faces of the kids who had gone missing. They were so young. She remembered herself at that age, living in Chatsworth, navigating her parents' divorce, which wasn't even that difficult, given how well they both worked to make it easy for her. Her mom was there to pick her up after school every day, even when Cassidy chose to live with her dad. But looking at the faces of the missing teens, Cassidy felt a disconcerting sense of dread, imagining how they lived alone every day on the rough streets of Hollywood.

"Here we have a small dormitory with five beds, but they fill up pretty quickly each night. We have showers and help the kids connect to public assistance programs. And we try to get them back into school, even to get their GED if possible. It's hard, some don't even have a certified birth certificate," Melinda explained, leading them down a narrow hallway.

Everything about the place seemed slightly run down, albeit clean. The walls were scuffed, and the plaster was cracked in several places. A makeshift tarp had been hung over a piece of the ceiling that was open. The dormitory room was clean and neat, with mismatched linens and an open cupboard of folded towels.

"We get most of our housewares from donations and local thrift stores. We have a washer and dryer, but both are in need of repair right now, so we use the Splash and Suds laundromat," Melinda said.

"Why don't we take police reports right now, and we can file them as missing persons cases. It will give us a place to start with a formal report, and we'll speak to people other than Captain Dykstra about starting a proper investigation," Cassidy suggested.

"Thank you. I've been so frustrated over this. Can we do it in my office?"

"We can take some notes on paper, but we'll need to use the MDT system in the patrol car to file the report. It's all digital and computerized now," Cassidy said.

"Thank heaven someone is finally doing something!" Melinda said, following them outside.

After filing the reports, Riley and Cassidy handed Melinda their cards.

"You can follow up with us directly, Ms. Drake. I will get on this right away today when we get back to the station," Cassidy said.

The three teenagers shuffled out the door, carrying their backpacks and a couple of plastic grocery bags.

"See you later, Melinda. Thanks for the mac and cheese," Clyde said, not meeting Riley or Cassidy's eyes. He was slight in stature, his gray backpack stuffed so full he resembled a potato bug as he moved up the street.

"Guess that was a quick lunch stop," Riley said.

"No, they're afraid of you. Normally they stay longer after eating," Melinda explained.

"We'll be in touch, Ms. Drake," Cassidy assured her as they got back into the patrol car. As they drove away, she continued, "I can't believe Dykstra just blew her off!"

"I can. He's a jerk. Do you think he gives a rat's ass about some missing homeless teenagers?"

"What do you think happened to them?"

"I think they met up with someone who said he could give them a place to live and buy them stuff. He probably took them to eat in a restaurant and let them get anything they wanted. And after a day or two of that, he turned them out to work the streets. Probably took them deep into the valley or out near Long Beach. And it'll be next to impossible to locate them," Riley said.

"I'd like to talk to that Aiden Howe guy that she mentioned."

"And that'll be like finding a teardrop in the ocean. If there's any heat, I'm sure he's left the area, even if he's not involved."

"Fucking hell . . ." Cassidy muttered. "I'm going to ask Ramsey and Carbone if we can do an investigation anyway."

Riley smiled. “Of course you are. Game Changer Cassidy Clarke to the rescue!”

She laughed. “Shut up!”

“Be careful not to catch your cape in the door when you get out.”

Cassidy rolled her eyes and looked out the window. “I can’t believe I missed you . . .” she mumbled.

Riley’s eyes lit up. “Really? You missed me?”

“Until this moment,” she replied dryly.

CHAPTER THREE

Bill Clarke stood outside the ring at Brickhouse Boxing Club, watching two teenage boys going through their paces. A young, short Latino kid was sparring with an older teenager who had to be six foot seven, close to three hundred pounds. Bill tried to hide a smile as the smaller boy swung aggressively at the larger one, unintimidated.

"You're doing good, José, go in for his body, that's your advantage. Nick is too tall for you to land much else," Bill shouted.

José crouched and then popped up with a swift uppercut jab, hitting Nick smack in the side of the head, stunning him. Nick stepped back, shaken despite the headgear. Bill climbed into the ring, taking him by the arm and leading him to sit down.

"He hit me really hard, Mr. Bill," Nick said, tears welling up in his eyes.

Bill patted his shoulder. "You're kind of a gentle giant, aren't you, Nick? That's enough for today, and José, this is just practice, just sparring. Don't hit that hard, especially at his face and head."

"Okay, Mr. Bill. Sorry, Nick," José said, taking off his gloves and gear.

"And stop calling me Mr. Bill! You're both too young to remember him on *Saturday Night Live*, but it's embarrassing!" Bill said, laughing.

Nick and José looked at him, confused. "Who's Mr. Bill?"

"Look him up online. He started back in the '70s. See you guys tomorrow."

As he walked away, he heard José whisper, "The '70s? Did they have television back then?"

On his way back home, Bill stopped to pick up a new propane tank for the gas grill. The weather in Los Angeles was so nice that he could cook outdoors year-round. He'd been cooking salmon and lamb chops of late, with a Lebanese potato recipe he found on Instagram. Cassidy had forbidden him to eat any more fast food, his staple diet when he was working as a homicide detective, pulling eighteen-hour days regularly.

Now he was cooking most nights and taking walks with a new Fitbit. The medication that Dr. Baruch had given him helped slow down his internal motor; gone were the major mood swings and the restlessness that once drove him. He still needed more tests, even if they had to wait until he died to confirm CTE. There were various degenerative brain issues he could have, but he didn't really want to know. He just wanted to live well, right now.

He pulled up at home and checked the mail, retrieving a letter from BSIS, the Bureau of Security and Investigative Services, which meant his private investigator's license had arrived. He ripped the envelope open and pulled it out; he felt like a kid again. Now he was a proper PI—he could take on cold cases, work for clients who needed help with problems that the police didn't have time to handle. He'd already made the decision that he would not take any adultery cases or help divorce attorneys get dirt on their client's spouse. That crap was beneath him.

After the situation with his neighbor, Alan Musselman, and Bill's obsession with the Min Sun-Hee case, he'd promised himself and his daughter that if he worked cold cases, he would have a license and follow the right protocol. As Bill hoisted the heavy propane tank up, Musselman was leaving his house next door and hurried over to help.

"Hey, Bill. Let me help you with that. It weighs a ton when it's full," Musselman said, taking the tank.

"I've got it, Alan. I'm not in the grave yet!" Bill protested.

"No one said you were, but there's no reason to risk hurting yourself. Should I set it by the grill?" Musselman asked as Bill opened the front door.

"Sure, man. Thanks," Bill said self-consciously while Musselman carried the tank to the yard. He always felt embarrassed around Musselman since the day he'd lost all perspective and broken into the man's house, trying to find evidence that he was Min Sun-Hee's neighbor twenty years ago and possibly her killer. Musselman had declined to press charges and seemed to have put the whole thing behind him, but Bill's face still flushed when they ran into each other. This little dance they did, of Musselman helping with the propane, Bill pretending they didn't have a troubled history, was an attempt to move past it. They both knew it, and they both followed the right steps; in time, perhaps, they would achieve their goal.

After Musselman left, Bill went to the office and looked at his cold case files, now stored in clear plastic bins with neat labels that Cassidy had printed out. He wasn't going to give them up, but he was going to approach them calmly and without the manic craving for resolution that pushed him over the edge. And prompted him to keep reaching out to convicted murderer Tyler Derby, dipping his cup into that poisoned well again and again.

Other detectives talked to convicted murderers from time to time. Their minds worked in distinctly different ways than normal people. He knew that Derby was toxic, but Bill had a connection with him, even if Cassidy dismissed him as a manipulative psychopath. Derby had given Bill information that had solved two long-cold cases, and that was no small thing. Bill opened the Min Sun-Hee file that he had laid out on the desk and looked over his notes. He hoped to solve it, and he'd keep asking for the DNA found at the scene to be run through CODIS every year, just in case. Maybe he'd get lucky.

He sat at the computer and logged in to the OurTime dating website. He'd set up an account the night before, when Cassidy was already asleep. He was too embarrassed to have his daughter see him do it. But his new therapist, Dr. Glass, told him that social isolation was a major problem for older people, especially after retirement. He'd never used any of the popular dating apps; they were too newfangled and strange. He preferred meeting women the way he always had, out and about in the city, working cases. Or maybe at one of the cop bars after work; there were always women who had a particular fascination with men in law enforcement.

But back then, he was a star detective with a demanding and rather glamorous life, at least to people looking at it from the outside. That was how he met his ex-wife. Now he was just a retired guy, taking medication for his moods and his blood pressure, working hard to color within the lines of his life. It brought him down sometimes. He missed the big bursts of emotion and energy, the late nights, the life-and-death consequences of police work.

And if he met someone he liked, he wondered if everything would still work the same with the SSRI medication—he'd heard that sometimes the old stiffy didn't cooperate the same way with those drugs, and that could make dating awkward. He closed the laptop, unwilling to think about that.

He saw that the 1980s-era answering machine that he insisted on keeping for the home line was blinking. Cassidy couldn't believe that anyone ever relied on such a "medieval contraption," but he pressed the message button to see who could possibly have called that line, which they rarely used. A choppy, staccato, automated voice left a message:

"You've received a collect call from an inmate at the Pleasant Valley Correctional Institution . . ."

Bill hit the erase button. He hadn't told his daughter. He didn't want her to know, but it was the third time that Tyler Derby had called him, and he fought the strong temptation to call him back. Just to see what he had to say.

As Evie approached the Clubhouse, an older blue Camry with an unpainted hood pulled up next to her. She kept moving, not looking at the driver; she'd learned not to make eye contact with the type of men who trolled the area.

"Hey, Squirt! What's up?"

She knew immediately that it was Aiden Howe; he was the only one who called her that. No one had seen him recently, and she had hoped he'd moved on. She didn't answer him.

"Come on, I'm just looking for Princess," Aiden said, with just a hint of pleading in his voice. Princess was one of his best money makers and his on-again, off-again girlfriend, but she had finally broken away from him.

"No idea where she is," Evie lied.

"You're her best friend, tell me. I miss her. You know how important she is to me," Aiden said.

"Right. That's why you kept her locked up in your apartment for a week as punishment. 'Cause you care so much about her," Evie replied sarcastically.

Aiden smiled apologetically. "I said I was sorry, and I promised I'd never do it again. Love can make you do strange things, Squirt. You ought to try it."

"Sorry. Gotta go," she said, pushing the door to the Clubhouse open and disappearing inside as he drove off in frustration.

She'd kept her cool, but she was afraid of Aiden; a year earlier he had cornered her in the bathroom of the Mobil station a few blocks away and clearly intended to rape her in a stall. She'd escaped by kicking him hard in the groin when he had his pants down at his knees. As he fell, she made her escape, but she knew he held a grudge against her. She texted Princess a warning.

just saw Aiden near the clubhouse. keep an eye out

She got no reply.

Inside the Clubhouse, Evie dropped her backpack into the big plastic bin, where kids left their belongings. She pulled her charging cord for her phone from the front pocket and plugged it into one of the outlets in the community room. Pebble Smith was there, sitting at a battered laptop. They exchanged a wave. A few other kids were crashed out on the couch, playing video games on a beat-up PlayStation 2. Evie saw Melinda in her office and stuck her head in.

"You got a minute?" she asked.

"Sure, what's up?" Melinda said.

Evie entered and sat on one of the overstuffed easy chairs, the big cushions swallowing her small frame.

"It's Layla. She called me and said she was coming back to Hollywood. That there was some creepy stuff going on with that boyfriend at his house in Atwater and she had to tell someone. She got to Sunset and Western, said she was in the alley by Home Depot, and she felt weird. Then she stopped talking, it sounded like the phone fell or something."

"She never responded again after that?" Melinda asked. Her internal alarm bells went off; this was completely out of character for Layla Waters.

"No. I took the bus and went to the alley, but it was empty. But I found this." Evie held up the silver bracelet. Melinda took it, recognizing it as Layla's. Evie continued, "I called the cops, and they showed up with an ambulance, but then they left."

"Did you talk to them?"

Evie looked at her dirty tennis shoes, thinking she really needed to wash them soon at the Splash and Suds on Franklin. Then she said quietly, "Nope. I hid under an appliance box. I didn't want them to find me. You know why."

Melinda nodded. She knew Evie's story, how she'd been picked up by CPS a few months after arriving in LA, how her foster family only fed her microwave meals by Hormel that they bought in bulk. And how their twenty-something son would come to visit and creep into her bedroom when everyone was asleep.

"I spoke to two police officers today about the other kids who've gone missing. They said they're going to look into it," Melinda said. "I'll tell them about Layla as well. What do you think happened?"

"I don't know. She sounded really out of it, and when I got there, she was gone."

Melinda nodded, trying to hide her growing concern. Evie was upset enough; the last thing she wanted to do was make her feel worse. "What do you know about Layla's new boyfriend? She never brought him around here," she asked.

Evie shrugged. "I never met him in person, but I saw some photos of him on her phone. He's from another country, maybe Germany or something. She just started hooking up with him, she met him at the library. She said he has a house near Atwater."

"So, he's not on the street? How old did he look?"

"Twenties maybe. She said he went to college. I'm sure someone met him in person. What do we do if she doesn't show up?" Evie asked.

"Don't worry, Evie. I'm sure we'll figure out what happened, and Layla is okay. Were you out in the rain all night?"

"I had a good spot, at Cahuenga and Franklin, where the cops can't see us very well. But when Layla called, I went to meet her. After that, I stayed near the Home Depot, in case she came back. I hid in the parking structure for Target, in a stairwell."

"Do you want me to assign you one of the beds tonight? They're not all taken yet, and I'd feel better if you were here," Melinda suggested.

"Okay. But I'm going to go out and look for her. Oh, and Aiden is back. I saw him just outside."

Melinda made note of his reappearance and to notify the police officers who took her report.

"Did he bother you?" Melinda asked.

"No, he was looking for Princess. I sent her a text to let her know."

Evie stood up and grabbed a protein bar from the box on Melinda's desk, then hurried out the door to begin her search for Layla. Melinda feared it would be fruitless, and she'd come back at the end of the day even more scared and disillusioned. Of all the kids that had passed through the doors of the Kidz Clubhouse, there were some that got around the professional distance Melinda had to maintain as a social worker.

It was hard, working with such vulnerable kids; she'd been doing it for twenty years, at the Clubhouse for twelve. At first, she'd wanted to take them all home and fix their broken lives, but she had learned to suppress that desire, to keep a healthy distance to offer a clearheaded perspective on their problems. It was also about self-preservation; if she lived out on that raw edge of empathy, she would not be able to get up each day and move forward.

But Evie Peacock was one of the kids who got around her defenses. She'd arrived at fifteen, not a typical runaway from abuse but because of her father's death in Corvallis, Oregon. He was her only parent; her mother had taken off years before. His battle with Merkel cell carcinoma had bankrupted them, and with no resources, Evie entered the foster care system only to bolt as each placement was worse than the last. She'd come to Los Angeles, believing the shows she saw on television that depicted it as a golden city, full of excitement and glamour. The reality was far more dismal and difficult.

Now seventeen, she looked younger, with a smattering of freckles across her nose, and her petite frame. She'd been a good student, an aspiring artist before her world imploded. Melinda had even considered becoming her foster parent before her own mother's health declined and she took over her care. Evie was one of her promising kids who might get her high school diploma and maybe even make it to community college and have a real life.

Melinda watched Evie as she crossed the busy street, dodging cars to arrive at the bus stop, pulling her bus pass from her belt bag and gripping it tightly in her hand. Next to her, a grungy, deranged man overturned a trash can and began kicking the garbage across the sidewalk, screaming obscenities. Evie hunched her shoulders but ignored him.

Melinda turned away; something in Evie Peacock broke her heart.

CHAPTER FOUR

"Did they come in through another entrance when you wouldn't open the front door, Mrs. Adamyan? Do you know how they gained entry to your home?" Riley asked a distraught Seda Adamyan, a sixty-ish housewife who was seated on a patio chair outside her home on Gramercy Avenue as Cassidy did a walk-through. It was another midday residential burglary, smack in the center of the Hollywood neighborhood where a string of similar crimes had been committed.

Seda shook her head, barely able to speak. "I don't know how they got inside. Maybe I left the back door unlocked when I put Shareek outside. I was cooking, and I didn't pay attention . . . and then they were inside the house!"

She began to cry again, while Riley jotted down the scant information he could get from her to make a report. Cassidy came back, wearing plastic gloves and holding an empty glass jewelry box.

"I found this on the back porch. It was discarded with some other small boxes," Cassidy said. At the sight of the box, Seda began crying louder.

"This was my grandmother's! It had her wedding pearls in it . . . and these boxes, I had them hidden under the dresser . . ."

"We can pull the security camera footage, but can you tell us what they looked like? How tall, what ethnicity, hair color, that type of thing," Riley asked.

Seda twisted her hands together. "They were kids, just kids! A boy and a girl, white. But they didn't seem scared of anything. They knew exactly what to take. They were in and out so fast, I barely had time to think!"

"Could you show us how you access the playback feature on your security cameras?" Cassidy asked.

"Usually, my son does this for me . . ." Seda said, opening the app on her phone. It used face recognition to log in, and she handed the phone to Riley. "I don't know how to see it, but it's open now."

Riley scrolled through the app features to find video playback and opened it. Cassidy watched over his shoulder as the screen showed two figures, dressed in oversize hoodies and sweatpants, come in through the unlocked back door. An interior security camera revealed them pushing Seda Adamyan onto the couch as she covered her face with her hands. One ransacked the curio cabinet but left behind the decorative ceramic figurines and colored marble eggs in crystal bowls. He grabbed small electronics and as many pieces of the silver flatware set that he could jam into a canvas bag.

From the bedroom, the girl emerged with the glass jewel box and a grocery bag containing unknown items that weighed it down. They shouted once more at Seda and left the way they had come in. The entire burglary took less than seven minutes. The exterior cameras showed the two thieves disappearing over a low concrete retaining wall in the yard, and they were gone.

"Could you replay that, Sean? I want to see if there is a decent shot of their faces," Cassidy asked. Riley replayed the video. When the boy reached into the drawer with the silverware, the camera caught a clear image of his face beneath the large hoodie. He was young, most likely under eighteen. When the girl entered the frame, her face was not visible but her long, thick hair was pulled to one side and spilled out over one shoulder.

"Mrs. Adamyan, I'm going to send this video footage to my partner's phone so we can analyze it at the station. We may need to come back and take your phone for a few days," Riley said evenly, trying to calm the terrified woman down. "Do you want to be checked out by paramedics? We saw the thieves push you."

Seda shook her head. "No, no ambulance. I was not hurt; they just scared me. They did not seem violent; they just wanted things to sell for money . . ." Her voice trailed off, and she began to cry anew. A stocky, older woman arrived and pushed Riley aside to sit next to Seda.

"Are you okay, Seda? Was it like the others?" she asked.

"Excuse me, who are you to Mrs. Adamyan?" Riley asked.

The woman glared at him. "I'm her cousin, I live just two doors down. I'm asking if it was the same as the other neighbors who have been robbed lately. It's too much, all the time these days!"

"We've made a police report, and we're going to analyze the video footage to get an idea who the perpetrators are," Cassidy said.

Seda's cousin narrowed her eyes at Cassidy. "Talk! Talk! That is all the police do. We've had many of these robberies. People don't feel safe at home anymore! These kids, these kids are out of control!"

"We'll drop this video off at the station and follow up with you in the next day or two," Riley said.

As they approached their patrol car, Cassidy asked, "Do you think this could be connected to Melinda Drake's missing kids?"

"I don't know. She said they're street kids, but this seems a little more organized, right? They've hit several houses, all with the same MO?" Riley responded skeptically.

"What if it's like you said—they met someone who gave them a place to stay and all that, but they're being used this way?"

"Like in *Oliver Twist*? The old guy, the one who had the pickpockets work for him?"

"Exactly. Seda said they were young. Most teenagers don't operate this way if they steal something. They go for the easy stuff, not breaking into a house in the middle of the day," Cassidy said. "How about we swing by the Clubhouse on the way back to the station, just to check if Melinda recognizes them?"

Fifteen minutes later, they sat at Melinda Drake's computer in her office, watching the video footage. She froze the frame on the boy's face as he reached for the silver.

"That's Kyle Christiansen! He's one of the kids who's gone missing!" she exclaimed.

"Do you recognize the girl?" Cassidy asked.

"From the hair, I think it's Zephyr. She has long, thick red hair, and she always wears it to one side over her shoulder. It's her signature style, you know? And they are very tight, always hanging out together. But they would never have been able to plan and instigate something like this!"

"We're heading back to the station, and we're going to ask our lieutenant to authorize a targeted investigation into this. I think it's clear this is related, and maybe someone is using them for this purpose," Cassidy said.

"You received my message about another missing girl, right? Layla Waters? She's nineteen, kind of a leader to a lot of these kids, and now she's gone too. And Aiden Howe is back in the area as well. He's a tall, well-built kid. Midwestern, sandy hair, he looks like a million other young guys. I don't know that he'd be able to get these kids to commit robberies. That seems a bit beyond his reach with them," Melinda said.

"Yes, we got the message and Layla's photo. We'll keep an eye out for Aiden as well. We'll get back to you as soon as we have some information," Riley said.

Melinda followed them to the door of the Clubhouse, her concern turning to full-blown fear.

"Kyle and Zephyr could never have instigated something like this. Who could have this kind of control over them?"

Tyler Derby sat in his cell; his body racked with pain as he shifted his weight from one side to the other. Cancer was a bitch, complicated by Addison's disease, which was all he thought he had. Until they discovered he had stage four liver cancer with a 3 percent survival rate if it was caught early. Which it wasn't.

He never got his transfer to San Diego. He never got away from the inmates at Pleasant Valley who made his life a ruinous hell every single day. Now he didn't even get to go out in the exercise yard to walk around because he could barely stand up. He was released from any work duty and just stayed in his room alone all day.

But he had called Bill Clarke, even if he wasn't supposed to, even if his cop daughter had warned him to stay away. He did it because what could Cassidy Clarke take from him now? When he had something to give to her father that would heal one of the dark and broken places within him? She was a kid; she didn't understand about those places yet. She didn't have any of her own, but she would, with time.

Lately, Derby often thought back to his childhood in rural Oklahoma. How his father, Harland, would force him and his younger brothers to go noodling with all the boys in the local river, slapping the water with sticks to drive the fish toward a big net. The river that was filled with deadly water moccasins, and every year at least one kid would die from a lethal snake bite. Derby feared each summer that it would be him, and he'd beg and cry to avoid going, but that only enraged his father more, and he and his brothers would get the beating of the season out behind the barn.

Until the day that Derby grabbed an iron baling hook and slammed it into his father's neck, plunging it straight and deep into his carotid artery. He bled to death on the dirty straw, to the faint clucking of the chickens in their coop. Derby smiled as the thought of his skinny, careworn mother with ever-present bruises on her arms looking impassively at her husband's dead body.

How she tapped him with her toe to be sure he was dead and used an old rag to pull that baling hook free and dropped it into a bucket of bleach in the kitchen. How they had dragged his father's body and dumped it into the pigsty. And then she'd taken Tyler into the kitchen to give him a big steaming bowl of peach cobbler. Two whole servings heaped together and freshly made. A few days later, when all signs of Harland were gone, she told the neighbors he'd run off with another woman.

Derby thought more and more about heaven, knowing he'd never get there if it really existed. He'd done too much harm and enjoyed doing it too. He knew there was something wrong with him, but he didn't have the will or patience to figure out what it was. But it kept him awake at night now, a needling companion to his withering pain. He still had some secrets to give up. Perhaps he could barter with whoever was up there, pulling the strings. Maybe he could get a spot in the middle, in that place of blustering winds and hovering shadows that his mother warned him about. That purgatory where you just might get a sliver of a chance at some bargain-basement redemption.

Before he was confined to his cell, when he could still eat in the dining hall, he sat at a table with a new arrival, a transfer from San Quentin. A lifer who'd killed almost as many women as Derby had. Killed them crazy, too, like BTK. His name was Sonny Harris, and Derby listened as he bragged about his brother, who was the smart one, the one who never got caught.

The one who killed that little slanty-eyed girl in Los Angeles years ago and that housewife up out in Hacienda Heights. Sonny Harris looked up to his big brother, who was still on the outside, who didn't need to keep killing. He had self-control. He had inner strength, that's what Sonny said. Sonny even remembered their names. The fat, lazy-ass housewife was Tammy Hotchkis. And the slanty-eyed girl was Min Sun-Hee. Sonny had laughed at that name, but Derby remembered it.

He knew Bill Clarke did too.

CHAPTER FIVE

Cassidy and Riley finished their shift and found Lieutenant Carbone in her office, meeting with Commander Joyce Ramsey. They waited dutifully in the hallway until they were invited in. Ramsey greeted them with a smile and a handshake; she was planning to develop Cassidy into one of her protégés after the success of the Hollywood Hit Men case.

"We took a call today for another residential break-in. The perpetrators appear to be teenagers, and one of them has been identified from security footage as a missing, homeless teenager named Kyle Christiansen. The director of the Kidz Clubhouse identified him," Cassidy explained.

"Evidently she's called several times about missing kids, and she spoke to Dykstra, who never followed up with her," Riley added.

"They're homeless, how does she know they're missing?" Carbone asked.

"She said some of the kids are regulars at the Clubhouse. They rely on the place for a lot of services," Cassidy said. "We think there might be a connection, that someone has lured these kids off the street and coerced them into committing these robberies."

"Or they've organized themselves into a criminal ring," Carbone suggested.

"Maybe," Ramsey said, weighing the political pros and cons of launching a formal investigation. The burglaries were causing a lot of tension in the community, and they hadn't yet migrated to the wealthier neighborhood of Los Feliz, but it was just a matter of time. If that happened, there would be a lot of pushback. Homeless minors generated a lot of sympathy, significantly more than homeless adults. Helping them could raise her empathy quotient when divided by her tough-on-crime positions.

"We'd need to put a detective team on it; they could coordinate with you since you're out working those streets every day. You worked well with Postiff, right?" Ramsey asked Cassidy.

"Yes, I did."

Carbone concurred, "Pete Barrera's back, and he only has a few months left before retirement. They work homicide, but this might be a fairly easy one for him, not like the Hit Men, no murders or dead bodies. We could let him coast through these final weeks."

"Okay, we'll let Postiff and Barrera know. I also think it would be good for you two to speak to the kids at the Clubhouse. We can try and set it up right away. Just give them a warning, what to look out for," Ramsey said.

"Thank you," Cassidy replied.

"And as a heads-up, we will have local press there," Ramsey added.

As they walked toward the locker room, Riley said, "Of course she's going to have the press there. She'll show up with her helmet hair and a big fake smile, to show everyone how great she is."

Cassidy nodded in agreement. She had lost all illusions she once had about Joyce Ramsey. Dealing with her on the Hit Men case had revealed her as a self-serving manipulator, and Cassidy knew that Ramsey had pushed to pin the Balcomb murder on her dad. He referred to Ramsey as a political hyena, and he was right. But Cassidy didn't care what Ramsey's agenda was. She'd gotten what she wanted; they were going to open an investigation into Melinda Drake's missing kids.

Jeppe Lind sat back at the big wooden desk that dominated his office at home—the third-story loft of the rambling Craftsman home he called the

Raven's Nest that his parents had rented for him when he began graduate school at USC the year before. A chemical engineering student, he had chosen the Mount Washington area over the neighborhoods closer to campus. No matter how many homes the university bought up or converted into student apartments, the school community pushed up against the low-income, crime-filled streets of central Los Angeles.

Jeppe didn't want any part of it, nor did he romanticize poverty the way some of his wealthy classmates did, showing up to school in thrift store clothes, shopping at the local swap meet. He had no time for playing poor to present himself as someone with real-world problems. They all knew that a year's tuition cost ninety thousand dollars.

No, Jeppe chose the big, sprawling house that sat at the top of a long driveway, with a double lot. Tall hedges grew all around the perimeter of the property. He had a view of the city below, and few people would venture up the steep approach to knock on his door or make inquiries, which was just the way he wanted it. There were too many close neighbors near campus, and students didn't respect privacy very well. They were always showing up, looking for someone to hang out with. But he hadn't really made many friends at school. He'd always been that way.

At twenty-three, he was tall and lanky, with a loose-limbed gait and carriage that made him seem like an eighteenth-century aristocrat paying a visit to the servants' quarters when he walked into a room. His reddish-blond hair and dimpled baby face disarmed people when they met him; he looked like Leonardo DiCaprio's sweet younger brother. He'd been a brilliant student but prone to intense emotional upheavals. His parents back in Norway were professors and expected him to return home with a PhD and the well-rounded life experience of living abroad for a few years.

He hadn't told them that he'd started hearing odd voices, as if a person were standing directly beside him, whispering into his ear. That he rarely slept and instead roamed the halls of his big house, sure that there were ghosts inside the walls. Or that he'd stopped attending classes. Jeppe spent his days visiting the library, poring over old books on American history and watching porn. He saw every documentary on Charles Manson and marveled at how he had achieved complete control over a group of disaffected middle-class kids living the American dream and turned them into agents of an American nightmare. He fancied his big Craftsman as a kind of urban Spahn Ranch, where he could promote his developing philosophies about humanity and have sex with a lot of young girls, if he could entice them into joining him.

He never had trouble attracting girls; he had trouble keeping them. He wondered if once they got close enough to him, they could sense something was off-kilter with his internal wiring. Maybe they felt the chill of the dark, cold, empty place inside of him that nothing seemed to be able to fill. Perhaps assembling a loyal group of devotees, manipulated by drugs, lack of sleep, and mind-fuck pseudo intellectualism, would gain him steady access to companionship and sex. He could play that role; it was as if it were written for him.

He'd gone to a Hollywood hot spot, Dray's Billiards and Brews, with some frat guys he knew casually from school, and there he'd discovered a whole world of possibilities. Dray's regularly had young, pretty teenagers present, and he'd learned that they found most of them trolling the streets of East Hollywood. There were young men and women, adrift and alone, struggling and susceptible. At Dray's they were window dressing; with Jeppe they could be so much more.

The power was potent; he already had a small group he'd picked up near Gower and Franklin. It was so easy. All he had to do was give them a place to live, a bed with clean sheets, and a hot shower with a door that locked. And some fun drugs to help them relax and forget whatever led them to the city of lost angels. That was what he called them, his lost angels.

He'd found a good drug connection during his first week at school; that was easy at a place like USC. The undergrads had more than a few local entrepreneurs ready to meet the market. Students regularly picked up whatever they wanted from various dealers, all with a fat cash advance on Daddy's credit card. Now, with his lost angels, he was buying more psilocybin, salvia, MDMA, and others, since everyone enjoyed them so much and the drugs made them so willing.

He laid out the treasures that Kyle and Zephyr had dutifully brought home to him. They were proving to be two of his best workers. He took photos of the items and sent them to his resale connection, Toddy. The jewelry was real and valuable. But it wasn't the money, for Jeppe. It was the thrill. And as a reward, he'd give Kyle and Zephyr the fun gummies that would render them dreamy and doped up for the rest of the day. He liked how the girls would talk and talk, barely noticing when he gingerly reached under their clothes to touch them; sometimes they didn't even wake up. But he'd stopped himself from going too far.

The voices he heard could be maddeningly perverse and conflicted when it came to sex. Urging him on and then punitive and chastising. He'd tried tuning them out, but that only made them louder inside his head, like banging a pot with a metal spoon.

But then there were the parties. He had carefully assembled a growing group of like-minded grad students, club-hoppers, and even one professor, who found his Mount Washington hideaway enticing, and every new street recruit was like a toy, still in the box and ready to be played with. His guests liked them the best. He never associated much with the guests outside of the parties. They were like a cast of characters in a movie whose presence completed the scene.

Jeppe could watch from a darkened corner, building up the courage to participate but getting a thrill, nonetheless. Safe in the Raven's Nest, where everything was allowed and nothing was exposed. A hedonistic wet dream fueled by ketamine, Molly, and a handful of professional sex workers to round the evening out.

There was a knock at the door of his office. A petite girl named Anya stuck her head in.

"Jeppe? Did you need me on kitchen duty tonight? Zephyr is on the schedule, but she's kind of out of it," Anya said, referring to the schedule that Jeppe printed out each week to show what everyone's duties were.

"Yes, that will be fine, Anya. Remember, we have a party tomorrow night, so we must prepare everyone."

"Yes, I remember," she said with a smile, her eyes lingering on his.

Anya was tiny, with a blond bob haircut and dark-brown eyes. She was like the others, sweet and in desperate need of validation. Even the boys sought his approval constantly. It was as if they were caught in the space where their lives began to shift into something that hurt so much, they got stuck there: wholly unintegrated; part young adult, part broken child. Which made them all so easy to please. And control.

But there was one who was not easy. The girl he found in an unexpected place, with eyes that had seen so much that now she saw everything: through him, into him, beyond him. Those dark-green eyes that would flash at him in anger and turn to soft velvet in surrender. Never afraid of a fight, able to string together a life from just the meager threads and remnants she'd been given. Stronger than he was. More courageous, more astute.

He wanted to be like her. He wanted to possess her, and like all spoiled children, he wanted to break what he couldn't control. She was the only one he took to his big bed in the middle of the night, who sat at the window looking at the city below, gently stroking the back of his hand, quieting the whispering voices in his head.

His Hekate. His Morrigan. His Atalanta. Even her name sounded like music: Layla.

What was he going to do with her now?

CHAPTER SIX

Layla woke from an afternoon nap in Jeppe's bedroom to find the door locked. The clock read 11:18 p.m. How had she slept so long? She'd called out his name but got no answer. She could hear people and music in the hallway. What the hell was going on? She'd slept heavily. Jeppe had given her one of his melatonin capsules, but she hadn't checked the bottle; maybe it was something else? She was sure it was. Her head felt too heavy and groggy. Too much time had passed. She tried the door again, but it wouldn't budge. Why would he have locked her in if he was having people over?

She climbed out onto the gentle slope of the Craftsman roof outside his office and made her way to the side of the house where there was an old-fashioned fire escape. She climbed down and walked in the front door.

The lights were dim, deep house music played loudly, and each room was filled with people in various stages of undress and intoxication. She pushed through the guests, their hands reaching out to touch her arms, her face, her neck. Squeezing her flesh, clinging to her as she pried their fingers off. Some wore party masks, some were unrecognizable in glittering face paint that made them look like nymphs and woodland creatures.

She pushed open a door off the living room and saw two men and a young woman on a bed . . . Was that Anya? Her blond hair was iridescent lilac under the black lights. She waved at Layla and gestured for her to close the door. She found Jeppe and his guests in a circle, clapping as several people in the middle of the group writhed and climbed over and under one another. She couldn't see what they were doing or make out their faces, but with the spectators' show of lurid excitement, she knew it was something deviant and degrading.

She looked hard at Jeppe; he didn't see her, his eyes glistening. She realized in that moment what this was, what he was. She scanned the party guests for the kids she knew from the Clubhouse who Jeppe had taken in. They were nowhere to be found. She feared they were behind the locked doors on the upper floor with the types of people she had tried to protect them from.

She hurried along the corridor to the back of the house. Everywhere bodies pressed up against bodies. The sounds of pleasure and pain. She ran to the outside, fearing she would be dragged into a room or darkened hallway, by hands, too many hands, all reaching, greedy, grasping. She knew that Jeppe had drugged and locked her in to keep her from witnessing this scene, his hidden self, his true intentions. She moved to the far end of the yard, where the shadows were deep and the hedges were thick with foliage and flowers. She tucked herself in among them to wait until the house grew quiet. She stared up at the windows, the silhouettes of people dancing, intertwined, pulsing, rising and falling in the strobing purple light, like a grotesque fun house in a traveling carnival.

She had to get away from him. She had to get the others away . . .

Judson Postiff and his partner, Pete Barrera, sat in Lieutenant Carbone's office, getting briefed on the new investigation.

"There might be a connection between the residential robberies and a group of homeless kids who've stopped going to the Kidz Clubhouse for services. Officers Clarke and Riley were there today, speaking to the director, Melinda Drake," Carbone said.

Barrera shook his head. "We're looking for missing runaways, right? They're always homeless. Been that way forever. There's always going to be more of them."

"They could be runaways; we've always had a problem with underage kids on the street. But there could be a link to these robberies, which we're getting a lot of complaints about. It's a stone's throw to Los Feliz, and we don't want them spreading to that area," Carbone said, her inference clear. No one wanted to deal with Jules Johnson, the head of the Los Feliz Neighborhood Alliance. A frustrated actress with no talent, she'd turned the monthly community meeting into her own piece of performance art. And the residents hadn't paid multimillion-dollar prices to live in an area where brazen daytime robberies took place.

"Are Clarke and Riley going to be on this with us?" Postiff asked.

"Not exclusively," Carbone said. "But they are the point of contact for Ms. Drake from the Clubhouse, and that is their beat. They're all over those streets every day, so they'll be keeping an eye out. I know you two work homicide, but this should be an easy one. No dead bodies for you, Pete, in your final months on the force."

"Okay, we're on it," Postiff said.

Carbone handed them a piece of paper with names and photos of six missing kids. "This is the short list that Melinda Drake gave us."

"Six kids are the short list? How many more are there?" Barrera asked.

"Evidently she said there could be up to ten or maybe more," Carbone said.

Barrera rubbed his eyes. They were still bothering him post COVID, itchy and red. His vision was still blurry sometimes.

"Why are we just hearing about this now if this many kids could be missing?" he asked.

"Because Melinda Drake spoke to Dykstra, that's why," Carbone said.

Postiff and Barrera left Carbone's office and went to their desks to see what information they could find on the missing kids. Postiff began searching the database from the National Center for Missing & Exploited Children. Barrera checked the missing person reports filed in California. Several kids on Melinda's list had been reported. Some had not.

Barrera exhaled deeply. "Who are these parents? Who doesn't report a fourteen-year-old kid missing? Several of them have nothing filed. No one is even looking for them."

"I guess they prefer them gone. Or they've got shit to hide and they don't want them talking to the police about it," Postiff said. "We'll follow up with the local police in the cases that do have open files on them. Kyle Christiansen is from Utah. Zephyr Star is from the Bay Area. Anya Atwell is from Tucson."

"And Autumn Lindo and this Zeno kid are just in the wind. No one cares what happens to them. I hate people sometimes, you know?" Barrera said, coughing.

"Are you feeling okay? Maybe you came back to work too soon?" Postiff asked.

"Nah, I'm just tired. This fucking virus does a number on you, but you can't give in. You've got to get back up and in the game."

"Yeah, but did your doctor clear you to come back to work?"

"He did. I tested negative three times, and I had to get out of the house. Gloria has those Netflix Korean shows on all the time," Barrera complained.

"I've never watched them," Postiff said.

"Don't get started. They're addictive, like crack," Barrera warned.

Postiff pulled up the security footage they had obtained from the robberies.

"These perps do look awfully young, just from the size of them. And they all fit the same MO. It's definitely a coordinated effort," he said. "Let's start with the robberies, go back and talk to the residents. A few of them were home when they were hit," Postiff said.

"That's the same neighborhood where that fourth Hit Men victim lives, isn't it? The cute one who survived?" Barrera asked.

"Yeah, Millie Grace," Postiff replied.

"Weren't you going to follow up with her? Dykstra told me you're dating her."

"How would he know? We've gone on four dates," Postiff said with a smile.

"Four dates? So that means you guys have already done the deed . . ."

"Not everyone is an old hippie boomer who believes in free love, Barrera. I happen to be a ten-date guy," Postiff said, heading out.

"I was never a hippie. I listened to Earth, Wind & Fire. And ten dates? What're you, Dudley Do-Right?" Barrera called after him as they left.

Cassidy left work, pulling her MINI Cooper onto Wilcox, heading toward the 101 freeway. Rather than follow her normal route up the Cahuenga Corridor, she hung a right turn toward Gower and the Kidz Clubhouse. The traffic was beginning to build as people arrived to try the newest restaurant or go club-hopping. Cassidy drove slowly, her eyes searching for the spots where kids might hide themselves from the revelers enjoying nightlife as entertainment, not the rough game of risk and survival.

In the spaces between buildings, alleys behind shuttered businesses—those were the places she imagined they might be. She stopped at a light and saw two teenagers scurry across the street and disappear among a crush of trash dumpsters by a strip mall. As she neared the Hollywood Freeway, there were telltale signs of life below the freeway overpasses.

Gone were the big encampments filled with tents, makeshift and discarded furniture, random collections of broken-down bicycles. Now that it was a crime to be unhoused, the homeless had to hide their existence more creatively because the city certainly hadn't made more beds or shelter available. It just wanted them out of the way, not visible in the rapidly gentrifying area of East Hollywood.

She wondered how they slept at night, with one eye open and their senses always in a state of fight or flight, the strain of never being able to fully relax under the threat of very real danger. That existence was impossibly difficult for adults, but for teenagers, it must have felt like a war zone. Carbone and Ramsey had scheduled a visit for her and Riley to the Clubhouse to speak to the kids about the current situation and what signs to watch out for. She had an instinct that there was a puppet master behind the whole enterprise, and petty theft might not be the most dangerous thing they were involved in.

Forty-five minutes later, she pulled up outside the New Life Rehabilitation facility where her best and oldest friend, Kylie Keyes, had resided for the past seven years. A paraplegic after a family shooting, Kylie had been through years of every imaginable therapy to regain her mobility.

A few weeks earlier Kylie had asked her not to come for regular visits any longer. Hurt and confused by the request, Cassidy had nonetheless honored it, although she still had no idea what motivated it. She wholeheartedly rejected her ex-boyfriend's interpretation that Kylie didn't want to be a burden to her any longer. His clueless lack of emotional intelligence was one of the many reasons he'd been unceremoniously dumped. She had to admit, she didn't miss him at all.

But tonight, she would walk into Kylie's room and resume their routine. Returning to work after a break to regroup, she was ready to step back into her life. She entered the main lobby of the facility and signed in. As she made her way down the hallway to Kylie's room, she bumped into Jaretta, Kylie's primary attendant.

"Coming back for a visit?" Jaretta asked.

"Yeah, I think the break is over," Cassidy said with a smile.

Jaretta took her arm and pulled her into the reading room off the main hallway.

"I need to speak to you before you go in. I know you're wondering why she asked you to stop coming so much."

"Yeah, I'm hoping she's over that by now."

"She's trying to find the right way to tell you, and I know she'd be okay with me sharing this. She's considering euthanasia-assisted suicide. She wanted you to start to get used to her not being here," Jaretta said quietly.

Cassidy stared at her, shocked and uncomprehending. Finally, she spoke. "You're kidding, right? I mean, that's a pretty weird joke—"

Jaretta interrupted her. "It's not a joke. She's been talking about it and researching it for the past few months. She asked me to help her . . . and it's been difficult. I'm a Christian, and it goes against my religious beliefs, but I also know how hard it is for her to be trapped in that body that doesn't work properly. She hides it from you, but she's in pain, and it's getting worse. She just sits and watches television all day, and she knows that's no kind of life."

Cassidy suddenly felt nauseous, as if her body were rejecting a toxin. She and Kylie had been best friends since before the accident, as they called it. But it was no accident. Sixteen years earlier, her father, Marvin, had suffered a mental breakdown and murdered his wife and children—only Kylie and her brother Kevin escaped alive, albeit with the physical and emotional scars that would impact their lives forever. When a bullet tore through her brain stem, Kylie lost her ability to walk and lost control over many functions of her body, but this was the first time Cassidy had ever heard even a whisper of what Jaretta was telling her.

"Is her brother encouraging this? Is it about the cost of her care?" Cassidy asked, searching for any explanation other than the truth she didn't want to face.

"No. She just doesn't want to live this way any longer. I want you to know before you go in there to see her, so you're not blindsided. She needs someone to listen and to help her, not to get upset and try to change her mind. She might change it on her own, but she needs support right now."

Cassidy shook her head vehemently, unable to accept what Jaretta was saying.

"How can I support something like this? There are breakthroughs all the time for spinal cord injuries. She's so young!" Cassidy protested.

"I know. I just wanted you to be aware of it."

Cassidy took a deep breath, trying to pull her emotions back. "I'm going to wait to see her for a few days. I have to get my head around this so I don't upset her."

"Good. She won't want to see you upset."

Cassidy left and walked to her car in a daze. Euthanasia-assisted suicide. She never even considered what that decision would be like for a human being; it had been hard enough for her to put their family dog down seven years earlier. She figured Kylie had to be depressed; how could she not be? They needed to get out and engage in more activities together. Kylie had been a talented artist; maybe they could take a painting class or join a group.

But even as she sat in her car, frantically foraging for solutions, she knew that there were no games or classes or special sports that could give Kylie back what she had lost. Cassidy struggled to imagine what it felt like to live every day, trapped in a body that fought back at every single thing you wanted it to do. She had avoided facing that. It was too painful to think of Kylie living that battle and frustration every day. It was easier to stick to the hopes and the possibilities when the reality was crushingly bitter and sad. She would prepare herself and walk into Kylie's room, putting her own feelings aside. She just wasn't sure how long that preparation would take.

When she arrived at home twenty minutes later, she saw her dad's car in the driveway, which meant that he had most likely made another one of his Green Chef meal kit dinners. She could smell something cooking from the driveway and went in to find him wearing an apron that read **Kiss The Cook and Bring Him A Beer**, standing over the CharKing, stainless steel, double-decker grill he had recently purchased.

"Hey, Binkie! I'm making salmon marinated with soy sauce, garlic, and harissa, with a side dish of couscous with white beans and broccoli!" he said.

She smiled, happy that he had fully embraced the changes his doctor suggested since his retirement and that he was describing ingredients he hadn't known existed a few months before. She tossed her duty bag on her bed and took a quick shower before grabbing a beer to meet him outside.

She plunked herself down into an Adirondack chair and asked, "How were the young boxing protégés today?"

"Good. I have a kid who's six foot seven at fifteen years old. He's a giant. And he spars with a kid who's five foot three, maybe a hundred and twenty. But it works."

"Were you able to set the appointments that Dr. Baruch recommended?" she asked.

Bill shook his head. "I've got the letter he sent. It has a whole bunch of tests that I don't think I need. A special PET scan, some kind of neuropsychological testing, and other stuff. I've called to schedule them, but the insurance hasn't approved any yet."

"I'll call them also. You have to get really tough with these fuckers," Cassidy said darkly, taking a swig of her Pacifica.

Bill laughed softly. "Look at you! Binkie's become a badass."

She smiled. "I know you, Dad. You don't want the tests, so you won't push as hard as I will. They're going to meet the angry daughter, and then we'll see what happens."

"How was the first day back at work?"

"It was fine. We're starting an investigation into missing homeless teenagers. Riley and I got flagged down by the lady who runs the Kidz Clubhouse to tell us about a bunch of her kids who've disappeared recently."

"That place has been there for years. The kids take the bus from downtown to that little park shaped like a triangle. That's also where they dropped off the people when Reagan closed the state mental hospitals," he said, flipping a thick salmon steak.

"Wait, they just closed the state mental hospitals and dropped mentally ill people off? With no supervision?" she asked, horrified.

"Yep. Then there were suddenly all these people living on the streets, talking to themselves, no idea how to function. And the runaway kids ended up in the same area."

"I think someone may have taken those kids in and, in exchange, has them doing robberies and car break-ins. Riley and I are talking to some of them tomorrow at the Clubhouse, to tell them to keep an eye out, see if they know anything."

"You know, I might like volunteering there. That place always looked like they were doing good stuff. They kept it nice even when the area went to crap. I know that area like the back of my hand, and I could give them some good advice," Bill said with sudden interest.

"Show up when we do. We're meeting them at eleven a.m. It'd be good for you."

He stirred the white beans and couscous, hesitant for a moment before deciding to take the risk and confide in her.

"And I need your help with my dating profile. I wasn't going to tell you, but I'm not sure what to put in some spots . . ." He shrugged and gave her a crooked smile.

"Oh my god . . ." Cassidy groaned. "You're on a dating site? Which one?"

"A couple. I haven't actually completed the process. I'm just getting ready. My very nice shrink says I should," he said, trying unsuccessfully to cover his embarrassment.

"Please tell me it's not one with young bimbos looking for sugar daddies?"

"Right. Binkie. On my pension and social security, I don't qualify as a sugar daddy. And no one under fifty. I'm not an idiot, you know. You can open my laptop to check it out. I bookmarked the page," he said.

She got up to retrieve his laptop. "Why have you suddenly become so cute for an old man?"

He grinned and flicked his kitchen towel at her; it felt like old times between them. "Just give it the once-over and tell me if it sounds good."

She sauntered to the house, breathing in the smell of the night-blooming jasmine that covered the back fence of their yard. It was so quiet out in Chatsworth, miles away from the freeway. It felt like a different world from the streets near the Hollywood station.

When she returned a few minutes later, Bill asked, "Any updates on Acevedo?"

"Nope. Kriss mentioned it in roll call. Postiff said the last they heard, he had crossed into Mexico and he hasn't come back. They have an Interpol alert with his ID and passport number. He can't stay down there forever."

"Son of a bitch . . ." Bill grumbled. "Just give me five minutes alone with that motherfucker. Just five minutes!"

He was struggling with Eden's death and the way it happened. Cassidy considered telling her dad about Kylie's situation but decided against it. He had beaten himself up for years with wondering if only he had been home that day from work, if he could've stopped Marvin Keyes before he hurt anyone. He said that even now, he couldn't think back on that day without the cold, heart-stopping fear that something could've happened to her. What if Marty hadn't pushed Cassidy out the door when he returned home, bent on the destruction of himself and his family.

Cassidy didn't need to burden him with what Kylie was going through; he was on an even keel these days, getting enough sleep and working out. She would need to come to terms with Kylie's plan all by herself.

Princess climbed out of the big blue Escalade a few blocks from the Clubhouse, near the on-ramp to the 101 freeway. One of her regulars, a firefighter who said his name was Brandon, had cruised her earlier as she walked west on Franklin. She met up with him at least once a week, before he headed home to his wife and kids in Woodland Hills. He was nice enough, never wanted super weird stuff, other than her calling him "daddy" and keeping her retainer in when they did it. And he had a really big car, which made things easier. But he wasn't a trick that she could spend the whole night with, in a motel, like some of the others. She needed to find a place to stay, or she'd have to get her backpack and tent from the Clubhouse storage locker. She hurried, knowing the doors would soon be locked.

She heard Aiden's car before she saw it; she knew the knocking sound his old Camry made. He pulled up alongside her and got out, blocking the sidewalk.

"Why're you avoiding me, Princess Pea?" he asked with a smile, but his eyes were hard and angry.

"Like you don't know," she said, trying to figure out a way to get around him and move on.

"I said I was sorry. You can't be doing that well out here without me," he said.

"I'm doing fine," she said, watching the cars that whizzed by, not paying any attention.

"Really? Who's helping you when those jerks don't want to pay?" he insisted, stepping closer to her as she stepped back.

"I'm not getting back with you. You dislocated my shoulder and handcuffed me inside your apartment like a fucking prisoner!" she shouted, hoping to attract the attention of a group of people approaching. It worked; two of the guys in that group noticed and walked toward them.

"Are you okay, miss?" one of them asked. He was in his late twenties. His friend looked older.

"No, this guy isn't letting me pass to go home," she said as Aiden backed up.

"I'm her boyfriend, okay? We just had an argument, it's none of your business," Aiden said, trying to play it off, but the older guys weren't fooled.

"Why don't you let her go on her way? Or we can call the police," the older guy said, making it clear he wasn't leaving until Princess did.

"Whatever. Do what you want, baby," Aiden said, getting back into his car. "I'll be seeing you around."

He gunned the engine in macho frustration and drove away. The twentysomething turned to Princess and asked, "What are you up to? Want to go hang with us? Ever been to Dray's?"

She smiled; she knew Dray's well. She always made good money when they had her there, and she'd probably be able to stay in the fancy back room all night, with free food and drinks.

"Sure. Let's go," she said, slipping her slender arm through his.

Two blocks away, Evie pushed the door to the Clubhouse open, just minutes before it was closed and locked for the night. Melinda or her staff stayed on the premises and would open it if someone needed to come in, but they could no longer leave the Clubhouse front doors open after dark. The place had been burglarized too many times, and mentally unstable street people came in and caused problems.

Evie had not had any luck in tracking down Layla or any information about her. She'd gone to the Goldwyn library right there in Hollywood and even taken the bus to the one in Los Feliz because Layla spent most days there. They used to go together; Evie would lose herself in art books, and Layla would read novels. Evie had hoped to talk to the librarian in Los Feliz, but she was out on maternity leave. After signing in at the Clubhouse, Evie took her backpack to the small dormitory room and sat on one of the beds.

Evie knew the other kids there, like Pebble Smith, who always tried to spend the night since she was so small she looked younger than sixteen. If she slept out and was seen by some do-gooder, they'd call the police, thinking she was a preteen. And if she ran into a different type of creep, they'd think the same thing but with bad intentions.

The other kids were Steve Trejo, who wanted to be a singer; Dominique, who only used one name and was going to be a game show contestant; and Nelson Simmoge, who had no plans as long as he didn't have to go back to a group home in Seattle. They were all buried in their phones and simply nodded to her in greeting.

Evie put her dirty clothes into a grocery bag that was almost full; she'd have to hit the Splash and Suds tomorrow if she could find the cash for the washer and the box of soap. She usually skipped the dryer and hung her stuff up on a fence or a pallet to dry. She took a quick shower and grabbed a clean towel from the pile by the door. It felt good to have a shower and not a baby-wipe cleanup like she did most days. Once she turned eighteen, she'd be able to get a real job and join a gym so she could shower every day. She plugged her phone into one of the outlets and climbed under the mismatched sheets.

From the open second-story window, she could hear the street below, cars honking and the jingle of voices laughing, yelling, fighting. A siren whined somewhere in the distance. It felt good to be inside a locked building, but she couldn't stop imagining the worst possible scenarios about Layla. It was a habit now. It was what she expected. So many had already come true for her.

Jeppe drove past the Kidz Clubhouse, hoping he'd find something pretty out on the streets, in need of shelter for the night. He'd considered going to Dray's to see who they might have on the menu, but the parking was a nightmare, and he didn't want to deal with it. Plus, he'd have to buy at least two drinks, and the monthly deposit from his parents into his bank account was running low.

He could easily text them to send more, but he didn't want to engage with them for a few days. Last time they'd spoken, his mother, Linnea, had asked too many questions, and he sensed that she might know something was wrong. He'd gotten a call from his academic adviser at USC regarding his absences. He'd have to deal with that in the next few days.

It exasperated him, having to manage such pointless things in life. He didn't want to get a PhD. He didn't want to be an academic like his parents. He didn't know how he'd ever do that with the voices in his head so often these days. Even now, driving the streets, they were like a constant, electrical hum in his ears.

Something sour, something sweet, give me something good to eat!

Ding dong bell, the pussy's in the well, who put her in, Little Jeppe Lind!

He shook his head and gripped the steering wheel tighter. He hated it when the voices toyed with nursery rhymes. They were mocking him, testing him. Challenging to see if he was an effective fisher of men, like Jesus, bringing lost souls home to safety. And the rhyme about the pussy in the well? It was the old man's voice, the gravelly rumble that was always thick with judgment and accusation. How was Jeppe to know that the freezer in the shed had stopped working? He didn't go out there every day to check on Layla's body, wrapped tightly in heavy trash bags. The Raven's Nest was so old, it had a dried-up well at the back of the property. Cool and dark, it was a good place to store things that needed to be kept hidden. It would do for a day or two.

But he already had plans to do away with any sign of his beautiful, perfidious Layla.

CHAPTER SEVEN

The morning sun was beginning its slow burn through the marine layer as Postiff and Barrera stood in the cramped kitchen of a middle-aged man named Spencer Ogilvie. He lived in a small bungalow from the forties on Serrano Avenue. He'd been robbed by two young men who entered and threatened him but, ultimately, just took the easily available cash and what they could carry in their pockets.

"I was surprised when I saw them. I thought they'd be older. They looked like kids, made a lot of noise to intimidate me once they were in. They sounded like they've watched too many of those reality cop shows. They must be casing the area. Everyone they've hit has been older and lived alone or with one other person. They haven't robbed the apartments or houses with multiple residents. Just FYI, I pay attention to those types of details," Ogilvie said.

"Thank you, Mr. Ogilvie," Postiff said. "What would you say the total value is of what they took?"

"Not much, maybe three or four hundred dollars."

"How were they dressed? What I mean is, did their clothes look scruffy or raggedy?" Barrera asked.

"Now that you mention it, their clothes looked kind of new. Not fancy but like thick hoodies, the kind that hadn't been washed a bunch of times. And their shoes were definitely new. What do you think that means?" Ogilvie asked.

"We're just putting together some similarities in the crimes. We'll be in touch if we need any more information or if we get a lead on your personal property," Postiff said.

Once they were back in the car, Barrera said, "They aren't taking anything of high value. Every place we've been had more expensive stuff that they left behind."

"Yeah, it's like the whole thing is about something else. Weird, especially if some predatory type has put them up to it. And the new clothes and shoes . . . If the kids we saw on video today are from the Clubhouse list, then someone is buying them new stuff. Maybe it's some kind of initiation?" Postiff mused.

"Or maybe the guy is starting small, building up to more serious stuff," Barrera suggested.

"Let's check security camera footage on major cross streets to see where they went. In each case, they take off on foot, but they've got to have some kind of transportation ready. They didn't walk around the neighborhood with bags of stolen shit," Postiff said.

"Right, where'd they go?"

Cassidy and Riley had been on patrol for a few hours when they pulled up to the Kidz Clubhouse for their scheduled meeting. A local news crew was already set up, and Joyce Ramsey was there, ready to be interviewed on air. Melinda Drake had called as many kids as she could and told them to spread the word. Now a group of about fifteen teenagers was assembled in the community room. Cassidy's first thought was how young they all looked, even the ones with a noticeably hardened attitude. They were intrigued by the news cameras, jockeying for positions to be seen. The reporter, Jen Liu, began interviewing Ramsey.

"Commander Joyce Ramsey is here at the Kidz Clubhouse in Hollywood, where there is concern about missing teens being tied to the string of burglaries that have taken place in the area," Liu said. "What have the police learned so far, commander?"

"Well, Jenny, we don't want to jump to conclusions, but the main concern is what is happening to these young people in our community. Being homeless is not a crime, and we are committed to finding these missing youth."

"Do the police suspect foul play?" Liu asked.

"We hope not, but we have to get to the bottom of it. The director of the Kidz Clubhouse called our Hollywood station with her concerns, and we immediately put detectives and patrol officers on it," Ramsey replied, deftly avoiding any mention of a link to the recent spate of robberies. This exercise was meant to boost her compassion quotient in the eyes of the public, and for that, the missing teens needed to be innocent victims.

After several more banal, self-serving questions and answers, the crew moved inside but avoided filming the faces of any minors, which was against the law. Melinda introduced them to Cassidy and Riley.

"Officers Clarke and Riley are here to talk to you about possible dangerous activity on the street. As you know, some of our people have gone missing, and while there's an open-door policy here, I think we need to pay attention."

Riley took the lead. "Ms. Drake gave us the names of some kids who've stopped coming regularly, and she's concerned. We thought maybe you could tell us what you think? It appears that some of the kids who have stopped showing up are involved in a string of robberies in the area."

"We're worried that someone who is a predator may have lured them into a living situation that might be dangerous and could be manipulating them to commit these crimes," Cassidy said. "And since they haven't taken anything of significant value, it's a concern that this could be leading up to more serious crimes."

At that moment, Bill stepped in, drawing the attention of the kids, who regarded him with suspicion until Cassidy said, "He's okay. This is my dad, Bill Clarke. He was a homicide detective who just retired."

This stirred the kids' attention, and Clyde asked, "Are you like Benson and Stabler on *Law & Order*?"

Bill laughed. "I wish I had a partner like her. My partner was a fat guy named Pete. But yeah, we investigated murders."

"That's cool," Clyde said with an approving nod.

A small girl with a childlike, round face raised her hand to speak.

"Do you think someone is like the Pied Piper, but he's getting them to steal stuff?"

"Exactly, Pebble," Miranda said.

"We want you to be extra careful out there. If someone approaches you, offers you a place to stay, or wants to buy you food, think twice. And we also wanted to know, has anybody been coming around the areas where you hang out? Maybe a new face? Someone who's a little too interested?" Cassidy said.

Dominique laughed. "There's plenty of assholes out here who are *too interested* in a lot of us. The one you should ask about that is Princess, but she's not here."

"Where could we find her?" Riley asked.

The kids exchanged knowing looks, and Clyde said, "Right now, she might be up at Marjorie's place. It's up near where the dam is, where the water company has their station."

"Who's Marjorie?" Cassidy asked, taking notes with her phone.

"She's an old lady who lets us stay at her place if we do jobs around her house or help with her dogs. She's got a lot of dogs. Princess goes there when she's done working sometimes," Pebble said.

"Where does Princess work? Maybe we can talk to her later?" Cassidy asked.

The kids tittered, then a girl with spiky, two-tone hair named Joannie Valdez said, "She works on Western and Santa Monica, or Argyle and Yucca, wherever there's money to be made."

"I see," Riley said.

"There's been a few new people lately, like Little Leo or the Banana Van guy," Clyde said.

Melinda was taking notes, too, and asked, "Who's Little Leo? Have I met him?"

"He's not a kid, and he's not on the street. We call him Little Leo 'cause he looks like the guy from *Titanic*," Pebble said.

"Yeah, but younger. I think he was hanging out with Layla," a slight, Latino boy named Steve Trejo added. At the mention of Layla, Evie perked up.

"Was that her boyfriend? The guy she went to live with?" Evie asked.

"I think so. I saw her in a car with him a few weeks ago," Steve said. "But I haven't seen her since then."

"She said she was coming back, and I was supposed to meet her. She called and then she disappeared," Evie said.

"And the Banana Van guy?" Cassidy asked.

"He drives a yellow van that has banana decals in the back doors. Like maybe it was a fruit van at some point or something. He's always offering us rides, or he'll buy lunch, but he's weird. The back of the van is empty, it just has an air mattress," said Steve.

"Do you guys have any thoughts on Aiden Howe? Melinda mentioned him to us," Riley said.

"He's a dirtbag. But he's all over Princess like cat hair," Dominique said with disgust.

"He's got a little shitty apartment over on Argyle. He's just into working the girls. I don't think he even has room for a bunch of kids at his place, and no one who knows him like we do would go stay there. I mean, he handcuffed Princess and wouldn't let her out!" Clyde explained.

"Maybe you guys could write down for us the names of people in the neighborhood like Marjorie so we can go talk to them. And any details about people like Little Leo, what kind of car he drives, what time of day he comes around. That type of stuff," Cassidy said as Melinda handed out pads of paper and pens.

The camera crew withdrew, frustrated that they were not able to film the faces of the kids. Riley overheard them complaining to Ramsey, who suggested they do a more in-depth interview with her outside.

While the kids were writing, Melinda approached Bill. "Hello, I'm the director of services here. You're Officer Clarke's father?"

"Yes. Bill Clarke. I came by 'cause I was thinking maybe I'd do some volunteering here. I worked the Hollywood area for years."

"That would be great. We always need help, and we don't get that many men," Melinda said.

Cassidy and Riley moved among the kids, handing out cards with their contact information. Evie eyed them warily, turning the card over in her hands.

"We'll go through the information you've given us and follow up with the people you suggested. We'll be checking in regularly with Melinda and dropping by. And you'll be seeing more of a police presence on the streets. But be careful, especially with people who are new to the area, any unfamiliar faces," Cassidy said.

She and Riley left while Bill hung in the doorway, waiting for Melinda, who was preparing a pile of papers for him.

"These will explain the history of the Clubhouse and our mission. It has information about the services we offer. And there's a volunteer form in there as well. You'll need to be live scanned to work with the kids," she said.

"I volunteer at a youth boxing gym, and they live scanned me a few months ago. But I know I have to do a separate one, so I'll get that done today," he replied.

As Bill leafed through the papers, he became aware of someone standing next to him. It was the petite girl with the short brown hair and freckles.

"Can I help you, miss?" he asked.

"Maybe," she said. "I'm Evie Peacock. You used to be a detective?"

"Yes, and now I'm a private investigator."

"For real? Maybe I can hire you," she said.

"For what?" he asked.

"I don't want to talk about it here. Maybe we can go to the House of Pies?" she suggested.

Bill bit back an amused smile. "The House of Pies? On Vermont?"

"Yeah. I can buy my own pie; I got some money today for running an errand. But we can talk there," Evie said.

"Okay, you want a ride? You don't have to worry about me, I'm not a creep or anything," he said.

"Yeah, a ride would be good."

"Then let's go," he said.

Evie Peacock walked next to him, a large backpack on her slim shoulders and a stuffed duffel bag worn cross body. Bill reached for the backpack.

"Let me carry that, Miss Peacock. You've got your hands full."

"I can manage it," she said but didn't resist when he took it from her and slung it over his arm. "How long have you been a private investigator?"

"One day," Bill said. "But I was a cop for over forty years."

She gave him the side-eye. "One day, huh? So, I'm your first client?"

"Yeah, you are."

Evie nodded, and she climbed into his SUV. "Cool," she said, and nothing more.

The guard at the border crossing at San Ysidro looked at the passport that the driver of a silver Hyundai handed him. It read Roberto Lopez, and the photo more or less matched the guy behind the wheel. But he thought all Mexicans looked the same, so he couldn't really tell. The guy had dark-olive skin and some scars that weren't visible in the passport photo, but things happen. Nothing came up when he scanned it; Roberto Lopez had no criminal record.

"Could you show me your vehicle registration, sir?" he asked.

The driver nodded but didn't speak as he handed over the registration, which matched his passport information.

The guard handed back the passport and the paperwork. "Thank you, sir. Welcome back to the United States."

Ethan Acevedo nodded and slipped on a pair of sunglasses. He drove through the checkpoint and into California. He'd been in Mexico for almost two months, recovering in a clinic outside of Ensenada, where no one asked any questions when he showed up, beaten and bloodied, in the back of a flatbed truck. A man fishing in Rosarito had found him in the shallows of the water and put him on the truck, assuming he was a victim of cartel retribution. The fisherman didn't leave his name and didn't ask Acevedo's. He just dropped him off at the door to the clinic and drove away.

Acevedo had had his ribs taped and a cast on his left tibia, which had now been replaced with a metal brace. His right shoulder and arm were broken, still in a sling, but he slipped it off as he approached the border guards. One of his eyes would always droop, and he'd had several of his teeth knocked out, but he had a new bridge to replace them. The bruises had faded from deep purple to yellow, and a few would remain discolored for life. He was lucky to be alive.

After being left for dead by the men who attacked him on the beach, he'd lain in the shallow surf overnight, his head and his body throbbing with pain. He went in and out of consciousness and realized later that he could've drowned. He rented a room in the house of a lady near La Bufadora, a former convent that she'd turned into a cash-only boarding house for people who didn't want to be found. Deadbeat dads running out on child support payments, local drug runners who'd gotten on the wrong side of someone. And the occasional *tourista* who just wanted a cheap place to stay so he could hit all the hooker bars in the area and not leave a paper trail.

It was the landlady, Doña Ilda, who alerted him that Roberto Lopez, the guy from Borrego Springs who rented room six, hadn't been back in several days after leaving to visit the Paris de Noche strip club. He'd left his passport as well as his car and keys, which Acevedo took possession of to make an easy crossing into San Diego. He'd get back to Los Angeles, ditch the car, and go underground. He'd get his parents to give him money, and he had a couple of loyal cops who might help him out, the ones who'd done some compromising shit over the years that could cost them their jobs or their families. Or both. He always had his own special kind of insurance for times like these. It felt good to be back. He had some scores to settle.

CHAPTER EIGHT

Cassidy and Riley stood outside a big Spanish-style house perched at an angle on the hillside just below the Mulholland Dam.

"I'd hate to be in this place if the dam ever burst, like in a big earthquake," Riley said.

"If it burst suddenly, you wouldn't even know what hit you. This looks like one of the original houses when this neighborhood was established," Cassidy said.

"I think this one was the look-alike brothel, like in *LA Confidential*. I have a book at the station that has all this Hollywood history," Riley said.

"That was a real place? With prostitutes that looked like movie stars?"

"Yeah. It was very big back in the day. There were a bunch of them, and the big movie studios funded them. I have a book about the golden days of Hollywood and this area. Back then, there was nothing near this house. It was way up here, all by itself."

Cassidy looked up at the big house; it was a far cry from what it must've been in its golden era. Run down, with a sagging balcony on the second floor and window awnings that were faded and torn from the weather. Huge bougainvillea and plumbago covered the front of the house, partially blocking the walkway and stairs to the front door. A mud-brown GMC Jimmy with two flat tires was parked in the driveway of a two-car garage.

Cassidy followed Riley up the stairs, pushing the thorny bougainvillea branches aside to knock on the door. They were about to leave, then it was opened by a woman in her late seventies, wearing platinum clip-in hair pieces that made her head look like a fountain. She wore full glamour makeup and held a live pigeon in her hand. The bird was relaxed, clearly a pet.

"Yes, can I help you officers?" she asked with a perfect mid-Atlantic accent.

"Are you Marjorie Mellencamp?" Cassidy asked.

"Yes, no relation to the pretentious, aging rock star from the Midwest. What can I do for you?"

"We're following up with some names from a group of homeless youth who frequent the Kidz Clubhouse. A number of them have gone missing, so we're checking out the places and people that they associate with," Riley said.

"Oh, the youngsters. Yes, they come here from time to time, to visit, to eat, or to pick up odd jobs. Please, come in," she said, stepping aside and letting them pass as a pack of small dogs descended on them from upstairs. They yipped and sniffed, circling Cassidy and Riley, who moved carefully to avoid stepping on them.

"I have a rescue license, and I have a foundation. I'm not breaking any laws by having too many dogs over the legal limit," Marjorie said.

Cassidy was tempted to ask how many dogs Marjorie rehomed but decided against it since it was clear that any dog who arrived never left. And there was no good reason to razz an eccentric elderly woman with fountain hair.

Inside, the house was crammed with all manner of items: unopened bedding sets, newspapers and magazines, boxes of gold-painted plaster cherubs. A thick layer of dust covered most surfaces. It was a hoarder's heaven. On the walls, old, framed photos of a beautiful blond starlet hung next to fading magazine covers featuring the same girl. On a vintage 1968 cover of *Life* magazine, the blond girl stood by the shore in a lemon-yellow dress, the lead line read California Dreaming with television starlet, Marjorie Mellencamp.

"These are lovely photographs, Ms. Mellencamp. I didn't realize you were an actress," Cassidy said.

"No one does any longer. Memories are short and life is long. What is it you want to know about the youngsters?"

"We heard that some of them come here to work or hang out. How often do they visit?" Riley asked.

Marjorie set the bird down on an antique secretary, where it perched happily.

"I don't know. They're here every week, different ones. Some steal, so you have to be careful. There's Clyde and Steve, they're good at picking up the things that are too heavy for me. And the little ones, Pebble and Evie, they help me go through boxes. I have so much to get rid of, you know? I'm planning a party, a big one for my eightieth, and I need the place in ship-shape condition."

"How about Princess? We heard she comes here to sleep sometimes?" Cassidy asked.

Marjorie's face fell at the mention of Princess.

"That little girl should be home with someone who can take care of her. She's out there on the streets all the time. There are so many predators, whether they're in a run-down van on Hollywood Boulevard or an expensive suit at a studio party. They're all the same . . ." Her voice trailed off.

"From what the kids said, I gather that Princess is engaged in sex work?" Cassidy asked carefully.

"How are they going to survive out here? They've come from small towns or cities, with a stupid idea that this is the place where dreams are made. It's the Sodom and Gomorrah where dreams die, but they don't know that until it's too late. Princess does come here sometimes to sleep and shower. She's on her own these days, and it's very dangerous out there."

"We heard about a young guy named Aiden Howe," Riley prodded.

"Yes, he's a young thug who tries to turn all the girls out. But she said she left him. I help them out when I can. I pay them for odd jobs, and some of them come regularly to walk the dogs for me."

"Do you know where Aiden lives? We heard he has an apartment nearby," Cassidy asked.

"Not the exact address, no. Princess used to stay with him. Her real name isn't Princess, it's Charmaine Mendoza. She's from somewhere near Bakersfield. Horrible family."

"Is it just you here in the house?" Riley asked.

"Yes. I rarely go out; I have most everything sent in. I withdrew from the world years ago. I just stay here with the dogs. The youngsters know they can come here if they need to. Someone must help them. I'll show you around, I have nothing to hide," she said with a dramatic flair.

Marjorie led them into the kitchen that had huge casement windows that looked out over a weed-filled yard. Piles of unwashed plates were stacked on the counter and in the sink. Jumbo packs of Top Ramen and family-size boxes of Frosted Flakes filled cupboards that were missing doors. It was squalid, dirty, and disorganized.

"I don't know how I've ended up with so much stuff . . ." Marjorie said as they stepped over piles of clothing, unopened housewares, and plates of half-eaten, rancid dog food. They climbed a grand staircase with a carved banister to the second story. The floor was covered with threadbare carpeting that smelled of dog urine. Marjorie led them along the hallway, pointing out the different rooms.

"My master suite is here, and these are the extra bedrooms that the youngsters use sometimes," she said, holding a door open to a bedroom that had several thin mattresses on the floor, with piles of sheets and blankets strewn haphazardly across them. A second bedroom was outfitted the same way. The other rooms were in disarray, filled with every kind of imaginable junk. Cassidy and Riley took it all in without comment.

"The only time I go out is after dark. Occasionally I like to drive through the streets late at night, when the infernal traffic has died down. I love to drive through the park up by the observatory," she said, referring to nearby Griffith Park.

"I noticed that your car has two flat tires," Cassidy said.

"Oh, you mean my Jimmy. That's my work truck. My driving car is in the garage. It's a white 1955 Thunderbird. It's my baby. Do you think I should get the youngsters to clean up the yard? I plan to have a gazebo and a small orchestra out there for my party, some small tables with candles, very elegant . . ."

Cassidy and Riley exchanged a glance; it was clear that Marjorie Mellencamp was out of touch with the reality of her life. Her dilapidated house was a safe haven for the street kids in the barest sense. She followed them to the front door and gave each of them a dusty bag of Cracker Jack.

"I'll keep my eyes and ears open, and I'll contact you if something comes up," she said with a smile.

Back in the patrol car, they sat for a moment to take in the exterior condition of the house, now that they had been inside and seen the state of Marjorie's life. The backyard was completely overgrown, and the ruins of a wooden shed stood crumbling in a corner. They could see a tall concrete statue of Venus de Milo covered with a climbing vine.

"This must've been quite the place when she first bought it," Riley said.

"It's kind of sad to think of her rambling around in all that junk. And it's so dirty and unhygienic with all those pets."

"We could call animal control and elder protective services," Riley suggested.

"We could. But maybe that junk and the pets are all she has now. Let's wait on that, okay? Do you think she'd be capable of organizing a bunch of kids to commit robberies?" Cassidy asked.

"No way. I'd like to find this girl, Princess. She sounds like she needs help."

"Yeah, I'd like to find Aiden or at least know what kind of car he drives. Let's visit the other places on the list. There's Cesar's Auto Repair, Los Donuts, and Argyle Storage," Cassidy said.

The radio crackled with a robbery taking place on Edgemont off Los Feliz Boulevard, a few blocks away. Cassidy and Riley responded and hung a U-turn, their reds and blues flashing, the siren blasting as they raced through traffic to the call.

Bill and Evie sat at a booth in the House of Pies restaurant on the busy corner of Vermont and Franklin. The place was half empty. The lunch crowd had not yet arrived for mediocre coffee shop food, followed by their signature slices of pie, heaping with fruit or whipped cream. The decor had not changed in years—sterile, vintage-style tables and booths; a wide glass display case of the day's pies; and waitresses who wore old-fashioned corsage-style name tags.

Evie ate a coffee shop staple, spaghetti with chili and beans, digging her fork into it with gastronomic gusto. Bill ordered a grilled cheese sandwich, thin and greasy with bright-orange processed cheese, a sad sprig of parsley, and a curled carrot ribbon on the side.

"This stuff hasn't changed since I was a kid," Bill said. "They still give you this useless piece of carrot that tastes like the refrigerator."

Evie smiled fleetingly, then her face settled back into what had become its default expression: a tight, wary scowl meant to deter any unwanted attention or engagement. A police car roared by, hanging a turn onto Los Feliz Boulevard.

"So, what's this job you want to hire me for?" Bill asked.

"To find my friend, Layla. She's missing."

"Is she on the list that Ms. Drake gave to the officers?"

"Yes, Melinda added her to it. But I don't think they're going to do anything. I spoke to her the day before yesterday. She was coming back and said she had stuff to show me about some bad shit going on at the place she was staying, and she sounded weird. Then I think she dropped the phone and went silent. And when I got there, she wasn't there—"

"Okay, slow this way down. That's a lot of information you just gave me with no backstory or context. Explain this from the start, like I'm a five-year-old. Slow and simple," Bill said, taking notes on a pad of paper. "First, what is her full name and age?"

"Layla Waters, she's nineteen. She's been living on the street for four years. She's from some place in Nevada, but not Las Vegas."

"Right. And where was she coming back from?"

Evie explained how Layla had gone to live at her new boyfriend's place, and their strange phone call the night of the storm. How she'd taken the bus and found the alley empty.

"Okay. And you don't know the boyfriend? Is he the guy they were talking about at the Clubhouse? Little Leo?"

Evie nodded. "I think so. He's from another country, that's what Layla said. He has a house out in Atwater, I think. She said that other kids lived there, and when she went, I thought maybe I could go, too, but that . . . didn't work out," she said, suddenly getting very interested in opening the plastic wrapper of the crackers that came with her spaghetti and chili.

Bill watched her struggle with the wrapper and try to hide the pain and disappointment that he knew were probably her constant companions living on the street. When her eyes began to water, he looked away to spare her any embarrassment.

"But you said she left his place and was coming back?" he asked when she regained her composure.

"Yeah, she said there was bad shit going on there, and we had to tell someone. And then she disappeared. I can show you the alley where I went to meet her," she said.

"Finish up the pie first," he said as the waitress set down a big slice of banana cream pie.

"What's your fee?" Evie asked abruptly.

"We can discuss that later."

"I'll have to pay you in installments, like layaway."

Before he could protest, she dug into her fanny pack and pulled out a folded ten-dollar bill, sliding it across the table to him.

"This is my down payment for your services," she said.

He slid the bill back to her. "Keep it for now. You can pay me when I get some results."

She slid the money back again and said, "My dad always said to pay my own way, so I could keep my independence and not owe anyone anything."

Bill nodded, took the money, and put it into his wallet, realizing it represented a small, remaining shred of her pride. "Smart guy, your dad. Where is he now?"

"He's dead. Three years ago, on May twenty-fifth. That's why I'm out here." She cracked a bitter smile before taking a forkful of pie.

Bill nodded. "And your mom?"

"Gone with the wind, like that old movie. No family, no money, nowhere to go. Don't ask about foster care, been there. Didn't work. I'm just about eighteen, so I'm basically an adult," she said, scraping the plate clean. "You ready to go?"

CHAPTER NINE

Cassidy and Riley stood in the high-ceilinged living room of a mid-century modern home in Los Feliz. It was furnished in the minimalist style, all neutral tones; it looked like the lobby of a West Hollywood hotel. On the bookshelves, several gold Emmy statues were displayed as well as glossy posters advertising several top-rated television series. The homeowner, Jason Weizman, was tall and skinny, wearing jeans and a form-fitting black sweater, with plush slippers on his feet.

"I was in my office upstairs and I heard a noise, so I came down, and one of them was here, going through the sideboard. I shouted and she turned, kind of freaked out, and she called out to the other one who was in the den. Then she came out with a bag of stuff, and then they both ran out the slider," Weizman said, shaken up.

"Both of them are females?" Riley asked. "About what age?"

"Yeah, definitely both girls, which is kind of weird, right?" Weizman replied, shifting his weight from foot to foot.

"How old did they appear?" Cassidy asked.

"Young, like maybe teenagers. I'd never seen them before. They aren't kids on the block or anything."

"Description?" Riley asked.

Weizman ran his hand over his face, thinking. "The one that I caught going through the sideboard was tiny. Like, really petite, with blond hair. Not long, she wore a ball cap, and it stuck out a little bit. The other one was about average, maybe five foot four. I think she had darker hair in kind of a scrunched-up bun on her head. They both wore hoodies."

"Do you have security footage?" Cassidy asked.

"Normally yeah, but I'm getting a new system that's wireless 'cause these are shit. I only keep them up for show right now," Weizman replied with an embarrassed smile.

"And what did they take?" Riley asked.

"From the den, she took a bag of stuff. I haven't really looked in there to see what's missing. The drawers were open; I had some expensive cameras and lenses and stuff. I'm a television director. And the blond one took about twenty-five hundred in cash that I had in the sideboard. And a gun."

Cassidy and Riley exchanged a glance. A gun complicated the situation significantly.

"Is it registered to you?" Cassidy asked.

"Yeah, everything is on the up-and-up. I bought it out in North Hollywood, got the permit, did the background check. Smith and Wesson .38 revolver. Five shot. It's got a special green grip on the handle. So, I guess I have to report it as stolen, right?"

"We'll include that in our police report, and yes, it has to be reported in case it is used in a crime," Cassidy said.

"Oh, man! That's fucked up! I mean, like I could get in trouble? I'm the victim here!" Weizman protested.

"If it's reported as stolen, there shouldn't be any problems. We'll check back with you, and two detectives are looking into these cases, so they will contact you as well," Riley said.

As they walked toward their police car, Weizman double-checked the drawer of the sideboard. The cash and the gun were gone, and so was a stash of heroin that he had neglected to mention to the cops. It was for his personal use and to sell when he needed extra money. And something else was bothering him. He thought he'd seen the little blond girl before, but he couldn't remember where.

Bill and Evie walked the alley behind Home Depot, where Layla had disappeared from. It was filled with newly discarded trash and packing materials.

"It wasn't this crowded with trash when I was here. Layla said she was in this alley. She stopped talking, but the phone was still connected. I thought I heard her speak, and then the phone went dead. I got here about fifteen minutes later, and she was gone," Evie explained.

"And that was the night of the storm? Are you sure she was ever really here?" Bill asked.

Evie pulled the griffin bracelet from her fanny pack. "I found this. It's hers, she never takes it off."

"And her phone was gone too? Can you give me the number?" Bill asked.

Evie took his phone and entered Layla's number. A moment later, he dialed the number. He signaled Evie and they both waited for an answer. It rang five times before disconnecting, and when he tried again, the call went straight to voicemail.

"It looks like maybe someone turned it off after it rang," Bill said.

"The same thing happened to me the night I couldn't find Layla. You think someone has it? Whoever has Layla?" Evie asked.

"Maybe. I'll be passing all of this on to my daughter and the detectives on this case, because they'll be able to get information that I can't get as a civilian."

"Like what?"

"Phone records, to see what numbers she called, stuff like that."

"But they're doing a lot of other stuff, and you're going to focus on Layla, right?"

"Yes, I am. Because you are my first and only client right now," Bill reassured her.

"So, what do we do now?" Evie asked.

"I've got the list of places you gave me that Layla used to hang out, so I'm going to visit those and talk to whoever may have dealt with her. I'm going to run a background check on her to see if I can locate her family to gain more insight into her life. I'll check back with Melinda at the Clubhouse and with my daughter, who's working these cases."

"Okay, let's go!" Evie said.

"No. I work alone, not with an assistant. You should be . . . in school or something, right?"

Evie looked at him with teenage contempt. "I'm a dropout, bruh. I quit school when I came out here. You can do it at sixteen."

"You said you've been here two years, right? And you're seventeen now, so you were fifteen?" Bill pushed back.

"Whatever," she grumbled. Her phone pinged. She checked it and smiled.

"Good news?" Bill asked.

"Kind of. It's from my friend Princess. She sent me a photo of the license plate of the guy who just picked her up. So, I know she's safe. It's the Banana Van guy."

"The one who's doing sex work? The kids at the Clubhouse talked about her."

"It sounds really bad when you say it like that. But yeah. She has clients who pay for her time."

"Can you send me a photo of her and the license plate of the Banana Van guy? Just so I keep an eye out for her?" Bill asked.

"Sure, but you're not going to bust her or anything, are you?" Evie asked warily.

"No way. And I'm not a cop any longer, remember? So, what're you going to do now?" he asked.

"I'll go make some money doing errands and coffee runs for the guys at Cesar's Auto. And maybe the storage place will let me sweep up for some cash. I might walk the dogs for Marjorie. She pays twenty bucks if you take all of them. I have resources, you know."

"And Marjorie's the lady you mentioned at the Clubhouse?"

"Yeah, she's old and kind of crazy. Her house is a total mess, and if you spend the night there, sometimes she wakes you up at like three a.m. to clean out a closet or watch an old movie. But walking the dogs is cool," Evie said.

Bill nodded, trying to wrap his head around the fact that Evie's schedule consisted of scraping together money for one day's survival on the street.

He took some photos of the alley and said, "You want a ride?"

"Sure, drop me at Cesar's Auto."

They got into his SUV and headed east on Franklin. As they approached Argyle, Bill saw a faded sign that read Cesar's Auto Repair and pulled into the driveway. Evie jumped out with her backpack and duffel bag as Cesar, a compact Latino man in an impeccable mechanic's jumpsuit, walked out to greet her. Bill noticed that the legs of Cesar's uniform were creased to perfection, his hair slicked back neatly with gel. Bill left the car idling as he stepped out, not knowing exactly why but feeling the need to let them know that he was there.

Cesar eyed him suspiciously as Evie said, "This is my friend, Bill."

Cesar did not shake Bill's extended hand and instead asked, "What're you doing with Evie? How do you know her?"

"It's cool, Cesar. He's a retired cop," Evie explained.

"So what? Being a cop doesn't always make him a good guy," Cesar said, never taking his eyes off Bill, who stood a good seven inches taller than he did.

"I was a detective, now I'm a private investigator, and I'm helping Evie look for Layla Waters. My daughter is a cop. You may have talked to her in the past day? She's looking into some of the missing kids, like Layla," Bill said.

"Your daughter, does she have reddish hair, and her partner is a tall guy, dark hair? He looks like a tree?" Cesar asked.

"She has reddish hair, and her name is Cassidy Clarke. And yeah, her partner Sean Riley does kind of look like a tree."

Cesar nodded and relaxed his protective stance as Evie went into the small office to drop off her bags.

"It's good you guys are looking for those kids. It's odd the way they just went away. But we look out for Evie. She's one of the special ones, so if you're helping her, I hope you find Layla. Because Evie won't make it without her."

Bill got back into his car to leave but somehow found himself circling the block and adjacent streets several times. He passed by Cesar's Auto to see what Evie was up to. He tailed her as she hurried up Franklin Avenue to do a run to the Coffee Bean and Tea Leaf. He finally decided to leave and drop by the Kidz Clubhouse again to see if Melinda could give him any more information on Layla Waters.

When he stepped inside, he saw that Melinda and another staff member were helping several kids fill out online forms and log information into a screen on one of the beat-up computers. Melinda moved to greet him.

"We're helping them get signed up for EBT benefits. How did it go with Evie Peacock?" she asked.

"Fine. She wants me to help her find Layla Waters, so I figured I'd ask you for any other pertinent information."

She led him into her office, where she had several large trash bags piled up by the door. "Layla was the leader of the group. Some of these kids are very tight. Some don't have good chemistry, and they just tolerate each other. But there's a core group, and Layla was the one they followed and looked up to. It's not like her to just disappear like this."

"Evie said she went to live with a new boyfriend? Little Leo, they called him?"

"I never met him, but the kids saw her with him. I'm concerned that it might not be a casual lapse that he never met any of the kids in person or came by here with her."

"You think it could be deliberate? So that no one knows exactly who he is?"

Melinda nodded. "Yes. You'd be surprised how many adults try to get next to these kids on the sly."

"I might not be too surprised. I worked homicide for thirty years," Bill said with a rueful smile. "What do you know about Layla's family history?"

"Just that she had problems at home and ran off. She lived up in Victorville before she came here. She spent a lot of time at the Los Feliz library. She's a voracious reader, and she got her GED. She was looking into LA City College. She's very responsible. I call her the office manager as a joke."

"Thanks. I might need some more information later on, but I'll start with this."

They shook hands, and Melinda moved to pick up the trash bags.

"Do you need a hand with those?" Bill asked.

"Sure, thanks. It's the linens for the dormitory upstairs. Our washer and dryer are broken, so I'm taking them to the Splash and Suds over on Yucca," Melinda said, carrying two bags out to her car in the small parking lot behind the Clubhouse. Bill followed, carrying the remaining bags.

"Let me know when you can come by to help out. We'd love any extra hands, and with all this stuff going on with the missing kids, it would be good to have a retired detective around," Melinda said, climbing into her 2005 Honda CR-V.

Bill waved as she drove away, then he headed back to the Home Depot where he and Evie had gone earlier. He walked the alley again, trying to imagine a scenario in which an impaired Layla arrived there late at night and what might have happened to her in that small window of time between the phone call and Evie's arrival. Someone knew where to find her and that she was under the influence of something. Evie heard the cops say there was no sign of a struggle, so Layla knew the person who came for her. He had to find out where she had been living and who gave her the ride to Hollywood. And the identity of Little Leo.

He took a few more photos with his phone, then headed into the store to buy a new washer and dryer for the Kidz Clubhouse. He hoped they had same-day delivery.

Detective Sandra Moody of the Hollenbeck station waited on hold for a detective in Tijuana to come back on the line. Ever since they learned that Ethan Acevedo's blood was found at the scene of Eden Balcomb's murder and that he'd fled to Mexico, she'd been following up every week with the authorities there. She had family living in Rosarito, and she could speak Spanish fluently; her maiden name was Amezcua.

She knew Lieutenant Carbone and Commander Joyce Ramsey were involved in contacting the Mexican authorities regarding Acevedo, but she had worked with both of them in Hollywood. They were more concerned with self-promotion than anything else, and Acevedo was unstable and violent. He was a danger to anyone who had crossed him, and everyone who had been on the internal investigation team for the Balcomb murder was now a target. She wasn't going to leave her personal safety in the hands of two career cops jockeying for position all the time.

As long as Acevedo remained in Mexico, she and the others on the investigation were safe. His passport was flagged with Border Patrol and Homeland Security, to let Ramsey and Carbone know if he came back into the US. But Acevedo could easily find a way around that. She'd been in contact with a police lieutenant, Rubén Ledezma, in Tijuana regularly to see if there had been any updates on Acevedo's whereabouts, since his car was found abandoned in Rosarito Beach. Ledezma came back on the line.

"There's been no sign of him, detective. No new updates. We just know he was staying in Rosarito, and then he disappeared. There was a report of a man found badly beaten in the surf near his hotel, and a local man took him to the Clinica Familiar, but we haven't been able to find that man to follow up with him. Some witnesses saw him load the man into his truck and said the guy was in very bad condition. They won't give us any information from the clinic, citing privacy laws."

"Did anyone at the hotel have any recollection of him?" Moody asked.

"Yeah, the bartender said he drank heavily every night he was there, and he hooked up with a local girl who works the beachfront hotels, and she might have cartel ties in some way. But since Acevedo disappeared, he hasn't seen her either. He wasn't willing to talk anymore after that first conversation."

"And no John Does in the local morgue? Filipino, male, about thirty-eight years old?"

"Nothing. I think he's alive, he's just lying low. Or he crossed the wrong person, and he's buried in some remote location, on private property," Ledezma said. "If I hear anything that could be suspicious or linked to him, I'll call you."

Moody thanked him and hung up. She would keep calling every week. This type of thing fell too easily between the cracks, unless someone had something at personal risk. She had a loving husband, a teenage son, and a college-age daughter. She was planning early retirement; they had already researched buying a house in Portugal. She wasn't going to become a victim of a maladjusted psycho like Acevedo, nor would she let Judson Postiff or young officers like Montoya and Clarke get caught in any blowback that he tried to put into play. She was the senior detective among them, and she wasn't letting anything go down on her watch.

Jeppe knocked on the door of his elderly neighbor, Christopher Russo, a retired singing teacher. In the driveway, an older white Toyota Corolla was parked. Russo answered the door in pajamas, his curly buff-toned toupee sitting crookedly on his head.

"Hey there, Jeppe. What can I do for you?" Russo asked.

"I wanted to know if you'd like me to drive your car this week. I know you don't want the battery to die from sitting too long," Jeppe offered.

Russo rarely drove any longer, and he'd had to replace valves and hoses when they rotted and dried out, a repair that took six hundred dollars out of his monthly social security check. He'd had to eat canned ravioli for several weeks after that, and he didn't want to risk it again. He took a key from a hook next to the door and handed it to Jeppe.

"Thanks, son. It needs to be driven to stay in shape, so take it whenever you want. Keep the key," Russo said.

"I'll bring it back soon, all safe and sound," Jeppe assured him, pocketing the key.

Half an hour later he was cruising the streets of Hollywood in Russo's car, looking for some additional entertainment to show off at his evening soiree. The kids at the Raven's Nest had been preparing all day, setting up tables and hanging black lights inside to give the house a club-like feel. He'd had them outfit the upstairs rooms with hidden nanny cameras so he could watch what took place when his guests wanted private time.

He made a turn onto El Centro, passing the cramped parking lot of Pla-Boy Liquor Store. That's where he saw her. She looked like an Asian doll, with her short skirt and knee socks, a shiny tiara in her jet-black hair. He pulled in and rolled down his window. She came over and leaned in, like they were dance partners in an age-old cotillion.

"You want to have some fun? I'm having a party later with lots of food and drinks. There'll be a lot of cool people there," he said with a charming grin.

She smiled back; her teeth were straight and perfect, even if her eyes were dull and flat, a sign that she was high on something that numbed whatever her particular pain might be.

"How much?" she asked, wasting no time on social niceties.

"We can work something out. It's an all-night affair, unlimited food and drinks and even some stronger stuff if you're interested. And a place to stay overnight. What do you say?"

She considered for a moment, flipping her long hair over one shoulder.

Then she said, "Cool, I'm up for it."

"Okay. I'll go into the CVS across the street and leave the car unlocked. You can get in, that way no one will notice," Jeppe said, looking over his shoulder. The last thing he needed was a solicitation arrest. He crossed the street and parked. When he went inside the store, Princess sauntered over and settled into the passenger seat, closing her eyes. Luckily the Banana Van guy hadn't been able to do much, like always. She didn't know why guys who couldn't get it up paid for sex. It was just embarrassing, and she had to pretend she didn't notice, telling them how hot they were when they were just pathetic and gross. But he'd paid, and she had the fifty dollars safe in her knockoff Hello Kitty bag.

A moment later, the door was yanked open. She sat up and found herself face-to-face with Aiden.

"We need to talk, Princess. This setup isn't going to work," he demanded.

"Leave me alone. It works just fine," Princess said, not looking at him.

"You can't just be out working on your own. Someone worse than me will take you over," he warned.

"And now I won't be stupid enough to believe him, will I? I can manage my own shit, okay?" she challenged him.

He grabbed her arm to pull her from the car, but she set her weight against him and gripped the seat belt.

"Come on, we're going!" he said.

As Jeppe emerged from the store, he saw, with alarm, that a young guy with full tattoo sleeves was trying to pull the girl from the car.

"What's going on here?" Jeppe asked indignantly.

"She's mine and I'm taking her, that's what. Back off, asshole," Aiden said.

Jeppe felt a surge in his solar plexus and stepped in between them.

"I don't allow trash like you to tell me what to do. She's my friend, and I'm taking her with me," Jeppe said.

Aiden pulled back as if he were ready to strike at Jeppe, but he noticed a police car cruising by and stopped himself.

"I'm gonna find you, and when I do, you're gonna regret it," Aiden warned as he retreated, getting into his Camry and pulling out of the parking lot.

Jeppe felt a thrill course through him as he got into the car.

"Are you all right?" he asked. "What's your name?"

She nodded, putting her delicate hand on his thigh in gratitude.

"Princess," she purred.

As he pulled the car into traffic, she realized she'd forgotten to send Evie a photo of his license plate. But she didn't need to this time. He wasn't really a stranger. She remembered she'd seen him around before. He was Little Leo.

CHAPTER TEN

Bill walked into the Los Feliz public library, following up on Evie's information that she and Layla frequented it. It was a small library that appeared to have been made possible by a donation from Leonardo DiCaprio, who grew up in the area. He looked at a collection of movie stills of DiCaprio that stood behind a glass case, thinking of the guy who'd been hanging around near the Clubhouse, the one they called Little Leo, who might've been Layla Waters's new boyfriend. *Strange irony,* he thought.

He walked to the main desk. A skinny young man with a braided beard, who was at work on a library computer, looked up at him.

"How can I help you, sir?" he asked.

"I'm a retired LAPD detective and now a private investigator. I'm wondering if you've seen this girl here lately?" Bill asked, showing him a photo of Layla on his phone.

Braided Beard rolled his eyes and gave the phone a perfunctory glance. "Why do you want to know?" he asked.

"Because I have a client who's trying to find her. She's gone missing."

Braided Beard gave him a scathing look. "Okay, you old guys need to find another schtick. Right, you're a retired detective, now a PI, like this is an episode of some TV cop show. And all to track down a young girl who probably gave you the brush-off. Have some self-respect, man!"

Bill was taken aback but recovered quickly. "You think I'm trying to hit on this girl? Are you nuts? Here, I keep this with me, just in case."

He pulled out his wallet that held a folded photo of him and Barrera receiving a commendation from the police commission.

"See that? It's the police commission, that's the chief, the deputy chief, and my old partner, Pete Barrera. And here's my newly minted PI license. I just retired from the LAPD a few months ago."

Braided Beard examined both and pushed them back to Bill, newly contrite. "Sorry, man. We get so many weirdos in here. Yeah, I recognize her. That's Layla, she came in all the time. She was a volunteer, and she even applied for a clerk job here. Her application is still under review. She reads a lot, loved books."

"You know she's homeless, right?"

"Yeah, I know. She always has a backpack and other stuff that gave it away. She has that little friend, also. With the short hair."

"Evie Peacock."

"Yeah, Evie. But Layla hasn't been here in a couple of weeks."

"When was the last time you saw her?" Bill asked.

"Not sure, maybe two or three weeks. She was getting friendly with that guy who came in to read all the time. He had an accent," Braided Beard said.

"Did he look like Leonardo DiCaprio?"

"Yeah, now that you mention it, he did. But younger and not all drunk and boozy looking."

"Do you know his name?"

Braided Beard shook his head. "He never got a library card from me. The regular clerk might have known him, but she's out on maternity leave. Won't be back for three months."

"Do you have a roster of library volunteers?" Bill asked.

"Yeah, but I can't show them to you. Maybe if you were still a detective I could, but now you're just a PI, and that has no official . . . like . . . status, you know? Like, I could become one too. Right?"

Bill sighed. Braided Beard was right. Being a PI didn't carry the same weight as being a cop. He needed to see the names and information on other volunteers and possibly something on Little Leo, to uncover his name and address.

"Okay, thanks, man," Bill said, moving off to wander through the library aisles. He pulled out a few books in the suspense/thriller section and a fat book about Harry Truman in biographies. He was turning down the aisle that contained romance/fantasy when he heard a familiar voice.

"We're looking into the disappearance of a handful of homeless teenagers in the area . . ." Pete Barrera said to Braided Beard.

"Hey! Brother!" Bill exclaimed, and several patrons shot him angry looks.

"Shhhhh!" an old lady with a green pixie haircut hissed at him.

Barrera looked up and saw Bill walking toward him. "What's up, man?" he asked, with a combination of surprise and a hint of dismay.

"Just got my first client as a PI. The license came yesterday! And I'm searching out some information on Layla Waters," Bill explained. He noticed that Barrera didn't look very well. But he didn't ask in front of young Postiff; he knew Barrera was touchy about getting older and slowing down.

"That's your first case?" Barrera asked.

"Yes. Her pal hired me to find her."

"You know Cassidy and Riley are helping out with this, right?" Postiff asked.

"Yeah, I dropped by the Kidz Clubhouse when they were there earlier."

"We're meeting up with them later today to go over everything and coordinate," Postiff said.

Bill gestured for them to follow him and led them toward the children's section, casting a look back at Braided Beard.

"Can you guys ask this guy with the beard if you can see the volunteer information? Layla Waters volunteered here, and I want to see who the others were. There might be something there, but I'm no longer a detective, you know? I'm just a civilian," Bill said.

"Sure. We'll be giving this to Cassidy and Riley also, you know," Barrera replied. "She can probably give it to you."

"Thanks, man. I'm doing a deep dive on this Waters girl later when I get home, but I want to see who else she was in contact with here. Oh, and ask about the Little Leo guy too."

"Who's Little Leo?" Postiff asked.

"A guy who was hanging around with Layla and some of the other kids. Looks like a young DiCaprio, I guess," Bill explained. "And I'll send you a photo of the license plate of a guy they call the Banana Van man. He picks up underage sex workers, like the one called Princess. She met up with him a little while ago. I'll send her photo as well."

"How'd you get all this information?" Barrera asked.

"From the kid who's hired me to find her friend, Layla," Bill replied nonchalantly.

"Thanks, Clarke," Postiff said. "I'll get the volunteer info for you. Wait for me outside."

Bill left with a wave as Postiff spoke to Braided Beard. Barrera watched Bill through the glass doors of the library. He couldn't catch a break in getting away from his old partner. The Clarkes, Bill and Cassidy, were always right there, entangled in his cases. Cassidy interviewed Ron Whitty, the key Hit Men murderer, and got a confession. Bill knew about Little Leo before they did. And the Banana Van guy.

Barrera's eyes felt sensitive in the fluorescent lights in the library. His suit jacket felt too tight. He couldn't wait for retirement.

Rick Brittenham finished his daily three-mile run through the USC campus and back to his fraternity house on Twenty-Eighth Street. He had a marketing exam to study for, but he blew it off. He didn't need the grade; he would work for his dad's company when he graduated. He was at USC because his parents had attended, as did his grandfather. He laughed to himself, knowing he was lucky enough to enroll before

California outlawed legacy admissions at private universities. If not, his two-point-seven grade point average wouldn't have gotten him past the first admissions cut.

He hated school, always had. He only liked that it was a party school, especially if you were in Greek life. So many guys in his house didn't need to be there, it was just to say they attended and go to the football games and then later, show up as an alum in red sweaters and yellow golf pants wearing big Trojan Styrofoam hats at sport events. It was what you did if you lived in Orange County and hung with his group.

And he had to find a wife as well. He didn't really care who it was, just someone his buddies thought was hot and came from money, like he did. Her parents could help set them up with a house in Newport and a membership at Pelican Hill. He had two more years to find one who belonged to one of the good sororities and get engaged, but that would be easy. Until then, he could pursue his kinks and quirks.

He walked along The Row, passing sororities that looked like stately suburban homes and fraternities that looked like derelict German brewhouses. And smelled that way as well. He walked into the SAE house, a looming Tudor-style structure, and found his roommate, Jed Grainger, sprawled out on a worn leather couch, playing video games in the living room.

"Bro, party tonight at the Raven's Nest," Rick said, giving him a slap on the head.

Jed sat up. "The German dude? The freaky one?"

"I don't think he's German, man. He's from someplace else over there. But yeah, a party like the last one."

Jed grinned. "I thought my dick was gonna fall off after that. Jesus!"

"He's going to have all the usual stuff—Molly, mushrooms, X—so it'll be a good time. I'm going to tell Scott and Josh also, they like that kind of shit," Rick said, taking the stairs two at a time toward their bedroom. "Gotta nap to get ready!"

Jed settled back onto the couch with a greedy smile; he'd had a fight with his Pi Phi girlfriend, Kristy, the night before, and since they were on the outs, he could do whatever he wanted. She'd even taken off the frat pin he gave her, which was kind of like a preengagement. Taking it off meant they were split up, even if just for a day or two. It was a pattern for them. Go to a frat party, she'd drink way too many kamikazes, get blasted and belligerent drunk, and they'd have a fight. She'd walk home, barely able to stand up, and then he'd run wild for a few days. Then they'd make up, and it started all over again.

He'd hit the ATM before heading over to Mount Washington, then swing by his dealer's place off Hoover to pick up some MDMA and ketamine, just to liven up the party. If the same young girls and guys were there as last time, it was going to be fire.

Aiden Howe had followed the rich guy's car from Cahuenga and Franklin all the way north to Mount Washington. He'd kept a safe distance and several cars between them, so he wouldn't be seen. He didn't know the guy's name, but he was moving in on Princess, and Aiden wasn't going to allow that without a fight. He knew the guy wasn't like the rest of them, including himself—the hardscrabble kids surviving out on the street with no safety net. No, the rich guy had legit money, Aiden could tell just from the clothes he wore—slacks and those lightweight sweaters that fit just right. And his shoes too. They were neat, polished leather with thin rope laces. Only rich guys wore hard shoes like that during the day.

He'd seen him drive a different car, also. Some kind of German imported ride, not the little Corolla he picked Princess up in today. Aiden had noticed him on the streets, driving too slowly where the kids congregated. At first, he thought he was a trick, but that didn't seem to be his kink. Aiden worried that the rich guy might be setting up his own stable of girls and possibly boys, housing them out of the area to make it harder to track them down.

Princess was the only one he was worried about. He wanted her back under his control for obvious reasons; she made good money, especially since she started dressing like an anime schoolgirl. But he also wanted her back for himself. They'd started as a convenient situationship born of their business relationship, but it had started to turn into something more, for him at least. She was the prettiest girl he had ever seen, with her big dark eyes and delicate features. She was perfectly proportioned, like a doll with shiny black hair that hung down her back.

There weren't any girls like her in his hometown in Ohio, just boring, pan-faced white girls who came from farms just like he did, whose fathers raised a few cattle and a lot of soybeans, who all went to the same evangelical Church of Christ where they weren't even allowed to dance. He might have gone that route until his father, George, torched their farm when foreclosure loomed, and they lost everything. Aiden ditched the whole depressing town and came to LA, hoping to land a role in a Marvel movie or be a stuntman, but that didn't work out unless you knew someone to get you in.

But Princess made everything better. She was smart. And funny. When they just hung out, she made him laugh harder than he had in a long time. He'd made room in the closet for her clothes, when she came to stay. Since their fight, he'd even gone to the mall and bought a whole bag of stuff from Bath & Body Works, remembering she said she used to like to go to that store before she left home in Bakersfield. But she hadn't come back the way he thought she would.

He knew she would still see her regulars, and he wasn't too worried about them. The firefighter, the Banana Van guy, the owner of the Cochinito Al Pastor restaurant who always wanted him to drop Princess off when his wife made the Smart & Final run for supplies. They all had too much to lose to get too crazy with any of the girls. But Aiden worried about the wild cards out there in the streets. Like the guys Princess had walked off with the previous night; she had no idea who they were, and neither did he. No way to find them, no vehicle license plate. They were like spooks, and any one of them could turn into some sex-freak serial killer like the ones he saw on true crime documentaries.

He hated to admit it, but he was scared about Princess being out there on her own. He wanted her back safe with him. He would be nicer; he'd give her more money. Maybe they'd even make real plans. But none of that would happen if she took off with the rich guy who was now turning toward the hills above Highland Park.

Aiden almost lost him a few times but stayed on the Corolla without being noticed. He needed to see where she was being taken to. The streets got steeper and more twisty as they climbed higher toward the top of Mount Washington. When Aiden saw the Corolla pull into the long driveway of the big house on the hill, he kept driving past it without slowing down.

He turned around and parked out of sight behind a bougainvillea bush. He leaned over his dashboard to see Princess get out and follow the rich guy into a house that looked like something from an old horror movie. He took several photos of it with his phone and sat for almost an hour, but he never saw Princess again, just a few of the kids he thought he recognized from Hollywood, moving in and out, cleaning up.

He sat back and slouched down in his seat, keeping his eyes trained on the big bow windows of the upper floors. He would get Princess out of there. After all, she belonged to him.

Ethan Acevedo unlocked the gate to his parents' house in Windsor Square. He'd abandoned Roberto Lopez's car in the Pico-Union area and took the MTA bus to his parents' neighborhood. Once on the property, he slipped into the side door that led to the kitchen. He saw his big white Tundra truck still parked outside the guesthouse, just where he had left it before heading to Mexico. No way he was taking that beauty across the border. He'd rented a car in San Diego and ended up leaving it in Rosarito. He knew if they were looking for him, they'd find it and think he was still out of the country.

Once inside, he quietly padded up the stairway toward his father's room, where he knew the old man would be napping or watching television. The caregiver, Margaret, stepped out as Acevedo approached, and she almost dropped the tray of dirty dishes she was carrying. Acevedo put his fingers to his lips and shook his head to warn her to stay quiet. She obeyed and looked away, terrified. She'd been scared of him for months, seeing how he came in and out at all hours of the night and the unsettling way he looked at her while she was washing the dishes or folding laundry. She just kept her head down and did her work—she wanted no trouble. She was undocumented, and Acevedo knew it.

In his father's room the old man was asleep on the bed, the TV playing myTFC, the local Filipino station. Acevedo opened the dresser drawer and pulled out his father's wallet, grabbing a couple of his credit cards and a wad of cash, then jamming them into his pocket. He also snagged the car keys from a crystal candy dish. There would be no reason for the police to stop his father's Mercedes, and given how Acevedo's face had shifted since the attack in Rosarito, he doubted he'd be recognized while driving.

He passed his mother's room, hearing the same TV station playing, but he didn't want her to see him. He didn't want either of them to know he was back, and to that end he grabbed some staples from the kitchen and went down the back stairs to the basement. It was lucky to have the type of old house in Los Angeles that still had a basement, and theirs even had a utility bathroom. Once he got down there, he put the food in the extra fridge, laid out a rolled-up futon, and tore open a plastic bag of extra bedding that he knew his mother kept stored down for the guests she always expected that never showed up.

He was tired. He lay down to sleep, knowing the door was bolted against anyone entering uninvited. He chuckled softly, thinking of that fool, Roberto Lopez, who ran his mouth, bragging about how much cash he had on him. All Acevedo had to do was let the doorman at the Paris de Noche strip club know, and some locals had taken care of everything when Lopez drank too much and got in a bar fight over one of the girls.

Acevedo had firsthand experience in how wrong that scenario could go; he wasn't surprised when Doña Ilda alerted him to Lopez's disappearance. She needed his belongings and his truck gone before anyone came looking, and Acevedo was happy to oblige. He'd had his eye on Lopez's passport and truck since the day he arrived at the Bufadora boarding house.

Acevedo lay in the cool darkness of the basement, going through the names on his list, picturing their faces as he had every night as he fell asleep.

Judson Postiff, Sandra Moody, Cassidy Clarke, Diana Montoya, Bill Clarke.

Everyone who had been part of the secret internal investigation team for Eden Balcomb's murder. The people who couldn't just let it go. He felt the burning sensation of acid reflux—since the attack, his digestive system didn't work properly any longer. Constant burning in his stomach. His shit was like water from a faucet every time he went.

He kept his gun by his head, just in case. He could afford to catch some shut-eye. He needed the sun to go down to get to work.

CHAPTER ELEVEN

Postiff and Barrera sat at their desks with Cassidy and Riley, who'd spent the day on their normal patrol and were following up on the list of people and places that the homeless kids frequented.

"We spoke to Marjorie Mellencamp, at her house in the hills," Cassidy said.

"We saw her also. She's off her rocker," Barrera said, popping an antacid tablet and following it with a swig of Coke.

"That house is a mess, and she seemed like she didn't have the best grip on reality," Riley added.

"She's called us multiple times with crazy information and revelations. She's lonely, and I guess she wants to connect with people," Postiff added.

"Then she should join the fucking senior center and stop calling cops in the middle of an investigation," Barrera complained.

"Have you guys been to Cesar's Auto?" Cassidy asked.

"No, we haven't spoken to them yet," Postiff said.

"We did. The owner, Cesar Sarellano, seems like a good guy. He lets the kids run errands for cash, or they clean up the office for him. The other guys there seem normal, and none of the kids said they were weird or inappropriate," Cassidy said.

"Who's this Little Leo guy?" Postiff asked.

"Evidently, a guy who's been hanging around with some of these street kids. He's a new face in the area, and he might have been Layla's boyfriend, the one she went to live with near Atwater. We got that from the kid who's her closest friend, Evie Peacock," Cassidy said.

"And that's the kid who's hired your dad to find her, right?" Barrera asked.

Cassidy looked at him, surprised. "Hired my dad? Since when?"

"We ran into him at the Los Feliz Branch Library, where Layla and Evie used to hang out," Postiff said.

"This is the first I've heard about this . . ." Cassidy said as she picked up her phone to text her dad.

Hey! do you have a new client? R u looking for that missing girl Layla Waters? From the Clubhouse??!

He replied immediately.

Yep Evie Peacock hired me today. The kid with the short hair and freckles

A kid hired you??!

Yeah, I'll tell you about it at home. Got work to do!

She turned to the others in disbelief. "You're right! He has a new client, that kid named Evie Peacock. He's looking for Layla Waters!"

"Of course he is," Barrera said under his breath.

"Have you guys spoken to all the robbery victims?" Riley asked.

"Yeah, the final one was today. That TV director, Jason Weizman. There's something I didn't like about that guy," Postiff said.

"Hmm, what was it? Maybe his weird little keto body in that ridiculous sweater? He looked like Gumby going to a club." Barrera scowled.

"We spoke to him. Whoever robbed him took a gun," Cassidy said. "It's in our report."

"Okay, let's divide up the remaining places and people on the list for tomorrow. We'll take Los Donuts, Gus Pizza, the Yucca market, and Splash and Suds. You guys hit Dray's Billiards and Brew, the Hollywood Storage place, and the Goldwyn library. We're following up with the Los Feliz library," Postiff said.

"And keep an eye out for the Banana Van guy," Riley added. "He's another new face in the area, according to the kids at the Clubhouse."

"Yeah, your dad mentioned him," Barrera said.

"Did you guys see or hear from the one called Princess? Real name Charmaine Mendoza," Riley asked.

Postiff shook his head. "No. Bill sent us her photo. She's not missing, right? Just high risk."

Barrera looked again at the photo of Princess. "My god, she looks like she's twelve!"

"Evidently, she's seventeen, but she sounds like she's in a bad situation. Let's keep an eye out for her," Riley said.

Barrera added, "Your dad told us she'd met up with a john, the Banana Van guy. She sent that Evie kid a photo of his license plate. I guess they do that as a safety measure. But we didn't see his car out in Hollywood. I'd love to bust that guy."

Postiff looked at the photo of Princess, shaking his head. "What kind of sick creep wants to do something like this?"

Bill sat at his computer in the den, running a background check on Layla Waters and Evie Peacock. There were a number of girls named Layla Waters from all over the country but only a handful from Nevada but not Las Vegas, as Evie told him. He found one from Elko that was the same age, and took a shot. He had paid for software that enabled him to do advanced searches of public records, police reports, and other filings with city, county, and state agencies.

She was born Layla Louise Waters, the birth certificate listed her mother as Denise Scobie, occupation waitress. Father was listed as unknown. School and census records showed Layla as living with Denise and two siblings until February of 2020. A missing person report was filed six months later in Elko, when Layla was fifteen. She had no criminal record; she had just vanished. He made note of Denise Scobie's contact information.

Then he did the same search on Evie Peacock and found her birth certificate in Corvallis, Oregon. Her father was John Peacock, her mother was Geraldine Howser. The census reports showed Evie living with her father until his death in 2021. She was briefly in the care and custody of Oregon CPS, but she disappeared from their records in 2022. She was in the California CPS system briefly, but there was no record of her after early 2023. Her next of kin was listed as Arthur Peacock in Eugene, Oregon, a brother to John.

Bill took notes on Evie as well, determined to figure out how she ended up on the streets of LA. Her blithe, succinct explanation of "no money, no family" had to be more complicated than she presented it. He wanted to track down her mother, Geraldine, to see if she was aware that her daughter was sleeping in parks and under freeways.

Next, he combed through the volunteer information from the Los Feliz Branch Library that Postiff had handed off to him. With their contact information, he did background searches on all the names, in case any had criminal records related to minors, sex crimes, etc. He wanted all the information available before he started making calls. He felt good, energized, and engaged by his first PI case, even if his paying client was a homeless teenager.

He was in the kitchen getting a refill from his Westinghouse percolator when the landline rang. His gut tightened—he knew it would be Tyler Derby again from Pleasant Valley State Prison. He was the only person calling that line and leaving messages of late. He listened to the mechanical voice leaving a message and resisted the urge to pick up the receiver. He felt the need to know what Derby wanted like an itch, a niggling, irritating itch that he could not scratch for fear of slipping back into the abyss of obsession with the unresolved, with the haunting absence of closure, with the smiling image of a fifteen-year-old Min Sun-Hee staring at him from his desk like an accusation.

Evie laid her sleeping bag out in the office of Cesar's Auto. Cesar had agreed to let her stay overnight indoors, which he did from time to time. She could keep an eye on the place with the office cat, Sin Calzones, a calico who had wandered up one day and never left. The big outside lights illuminated the yard that was surrounded by a tall, wrought iron fence, and no one was going to try to get in over it. The bays had steel doors that were closed and shut at night with a side door that led to the office, where Evie made her bed. The Clubhouse was full, and rain threatened again. She didn't want to spend another wet night in the dirt under the freeway.

She leafed through the automotive magazines that Cesar kept in the place, not wanting to turn on any overhead lights to attract attention. All she needed was for some nosy cop to come sniffing around and find her. She sat with her back against the wall, her head not visible in the windows that faced the street. She wondered what Bill's daughter and her partner were finding, looking into the disappearance of Zephyr and Kyle, Anya and Autumn, Zeno and the others. If Princess was at the Clubhouse or still working the streets. Where Layla might be and if she was still alive. She had so many unanswered questions. Most of all, she wondered how she could've ended up in the place she was, untethered and adrift with no place to land.

She leaned against the wall, closing her eyes, hoping to sleep, but she could not get her system to settle down and relax. Being in a perpetual state of fight or flight had become her default in the past few years, and she could no longer control it. It controlled her. She could only hope that the night terrors and bad memories might give her a brief reprieve. But they rarely did, stalking her during the daylight hours, waiting until the world was quiet, with no distractions to burst forth.

Evie sitting with her dad in their house in Corvallis, the fireplace roaring as he tried to explain to her what was happening and what was to come.

"I'm sick, Evie, with something I didn't know I had. It's a tumor, and it's growing fast . . ." he'd said, his voice calm and steady but his eyes betraying the fear he felt.

"But they're going to cure it, right? The doctors can fix it," Evie had insisted, which made her father's eyes soften in a strange combination of sorrow and guilt.

"I don't think they can, Evie. We have to make some plans . . ."

Later that evening, she'd sat in her room with the door cracked open to listen to her father talking with his brother, Arthur, whom she barely knew. He'd come to visit once with his uptight wife, who was half his age and looked around their house as if it were a mud hut. She refused to sit on the furniture, preferring to stand with a posture that looked like she had a broom handle up her ass.

"I need to make arrangements for Evie, she doesn't have anyone else," her father said. He was calling from the landline, and Evie had slipped out to the hallway phone, picking it up so quietly that no one knew she was on the line. She heard her uncle's whiny voice mid-protest.

"It's just that we're not set up to take her, John. I mean, we've got the toddlers and our hands are full . . ." Arthur explained.

"You both have secure jobs, you have tenure. You have room in your house. She's fourteen, you're the only family I have, Art!" her father pushed, and Evie heard the uncomfortable sigh on the other end of the line.

"It just won't fly with Cristina, John. She says we can't do it. We'd like to, but we just can't. You know we can't take care of someone who has health issues," Arthur explained.

"What the hell are you talking about? Evie has no health issues."

"I mean, she has her appendix out, right? There can be problems later with that," Arthur said. His voice sounded like a rusted wheel on a gravel road.

"She had an appendectomy when she was ten, lots of kids do. I can't believe you're doing this!" Evie's dad exploded, his voice a furious whisper.

"Look, John, I wish we could, but we just can't. It's too . . . complicated," Arthur said.

Evie's dad hung up the phone, and she retreated to her room, wondering what her life would become when the inevitable happened. Her uncle was an asshole, and she didn't want to live with them anyway. She knew she'd become the babysitter for their bratty twins and the housekeeper for Cristina, who'd treat her like a servant back in Cebu City.

When her world imploded, it came so quickly, like a rock sliding into the river. She began her journey into foster care and her escape from it, Arthur sending her the money to get to California, expecting a big show of gratitude.

Her mind was like a hamster wheel, turning and turning over in the same loop again and again. She felt locked into it, unable to step off and change course. She knew she needed to, but she couldn't figure out how. She pulled her sketch pad from her backpack and grabbed a pencil from Cesar's drawer. The cat had settled in a ball at the end of her sleeping bag. The light from the yard streamed in through the window. She crossed her legs underneath her and began to draw.

Diana Montoya left the gym, her bag slung over her shoulder, one of her AirPods in, listening to the Casefile true crime podcast from Australia. The parking lot was well lit and there were other people coming and going, so she felt at ease. Still, as soon as she entered her car, she locked all the doors, as was her habit. She took a minute to get herself situated, putting the AirPods away and getting the CarPlay system engaged with her phone so she could listen to her show on the twenty-minute drive home to the house she shared with her parents, Fernando and Leonor, in Sierra Madre.

She texted her mom.

On my way home from gym want me to pick up a taquiza at vallarta?

Yes, mija make sure to get the salsa picosa

She knew her mom was extra tired this week from finishing up the details on her younger sister's wedding dress. Since she'd made her living for three decades as a seamstress in a Korean-owned dry cleaner, Leonor had insisted on making the dress, which meant that Diana bringing home dinner would be a treat for everyone. A *taquiza* filled with steaming, freshly made carnitas, rice, beans, and street taco corn tortillas was always welcome at the Montoya house.

Diana took Colorado from her gym in South Pasadena toward the nearest Vallarta Mexican market, taking the route that ran parallel to the freeway, alongside a deep ravine. It had less traffic than the freeway, and at this time it was almost deserted, except for the car behind her. She turned up her podcast, listening to the deep, dramatic voice of the show's anonymous host. She liked this podcast the best. It was straightforward with a good narrative to build tension, unlike so many others that had idiotic cohosts who bantered back and forth and made moronic commentary on criminal cases.

Suddenly, the car behind her slammed into the back of her Santa Fe, sending it veering into the next lane. She righted the car and looked in her rearview mirror in surprise and anger, signaling that she was pulling over. Before she could, the car rammed her again, this time pushing her across the lanes toward the edge of the road. Diana gripped the steering wheel as she felt the car's stability go off-kilter. One of her tires had blown.

In the rearview mirror she could not make out the driver of the other car nor the make and model, but it was riding her tail intentionally. She kept her foot on the gas as her Santa Fe began to lose traction and slow down. She needed to get to the main boulevard, away from the nut who was purposely driving her off the road.

"Get off my ass, motherfucker!" she yelled as she pushed her car, the blown tire making a nauseating, flapping sound as she felt it driving on the raw metal rim. The car behind her slowed down, thankfully. She moved forward steadily but then saw her pursuer accelerating, aiming directly at her. She tried to swerve as the impact hit, pushing her over the edge and into the ravine. She gripped the steering wheel as the car tumbled down the steep grade, and she lost consciousness when her head hit the windshield.

CHAPTER TWELVE

Cassidy arrived at home to find Bill at the stove, cooking a skillet full of mushrooms with garlic and white wine as he talked on the phone, beef patties sizzling on a grill pan.

"And you never learned the name of the fellow that Ms. Waters hung out with at the library? I'll definitely follow up with you again, Mr. Higginbottom," he said, before hanging up.

"That smells amazing! What're you making?" she asked.

"Angus beef patties with a creamy mushroom garlic sauce with a side salad," he said as he sprinkled some seasoning into the pan. "Did you have any luck getting a real name for Little Leo?"

"Let's back up. How did you start working with Evie Peacock?"

Bill shrugged. "She hired me. I met her at the Clubhouse, and she asked me to investigate the disappearance of her friend, Layla Waters. She's on the list that Melinda gave you."

"How did she hire you? She's not paying you, is she?" Cassidy asked.

"She made a down payment on my services today. So, yes, she is paying me."

"You took money from a homeless teenager?"

"It was a point of pride for her, to pay something. I'll give it back to her in some other way. But I've been digging, and Layla volunteered at the Los Feliz Branch Library with a handful of other people. And she used to hang out with Little Leo, whom she met there. That's how I think he became her boyfriend, of sorts," Bill said with satisfaction.

"And she was planning to meet Evie to tell her something that was wrong, something going on at Little Leo's house, but she disappeared. Evie found Layla's bracelet in the alley where she made her final call from. There could be some forensic evidence there, but it's doubtful, given the rain."

"You went to the scene?"

He nodded. "Yeah, no sign of a struggle. Layla knew the person who picked her up. I'm going to call Layla's mother after dinner and maybe check up on Evie's situation as well. She has an uncle who's married with kids right there in Oregon, where she's from."

Cassidy looked at him with admiration. He'd only taken the case that day and had been to the possible crime scene, compiled and contacted a list of suspects and witnesses, tracked down the family information on both Layla and Evie, and surmised that Layla knew the person who took her, which was probably correct.

"I guess that's why they call you the Big Dog," she said with a smile.

"Any sign of Princess?" he asked.

"How do you know all the players in this?" she asked, exasperated. "No, none of us have seen Princess, but we're looking for her."

"So, Postiff and Pete never found the Banana Van guy?"

"No one saw him. But I'm sure he'll be back," she said, moving to get the plates and cutlery from the cupboard to set the table. "So, what'd you find out about Little Leo?"

"The other volunteers said he was foreign, had a slight accent. And they all agreed he looked like a young DiCaprio," Bill said, turning the stove off and wiping his hands on his apron. "I've got to hit the john. Would you plate this masterpiece, please?"

"Sure. And I'll do the dishes since you did the cooking," Cassidy said.

As she set the plates out, the landline rang loudly. She had stopped answering it during the Hit Men investigation when reporters were scrambling to get information from her. But now, while Whitty and Pham were waiting for trial, the attention from the press had died down. She picked up the receiver, expecting a real estate cold call or someone selling solar panels. The recorded voice caught her by surprise.

"You're receiving a call from an inmate at Pleasant Valley State Penitentiary. Press one to accept the call, two to decline, or hang up . . ."

She felt a surge of outrage, knowing it had to be Tyler Derby, still trying to harass her father, to drag him into his twisted, predatory psychodrama. She took the call and heard Derby's raspy voice on the other end of the line.

"Bill? Is that you?"

"No, it's his daughter. I told you never to call him again!" she said.

"Okay, okay, officer . . . it's not what you think . . . I don't want anything from him . . ." Derby's voice was weak and faint; he struggled to get through a sentence.

"What is it you want?" she asked.

"I have some information I think he'll want. A guy in here says his brother killed that little Asian girl that your dad is always looking for. Says the guy is still out there, never been caught. I wanted to let your dad know, that's all," Derby said, sounding as if he would pass out from the effort.

"Right. You want him to get obsessed and go off the rails again. You encouraged the idea that our neighbor was Sun-Hee's killer. You told him to break into his house!"

Derby fought to breathe. "I did, I know it. I totally fucked with him 'cause I was mad. But I don't have much time left, got a bunch of shit wrong with me. If you want to tell him, go ahead, and if not, that's on you, Officer Clarke. I've done my part," he said before hanging up, leaving the terrible choice in her hands.

Jeppe moved through the crowd at his house, sliding between half-naked guests, enjoying the sensation of them brushing up against him. He'd hired several professional sex workers from OnlyFans, as he always did. They knew how to take everything up a notch and were well worth the money.

The house pulsed with music and black lights, giving everything a spooky, sexy glow.

He'd had the lost angels handing out the fun drugs from silver platters, their young, beautiful faces painted to look like Gothic fairies. He'd dressed them in the bare minimum of clothing, just enough to tease the imaginations of his adult revelers. On a table, he had Anya and Autumn dancing provocatively together, high out of their minds, not even knowing where they were or what they were doing.

He waved to the group of college frat boys he always invited. Their white, suburban, macho energy brought a certain jolt to the parties, when so many others came from the raw margins of society or from the freewheeling art and music scene in the city. Rick and Jed were like horny bulls set loose in a courtesan's Paris brothel. He bumped into Jack Ekhart, a USC theater arts professor with a history of dating freshman girls and handing out STDs like Halloween candy. When he heard about Jeppe's parties, he made sure to bring a supply of liquor and top-quality weed to have access to underage girls, wearing Gothic masks and little else, in the dark.

Jeppe was near the front door when Jason Weizman, the television director he had met at Dray's, pushed it open with two young, skinny blonds in tow.

"Jeppe, man! Great party, right? I brought two of my protégés along. They're working on an episode of a show I'm shooting this week! Both super talented!" Weizman said, his eyes already bloodshot. The two girls looked barely legal and had the slightly frightened look of children who wandered too far from home after making a petulant threat to run away when Mom asked them to pick up their toys.

Jeppe ushered them inside and signaled for Kyle to bring a silver tray of drugs over for their choosing. Weizman grabbed the magic mushrooms, pushing them on the two girls aggressively before leading them into the depths of the crowd. When he passed Anya and Autumn dancing on the table, he remembered where he'd seen them the day of the robbery at his house. They were Jeppe's girls, and he couldn't remember if he'd had sex with one of them, but he thought he did. It didn't matter, no one at the party knew what was going on, and no one would remember anything the next day, just the way he liked it.

Jeppe climbed the stairs and looked out over his soiree, knowing that he had one of the best treats of the evening waiting on the second floor for his extra special guests. He'd given Princess a good dose of ecstasy, and he'd decked the bedroom out in pink tulle and roses, with her seated on the big bed on top of a pile of fluffy pink cushions, like a doll. And that was what she would be for the people who earned the right to play with her. In his head he heard the voices, giddy with joy, ringing like silver bells.

Bonfire, bonfire burning bright . . .
What shall we do on this dark, dark night?
All the pretty kitties staring at the sky . . .
When the moon comes out, they will cry, cry, cry . . .

He felt a giggle rising up in his throat and a surge of energy shoot through his legs, forcing him to rock from side to side. Then, like a whisper, the old man's voice, approaching from someplace far away, getting louder.

Ding dong bell, pussy's in the well
Who put her in? Little Jeppe Lind . . .
Ding dong bell, pussy's in the well . . . in the well . . .

He turned away from the party guests, muttering, "Shut up!" but the old man's voice did not obey him. Jeppe stepped into an empty bedroom and closed the door, facing the wall with his eyes closed, his body stiff. Like an old eight-millimeter film, the scene played out against his eyelids.

Layla, locking herself into one of the extra rooms after the party . . . she'd woken up too early and seen too much . . . she wouldn't let him explain, no matter how hard he banged on that closed door . . . she had moved beyond his reach . . . he always feared the day would come when she would see through him with her green-glass eyes, her hair that glistened with a hint of copper. Like a mermaid, a siren turned fury, she shut him out, cast him away from her circle of light . . . how she'd ruined his euphoria, leaving him slumped against the locked door, pleading with her like a child . . .

Then, her false pretense of forgiveness, which he had believed . . . but not enough to prevent precautions, mixing her daily green smoothie himself, a show of his contrition . . . followed by the betrayal he suspected she might deal him . . . escaping in the night with the help of the foolish neighbor next door . . . until he sent the imbecile to retrieve her and bring her back to the Raven's Nest for judgment day . . . then the sound, the sound he could not forget or silence, the sickening thud of the marble candlestick crashing against her skull, the way it sank into what should have been solid . . . the spurting of the blood, the blood . . .

He banged his head hard against the wall, several times. Tonight, he would silence the old man's voice for good. He had a plan in place. He would use the brute strength and macho posturing of Rick and Jed to retrieve the bags from the old well and dispose of them, with the promise of private time with the pink confection that waited like a petit four in the upstairs bedroom.

Chris Russo glared from his upstairs window at the racket going on at his neighbor Jeppe Lind's house. Most days, he was a nice college kid, respectful, clean cut. Russo had met his parents when they rented the house. Quality people, both professionals. Jeppe was a USC student. Russo knew the family had to have money.

But lately Jeppe had been throwing these parties, too loud with a lot of lights and music. And plenty of sketchy people. Russo saw them drive up in fancy cars, dressed in odd getups like characters in a movie. And he saw the kids too. The young ones who lived there now, who were always doing yard chores, the ones who danced at night on the terrace overlooking the yard. They were altogether too young to be living there with a kid like Jeppe.

And there was the pretty one with the dark hair who he'd given a ride to the night of the storm. He had to go out to pick up some Borax, and she was coming down Jeppe's driveway, like she was running away. He gave her a ride into Hollywood, but Jeppe had seen him and was waiting at his door when he came home. Jeppe explained that the girl wasn't well, she was running a high fever, and he was planning to take her to the doctor the following day, but she didn't want to go, and she'd run off. Now she was out there in the storm, sick and alone. Russo admitted that she'd seemed out of it in his car, and he'd hurried back to bring her home, where she'd be under Jeppe's care. But Russo hadn't seen her since that night, and it worried him. She used to be like the queen of the castle over there at Jeppe's, and now she'd vanished.

And Russo smelled marijuana on a regular basis as well. He knew the smell; he'd been to Vietnam as a young man. Lately, it seemed like everyone everywhere was smoking it. Even in line at the local Yucca Market, there was always someone who had the telltale skunk, weed stench sticking to their clothes and hair. He could tell those kids were getting high. It carried on the breeze to his windows. He didn't like it, not one bit. Just like he didn't like the loud parties and all the crazy people over there.

He stopped short of calling the police, but he would definitely call the landlord, Mr. Smolin. He might even dig out that business card that Jeppe's parents had given him when he moved in. Russo figured they might want to know what their son was up to, living in that big house with all those kids. Could be a Michael Jackson type of thing, for all he knew. He closed his window against the sounds from his neighbor's house. He was going to call someone.

CHAPTER THIRTEEN

Bill had showered and put on his pajamas, planning to watch some vintage TV before bed, but now he stood in the yard, staring up at the sky. There was light cloud cover; the whole county was smack in the middle of May Gray weather, when the marine layer sits heavily over everything as far as San Bernardino, slowly burning off by midday. It settled again after dark, and now there was a slight chill to the air. He remembered his ex-wife saying that you always need a light sweater at night, even in the summer, in Los Angeles.

He thought back to his many years working homicide at the Hollywood station, how many times he'd driven by the Kidz Clubhouse, passing the scruffy teenagers on the street. While he was chasing down the people who committed murder, those kids were there, generation after generation, surviving in those back alleys and low-rent motels, and relying on the kindness of strangers that was often not kindness at all but predation and abuse.

He and Barrera had looked right through them; they were a fixture in Hollywood, where the faces and the names changed but the stories remained the same. Lost kids, abandoned kids, rejected and betrayed by people and entire systems that were supposed to work to protect them. Labeled the bad kids, the problem kids, the incorrigibles. The ones beyond redemption. How had he never seen them the same way he saw his own daughter?

He thought of Evie Peacock, wondering where she was at this hour. Was she indoors or was she sleeping rough, in an alley or an underpass? Was she hiding in a stairwell? Was she alone or in the company of others? Were those people safe or dangerous? It made his heart race just to imagine the possibilities. He dialed her number for the third time, but it went straight to voicemail. Was that because she didn't have a charger and it ran down the battery, or was it because of some more nefarious reason?

He knew he was supposed to keep his emotions on an even keel and avoid high-intensity situations and people that triggered him into the overdrive that caused him so many problems over the years. It helped capsize his marriage, and while it made him a great detective, he knew he had been so single-minded and driven that his behavior crossed the line too many times. But he didn't know how anyone was supposed to come face-to-face with kids like Evie and not get emotionally involved.

Maybe it was now that he was retired, and he had time to take things in and process them. Maybe it was his new approach to life, aided by psychopharmacology and therapy, but he had to face that he was not okay not knowing if Evie was safe. Part of him wanted to get in his car and drive to Hollywood and cruise the streets until he found her, but he knew that was crazy and it might frighten her. He decided to text Melinda first thing in the morning to arrange a schedule for him to volunteer at the Clubhouse. If he were there a lot, he could keep a closer eye on Evie.

He heard the glass slider open, and Cassidy stepped out in sweats. Without a word, she took a seat in one of the patio chairs.

"Can't sleep?" he asked.

"Not really. I keep thinking about all of them," she said.

"The kids at the Clubhouse?"

"Yeah. Did you talk to Layla's mother yet?" she asked.

"No, it's too late to call. I'm doing it tomorrow, same with Evie's uncle."

"Postiff told me that they ran background checks on the missing kids. Only some of them are in the database for missing and exploited minors. The others are just out there, like a boat without a rudder," she said.

"What did Ramsey say?" he asked.

"She okayed the investigation, probably to make her seem more humane. But she'll be upset that the robberies have spread to Los Feliz. A house was hit over on Edgemont. Riley and I spoke to the homeowner, a TV director. He had a gun stolen."

"Let's hope the kids don't use it next time. This thing is like trying to stop a leak in a dam holding back a river," he said. "Even if we find Layla and the others, if we catch whoever might be putting them up to these robberies, there will just be a different predator tomorrow. And a fresh bunch of kids as well."

Cassidy was silent. She couldn't find the words that would bring either of them any comfort. She considered telling her father about Tyler Derby's information, but she feared that bringing the Min Sun-Hee case back to life might push him over the edge. There was a rustling in the eugenia bushes at the back edge of their property. Two coyotes appeared, silent and sure footed, moving in quiet grace across the yard. Their coats blended in perfectly with the dusty landscape, their big ears alert, their eyes impassive but searching. They were on the hunt, like all predators who work under the cover of darkness.

She knew that somewhere, tonight in Hollywood, someone was doing the same thing, trolling the side streets and dark corners for his young prey.

Marjorie Mellencamp drove her classic white Thunderbird along Los Feliz Boulevard. She loved looking at the big houses behind tall gates. She remembered parties she had attended as a young actress in some of those houses. Back when girls were glamorous and men were charming and gallant, at least on the surface. There was nothing gallant about being pushed into a closet and groped by an aging producer or convinced to go skinny-dipping in the pool with a group of fleshy studio executives. But how the facade sparkled in those days!

At this hour, when the clubs were closed and the restaurants long shuttered for the night, the city was the way she remembered it. The wide boulevard, the looming shadows of the park and its winding roads, like something in a German fairy tale with a California spin. She rolled down her car window and inhaled the scent of wild sage that grew abundantly as she took a left on a street that led into the park. The Griffith Observatory sat atop the hill, like a white, domed castle. She loved her city.

The streets of Griffith Park were nearly deserted, except for a lone car parked by the side of the road every half mile or so. People were meeting and hooking up, like they had been doing for years. She approached the loop of the observatory parking lot. A city roadblock had been erected, and she could see the asphalt beyond the orange cones was being dug up. Rather than drive right up to the cramped work zone, she opted to make a U-turn a few hundred yards early.

She swung her car into a dirt turnout, the mouth of a fire road that people used for hiking and dog walking. As her headlights illuminated the path, she saw the back end of a car wedged into the fire road and three young men, two carrying what appeared to be heavy black trash bags and tossing them over the edge into the ravine below.

Litterbugs, she thought, *too lazy to dispose of their garbage properly . . .*

One of the young men turned to her car, his pale, round face bathed in a beam of white light. Marjorie took in a sharp inhale and quickly put her car into reverse and turned around. His eyes terrified her. Cold, blank, devoid of any emotion. She floored the gas pedal, her tires screeching as she disappeared, driving back down to the city streets.

Jeppe watched the white Thunderbird as the driver backed away and sped off. He had seen her, a blond woman wearing sunglasses in the three a.m. darkness. And she had seen him. Behind him Rick and Jed were busy dumping the black trash bags over the edge of the trail. They made a heavy thud as they hit shrubs and trees on their descent. The frat boys were still inebriated, just following orders, doing what they were told. They hadn't even noticed the lights of the Thunderbird. What was that woman doing out in the park at that hour? And why had she chosen that particular trailhead to turn around? It worried him. It was a bad sign.

An omen. He heard the whispering of the voices in his ear. Why did they insist on repeating her name?

Layla . . . Layla . . .

Ethan Acevedo drove the streets, unable to decide where to go next. He felt energized, wide awake after the rush of seeing Montoya's car go over the edge into the ravine. He'd dumped the stolen car he'd used out near Altadena. It had been so easy; there were many things that could've gone wrong, but they didn't. It was like fate was on his side, the way he'd gotten revenge on Montoya for making him live now like a hunted dog. He felt as if he could deal with all of them tonight, his own personal *Kristallnacht*, striking at his enemies in one brilliant blow, but he knew that would be too risky. He had to plan carefully and take them out in ways that seemed random.

A spasm of pain shot up his back. It hurt all the time now, and his neck felt as if it were in a vise, being tightened every hour he was upright. He grabbed a bottle of Norco he'd stashed in his dad's glove box and popped two into his mouth. He needed them every day now, but he had a good stash that he'd brought back from Mexico. Given his physical limitations, he considered that he might need a helper to finish up his work with the remaining targets. But he had to be careful who he approached.

It had to be someone he could easily blackmail, with too much to lose if Acevedo exposed him. Or an old-timer with a secure pension who hated the way everything had changed. Maybe Pineda, who lost his job at the LAPD and had to be bitter, seeing his life plans evaporate so quickly. Acevedo needed someone easy to manipulate and with an axe to grind with the department. Pineda might be perfect, and he was a lapdog anyway.

Acevedo headed back toward home, making a convenient stop by Detective Sandra Moody's neighborhood. She lived in Eagle Rock, a short excursion on the 2 freeway. He knew the house. It was a two-story Spanish style on a quiet residential street. She had an attached garage and no gate or fencing to the driveway.

Moody should know better . . .

He pulled up across the street from her house, under the branches of a big jacaranda tree. The street was so quiet. A stray cat sauntered across the sidewalk. Acevedo smiled, feeling a rush of power. He imagined Moody and her family, asleep in their beds, with no idea what was coming for them.

The next morning, Postiff and Barrera stood in the strip mall parking lot for Gus Pizza, the Yucca Market, and several other mom-and-pop businesses hanging on in the gentrification of the area. They were talking with workers. Postiff's phone rang—it was Marjorie Mellencamp, again. He ignored the call; since they'd visited her the day before, she'd called repeatedly with nonsense information that amounted to nothing. It was clear she just wanted attention, but he didn't have time for it today.

The morning traffic was still heavy. Cahuenga Boulevard looked like a parking lot heading into the pass. Barrera held out his phone and scrolled through the photos of the missing kids for one of the Yucca Market employees.

"Have you seen any of these kids recently?" Barrera asked.

The guy took the phone and looked intently at the photos. "I haven't seen these in the past few weeks. I used to see them all the time, but I saw this one yesterday," he said, pointing to the photo of Princess.

"Where did you see her?" Postiff asked.

"Right in the parking lot next door, by the liquor store. She was talking with a guy in a white car. And then he went into the CVS, and she got into his car when he was inside."

"Did you notice the make or model of the car?" Postiff asked.

"What'd the guy look like?" Barrera asked, fighting a cough that threatened to overtake him.

"The guy was just regular, maybe in his twenties. Blondish hair, kind of tall. The car? I don't know. It was a compact. Maybe a Corolla? Or a Fiesta. Then she had a fight with the other kid. The one who's like a little pimp or something."

"A street kid? He's a pimp?" Barrera said.

"I don't know if he's on the street like the others. He may have a crib. But he runs some of these super young girls. He came up when she was in the car and tried to pull her out, and then the older guy came out, and they argued. Then the little pimp kid backed off, but he was pissed."

"Do you know his name?" Postiff asked.

The guy shrugged and shouted to one of the workers from Gus Pizza. "Hey! Mario, you know the name of that kid? The one who runs the young girls?"

The Gus Pizza worker nodded. "Yeah, his name is Aiden. He likes thin crust with extra tomatoes and pepperoni."

"Yeah, that's his name. Aiden. And everyone knows the girl. That's Princess."

Cassidy and Riley were driving patrol near Gower and Melrose, debating whether to have lunch at Astro Burger or the dim sum place on Hollywood and Wilton that neither could remember the name of, when they saw a yellow van drive past them.

"Could that be the Banana Van man?" Cassidy asked, straining to see him as he folded into the other traffic. Riley hung a U-turn and followed. As they drew closer to the van, they saw the banana decals on the back doors.

"Yeah, that's him. Let's pull him over. I think he has a broken taillight," Riley said.

"No, he doesn't," Cassidy said.

"I didn't say he did, I said I thought he did," Riley said, putting on the siren and the flashing lights.

The van pulled over at Gower and Sunset, into the 7-Eleven parking lot. Cassidy and Riley approached and asked the driver for his license and registration. He was an overweight, balding man in his forties. His name was Darrin Meecham. The address on his license was a post office box that Riley knew was in a Mail Boxes Etc. business on Cahuenga and Melrose. The physical address on the registration was on Wilton, near Sixth, in Hancock Park adjacent.

"What did I do, officer?" Meecham asked, nervously. He was sweating, casting furtive glances to the back of his van.

"I think one of your taillights is out, Mr. Meecham," Riley said as Cassidy walked around the van.

"Do we have your permission to look inside your van?" she asked.

Meecham shrugged, stepping out of the van. "I guess. I don't have anything in there. I just use it to do grocery runs for my mom and get stuff from Home Depot. You know, plants and garden stuff. I live with her, she's elderly and needs a lot of help with stuff . . ."

As he rambled on, Cassidy opened the back doors of the van to find it was just like Steve Trejo from the Clubhouse had described; it was empty except for a mattress. And a grocery bag of energy drinks and pornographic magazines.

"What do you use this for?" she asked pointedly.

"I take naps sometimes . . . when I'm out. I have a medical condition; I get worn out easily . . ." he stammered.

"I wouldn't imagine you use it to pick up underage sex workers. Maybe this one in particular?" She held out her phone with a photo of Princess.

Meecham shook his head, protesting, "I didn't know she was under eighteen! I thought she was older!"

"How's that? She looks like a seventh grader. We heard from a number of kids in the area that you've been driving around, offering to buy them stuff, take them to lunch?" Riley grilled him.

"I just moved back here with my mom. I don't know the area that well, and I was just . . . trying to make some friends!" Meecham insisted.

"You're forty-three, and you were trying to make friends with homeless teenagers, and you have a mattress in the back of your van? Charmaine Mendoza, the young lady you thought was over eighteen, sent your license plate to a friend before you hooked up with her, which is why we have it," Cassidy said. "We're doing an investigation into the disappearance of a number of these minors. We have probable cause to think you could have something to do with that."

Meecham looked frantically from Riley to Cassidy. "I don't! I swear I don't! I just use hookers sometimes, okay? I'll admit to that. I'm a lonely guy, is that a crime?"

"Using the services of underage hookers is a crime, and it's also statutory rape. Your car will be impounded and processed by the forensics unit," Riley said, turning Meecham around and slipping cuffs on him. "You have the right to remain silent . . ."

As Riley read him his Miranda rights, Cassidy looked into the grocery bag and beneath the porn magazines, discovering several computer-generated pages of child pornography.

"I just found child porn in here, Riley," she said, texting Postiff about Meecham's arrest.

Riley grabbed Meecham by the arm and put him into the back of the patrol car. "You just like to take naps, huh?"

CHAPTER FOURTEEN

The party mess at the Raven's Nest was formidable, but Jeppe didn't put his lost angels to work on the cleanup, not yet. He had woken them early and herded them into the reading room, where they sat, hungover from drugs and alcohol, unsure of what had transpired the night before. He did a head count: Zephyr, Kyle, Anya, Autumn, Zeno. Princess was still asleep upstairs in the pink bedroom.

While they sat on the big couch and the overstuffed chairs, he stood in front of them, lecturing them on their higher truth and the need to transcend the binary limitations of their existence through physical freedom and mind expansion, which was his own brand of psychobabble that meant drugs and unrestrained sexual activity. He had taken the model of Manson, and this was a regular feature after his sex-infused parties. An hours-long lecture when they were exhausted, dehydrated, and vulnerable to his mental manipulations. He'd pored over websites and library books, honing and developing his message.

"You all are born with a wound, a deep and broken place inside of you that led you here. Why were you alone and abandoned, on the streets? What harm was done to you? You can only be healed here, in our circle. This new earth-mother chakral womb at the Raven's Nest, where you can be reborn to synchronize with your inner potential. Don't you all know you're meant for much more than this? Your basic, higher truth can only be accessed in this learning hologram that I have created for you. Don't I take good care of you, my angels? Don't you get enough food to eat? A warm bed to sleep in at night?"

They nodded and mumbled in agreement as he moved among them, stroking their hair lovingly. "You must reach outside the boundaries that society imposes on you, that's what we did last night. You had neuro-physical alignment, and I am the astral traveler meant to take you there. We are all avatars of the higher power," he said, with growing fervor.

The kids battled to stay awake, trying to show their allegiance to him, their spiritual guide and savior, as he rambled on, filling their drug-addled brains with his own personal cult philosophy. When he finally allowed them to sleep, satisfied with the potency of his message, he checked on Princess, who as his special party favor, was allowed to miss the indoctrination session. It was also her first time at one of his parties, and he wanted to bring her along slowly. She would remain at the Raven's Nest from now on. On his way upstairs, his phone rang. It was his adviser at USC, Professor Verhoeven.

"Hello, professor!" Jeppe said with false bravado. The last thing he wanted was a conversation with Verhoeven.

"Jeppe! Glad to hear your voice. I'm a bit concerned, you haven't been coming to class. Is everything okay?" Verhoeven asked.

"Yes, I'm fine, professor. I've been battling a bad case of the flu. It just keeps hanging on," he said, feigning tiredness.

"You've missed a lot of work. I want to make sure you keep up, so you stay on track for your PhD. There are some assignments you must get in by this week to maintain your credits," Verhoeven warned.

"I'll get to them this week, professor. Could you post them so I can be sure I have the right ones?" Jeppe asked, hiding his impatience.

"I'll do it now so you can get started. I want to make sure you stay in the program."

"Me, too, sir. I'll get caught up as quickly as possible. Thank you for your attention," Jeppe said, then hung up.

He had no intention of completing those missing assignments for Verhoeven or anyone else. He just needed to buy time before his parents discovered his academic status. He had to push his lost angels to cross the boundaries, to see how far he could make them go before his parents intervened and called him home. They could ruin all his plans. He hurried up the staircase to check on Princess.

In the pink bedroom he found her crashed out with the two frat boys in the bed. Jeppe's visual confection of the previous night was now a disheveled mess. Rick and Jed would be out until the afternoon. After they'd made the park run to dispose of the trash bags and returned, they'd taken a big hit of GHB. He was picking the soiled pink satin sheets up from the floor when his phone rang again and he saw the number of his landlord, Mark Smolin. He scowled; he hated it when people called him. He hated the intrusion and the way their voices sounded. He hated them for using up any of his valuable time and energy.

"Hello, Mr. Smolin! How're you today?" Jeppe asked in his best grad student voice.

"I'm fine, Jeppe. Listen, I know you're a young guy and there's lot of fun to be had in college, but I've had a complaint about the parties. I guess you've been having some people over, kind of late into the evenings?" Smolin inquired.

Jeppe's mind worked, wondering who could have possibly called his landlord.

"Well, I did have a few people over and maybe we played some music a little too loud. I'll be more considerate of my neighbors next time," he said amiably.

"I know, I was young once too. But an old guy like Mr. Russo just has a different view of things. So, yes, just keep it down in the future."

"Will do, Mr. Smolin. Thank you for bringing it to my attention," Jeppe said.

He hung up the phone and moved to the back terrace, where he could see Chris Russo out watering his vegetable garden. The old man had gone too far this time. Jeppe had overlooked when he gave Layla a ride the night she tried to flee. And the only reason he'd forgiven him was that Russo had driven him to pick her up and bring her safely back home. But now he would have to pay. Jeppe smiled; maybe the universe had presented him with the perfect test of his control over his lost angels. Maybe it was time to move the needle up a notch.

Cassidy and Riley were booking Darrin Meecham into the Hollywood station when Postiff and Barrera arrived. Barrera had just ignored another call from Marjorie Mellencamp, wishing they'd never gone to her house in the first place. She was driving him crazy with suspicions about her gardener, her neighbors, the mailman.

"What's up with the Banana Van man?" Postiff asked.

Riley gave him the information on Meecham about the mattress, the adult and child porn found in his van.

"What an upright citizen. He could definitely be involved in the disappearances. We'll get a warrant and see what we find," Postiff said. "Let's set him up in interview room one."

Watch Commander Steven Kriss hurried by. "Did you guys hear about Montoya? She's at Huntington Hospital in Pasadena. She had a bad accident last night, lost control of her car and rolled into a ravine."

"Diana? Was she in a collision?" Cassidy asked.

"Don't know. I just spoke to her mom; she hasn't regained consciousness yet."

"What does the police report say?" Riley asked.

"No report. Maybe it was a hit-and-run. Her car was found when someone noticed smoke rising from a ravine. Could've caught on fire," Kriss said.

"Where was it?" Cassidy asked.

"Not far from where she lives. One of those roads that runs parallel to the freeway, near Pasadena. Lucky they found her. I'll keep you posted," Kriss said, disappearing down the hallway.

"That's messed up. Maybe something ran out in front of her? A dog or a coyote, maybe she swerved to avoid it?" Postiff suggested.

"I'm going to go visit her when we get off," Cassidy said.

"I'll go with you, if you don't mind," Riley added.

"Give her my best. I'll try and go tomorrow," Postiff said as they headed back out to patrol.

A moment later, he and Barrera sat in the observation room, watching Meecham being brought in to be interviewed. He squinted at the overhead lights and shuffled his feet, as if the effort to pick them up was too much for him. He sat awkwardly, tapping his feet against the linoleum floor.

"Why are these guys always disgusting pigs?" Barrera asked. "Look at him! He probably hasn't showered in days, and I'm sure those clothes haven't been washed either."

"He probably has mental health issues as well as being a pedophile. He might be the lynchpin we're looking for with these kids," Postiff said, hopeful.

Joyce Ramsey arrived, her eyes shining with expectation as she blew into the room like the Santa Ana winds, bringing the unease and tension that always accompanied them.

"So, this creep that Cassidy and Riley picked up, he could be our Pied Piper with the missing kids, right?" she said brightly.

"Maybe," Postiff replied noncommittally. "Right now, he's just a creep who picks up underage sex workers and has child porn in his possession. We're pulling a warrant. I hope we find what we're looking for."

"Carbone said he lives in the area, near Hancock Park?" she asked.

"Yeah, lives with his elderly mother, he says. You live in Hancock Park, don't you, commander?" Barrera asked.

"Yes, in Hancock Park proper, not on Wilton and Sixth. But there are some big old houses over there. He could have a bunch of kids living with him. If his mother's elderly and out of it, she may not even know," Ramsey said. "Once we get a better idea of his involvement, we should schedule a press conference," she added with a satisfied smile as she turned to go.

"Is it my imagination, or has she gotten worse since the Hit Men case?" Barrera asked.

Postiff just shook his head. He had no time for Ramsey's posturing and premature theories. She wanted a quick arrest and a show of her ability to protect homeless kids who she never gave a damn about before there was some political advantage to helping them. But, like Ramsey, he hoped Meecham was their guy. He hoped they'd get a warrant for his house and find the missing kids, get them into social services, and lock Meecham up for a long time. He had a date with Millie that evening, and he wanted to have something good to share.

His phone buzzed; it was another call from Marjorie Mellencamp. Like Barrera, he'd begun ignoring her calls after the first three were about how she knew that her half brother in Cincinnati was somehow involved in 9/11 and had never been arrested. He sent her call to voicemail and prepared himself to interrogate the piece of human garbage waiting in interview room one.

Bill waited on the line for the representative from Golden State Care to confirm that his neurological tests had been approved. He'd been waiting forty-five minutes, being transferred to one automated answering prompt after another, each one insisting they needed a little more information to connect him to a living person. When he was married, his wife, Cathy, had handled this type of thing.

Once they divorced, he began skipping checkups and putting off problems because he simply didn't have the time to spend sitting on a phone on hold when he was working cases. Now, he was eager to start calling about Layla and Evie, but he had promised Cassidy he would get his appointments set on the calendar so she wouldn't have to do it for him. He still felt the sting of her words, telling him how he made everyone else adjust to his impulsive decisions, adapt to his wild mood swings. She'd played the role of grown-up too long while he lived too close to the edge. Finally, the representative came on the line.

"Okay, Mr. Clarke. I finally located your file and reviewed the notes with my supervisor, and unfortunately, we are still waiting for an approval. Dr. Baruch needs to send us some more documentation regarding your condition," she said.

"I've spoken to him several times. He assured me that he has sent you everything you need, twice. He said he's called you as well. It is completely in your hands at this point," Bill said, exasperated.

"I understand what you're saying, Mr. Clarke, but we do need some more information from the doctor. The requirements do change unexpectedly as the underwriters require more documentation."

"Do you get a bonus for denying approvals? For keeping customers from getting treated?" he asked.

The representative flustered and stammered in reply, "Of course not, Mr. Clarke. There is just a procedural protocol that—"

Bill interrupted her. "That you keep changing so you can deny referrals? You know, back in the day, Kaiser gave their operators a cash bonus if they limited the number of appointments that patients scheduled with doctors. And for how quickly they got off the call. Are you guys doing something like that?"

"Of course not. I'll make sure that someone gets back to you within twenty-four hours," she said quickly.

"Good, because that was a big lawsuit, and it would be pretty bad for another company to be caught doing it," he said, hanging up. He didn't believe he'd hear anything within twenty-four hours, but he enjoyed giving them a hard time. Now he dialed the phone number for Layla's mother, Denise Scobie, in Elko, Nevada.

"Hello?" she answered. Bill could hear the television on in the background.

"Mrs. Scobie, I'm a private investigator who's been hired to find your daughter, Layla. She went missing in Los Angeles this past week," he said.

"A private investigator? How did she go missing? I heard she might be in Los Angeles," Denise said.

"She didn't show up for a planned meeting with a friend, and there has been no contact with her since that day. Could you give me some background as to how Layla left home? I'm building a profile," Bill said.

There was a pause on the phone, then Denise said, "It was my fault. I'm the one who threw her out of the house."

"Why did you kick her out, if you don't mind me asking?" Bill asked.

"We had some disagreements, and I made a mistake," Denise said, her voice thick with remorse.

"How so?"

"I was dating a guy at the time. We'd been together for over a year, it was pretty serious. I thought we were going to get married. And Layla told me he'd been bothering her, coming into the bathroom when she was showering and stuff . . ." Her voice trailed off.

"And?" Bill persisted.

"And I didn't believe her. I said she was making it up, that she was jealous that I had a man and there was someone else in my life. But she dug in and said it was true, she said she'd call the police if I didn't get him out of the house."

"And you made her leave instead?" Bill said, not even trying to hide his contempt.

"Yeah. I did, and then six months later the guy was arrested for molesting a girl in the same apartment complex. They had proof, photos, all of it. And by then, it was too hard to find Layla. She'd left town, and I didn't know where she went. I filed a missing persons report and spoke to the cops 'cause she was under eighteen, but no one took it seriously."

"And you haven't heard from her since then?"

"Nothing. I even called police departments in other cities, I thought maybe she went to Vegas. I went there one weekend to look for her. But there was no sign of her. I heard from some friends of hers that she had gone to LA, but I never checked it out."

"I was hired to look for her. She's been missing for a few days now. We think she might be at risk. The police are also involved. I'll let you know if I discover anything, Mrs. Scobie."

"I wasn't a bad mother, really. I loved Layla, she was everything to me—"

Bill hung up on her protestations, unable to stomach one more word of her self-serving excuses for choosing a pedophile over her own daughter. He had a few other leads; tax records showed Layla had a job working at a Black Bear Diner in Victorville, California, prior to coming to Los Angeles.

It was an utterly forgettable town in the huge county of San Bernardino, off the freeway that connected LA and Las Vegas—a place of trailer parks, strip malls, and a flat, dusty landscape that only added to the sense of desolation. He planned to make the drive out later in the day to speak to the people who had worked with Layla, hoping that she might have been in touch with them or even gone out there to get away. He dialed Evie again; he'd been calling since the night before. This time she answered.

"Evie! It's Bill Clarke," he said, relieved.

"I know. I saw your number. Did you find Layla?" Evie asked.

"Not yet. I just spoke to her mother in Elko, Nevada, and I'm heading out to visit a place she worked before coming to Los Angeles. It's in Victorville, she may still have friends out there."

"Do you need me to come with you?" she asked.

Bill realized that she had nowhere to go and nothing to do, other than scrape together enough money to eat that day and try to find Layla.

Against his better judgment, he said, "Sure. You can fill me in on more details about her on the drive. I have a few more calls to make first. I'll get you at the Clubhouse in about an hour?"

"Okay! I'm leaving Cesar's now!" she said excitedly, like a little kid going to Disneyland.

Bill hung up and dialed her uncle, Arthur Peacock, in Eugene, Oregon. He answered after two rings.

"This is Dr. Peacock," Arthur said.

Bill winced. Arthur Peacock was a PhD academic who taught medieval history, not a medical doctor.

"Mr. Peacock, I'm calling from Los Angeles regarding your niece, Evie," Bill said, stressing the title "mister."

"Oh my god, is she okay?" Arthur asked.

"Other than the fact that she's homeless, she's doing fine, I guess," Bill said. "My name is Bill Clarke, I'm a retired LAPD detective and a private investigator. I'm looking into some missing kids here, and I met Evie at a teen resource center."

"Yeah?" Arthur asked, his voice wary and suspicious. "What is it you want from me?"

"I'm curious to know how your niece ended up in the foster care system and then homeless after your brother's death. You are her next of kin since we have no record of her mother, Geraldine, after 2009."

"That's because Geraldine moved to Europe. She's an artist, and she hooked up with a Spanish guy after she and John broke up, when Evie was a baby. I don't know where she is now. John never spoke of her after she left. I figured they would find her after John died, but I guess they didn't?" he asked, with false sincerity.

"No, they didn't. Her records show that she entered CPS in Oregon, which I assume you knew? You are listed as her next of kin in state."

There was a pause on the line. Bill heard Arthur shuffling papers.

"Yeah, I knew. I'm about to go to a class, Mr. Clarke."

"Sure, I just want to know why you and your wife didn't take Evie in when your brother died," Bill said bluntly.

Now Arthur sighed heavily. "I just couldn't do it, okay? My wife, Cristina, is a lot younger than I am, and she didn't want the responsibility of someone else's kid, especially a kid who was fourteen."

"Evie isn't just someone else's kid. She's your brother's daughter," Bill said.

"I get it, I do. And I felt really bad about it, but it just wasn't going to work. I had to keep the peace, and Cristina said no way. I mean, what did we know about teenagers? We had twin toddlers at the time, and we had our hands full."

"Since you both work, did you have a nanny?"

"Well, sure. Doesn't everyone?"

"Just want to be clear. You had a two-income family and financial security, a full-time nanny, and you still couldn't take in your only brother's kid, who was a good student, never in any trouble, who had become an orphan?" Bill asked, his anger and disgust evident.

"Look, I don't know why you're giving me a hard time. I did the best I could. I gave her money to get to Los Angeles!" Arthur whined.

"I'm giving you a hard time because you're a piece of shit, professor. Let me guess, was your wife your student?" Bill asked.

"What does that have to do with anything?" Arthur retorted, defensively.

Arthur Peacock was the second person Bill hung up on that morning before grabbing his keys to go pick up Evie at the Clubhouse.

CHAPTER FIFTEEN

Ethan Acevedo slept heavily in the dark basement of his parents' home. They still had no idea he was there, and the caregiver, Margaret, had avoided him since that first encounter in the hallway. Now he woke to footsteps above as they started their day, which consisted of watching television and taking a walk around the block. Margaret did all the grocery shopping and cooking.

He stared at the ceiling and relived the moment he saw Diana Montoya leaving her gym the night before. How he'd tailed her for several miles and she didn't even have a sense that he was so close by. He'd followed her a few times in the past. He'd even waited for her once and asked her to go out and get something to eat postworkout, but she'd given him a look like he was crazy and avoided him after that.

Just like Marilise had several years earlier. Like he was a creep or something. Since the attack in Rosarito, he wasn't the same physically, and he knew he'd have a hard time taking Montoya down—she was thick and as strong as a front loader. In the old days, he could've done it easily, but not any longer, which pissed him off. One day, he'd go back across the border and find that little whore and her buddies who had tried to kill him.

He'd had to rely on other tactics to take Montoya out, and he had succeeded, without being seen or noticed at all. His mole at the Hollywood station had filled him in on everything. They considered it an accident, that Montoya lost control of her car. Moody would be a bit more difficult, but he had already checked out her house and had a plan. After he took care of her, he'd move on to Postiff. Acevedo had been in the group of officers that waited outside at the school shooting where Postiff went in alone with just his service revolver. That had always pissed him off. Cassidy Clarke would follow Postiff, and his final act of revenge would be on Bill Clarke.

Bill was the one who should've taken the fall for Eden's murder. He was the one Acevedo was counting on being pinned with it. His fingerprints were there, the guy probably left semen behind as well since Eden was screwing him. But it was those damn blood drops, that's what his contact told him. They found the blood, and then they'd staked out his house to go through his trash. Cassidy and Montoya. It was two new boot bitches that caught up with him. He was curious to check up on Montoya, to see how badly she was hurt and if they thought she would survive. He even considered paying her a visit at the hospital in Pasadena, but it would most likely not come to that.

One down. Five more to go.

Princess woke up, groggy and stiff, unable to recall what had happened the night before. She remembered hearing people call Little Leo by his real name: *Jeppe.* And she recalled him giving her some really good X, and she felt incredible. She did her makeup super pretty and had the whole pink bedroom to herself, but later on, there were other people there with her. She didn't remember their faces or names, but they wanted her to do stuff, the kind of stuff all her tricks wanted, but it was different. And she felt sick after a while. That was when the two young guys showed up, but they were out of it and fell asleep right away.

Now, she slipped back into the clothes she'd been wearing at the party; they smelled of weed and alcohol. The room had been cleaned up a little, but the floor was still sticky and wet in spots. She pushed the door open and walked out to the hallway and down the big staircase. She found her friends from the Clubhouse sprawled out amid the wreck of the previous night.

Liquor bottles, drug paraphernalia, clothing, and undergarments were tossed everywhere; it looked like a tornado had blown through. She took several photos with her phone; she'd send them to Evie, who'd be shook.

She wanted a shower and a chance to sleep, away from the other kids and Jeppe. She wanted a big glass of water and Advil for her head. She wished she were at Marjorie's, where even if it was a mess, she never woke up there with no idea what had happened to her, with bruises and broken skin that she knew hadn't come from watching Hulu.

She'd been prepared for a night of partying. She'd been hired for that before at places like Dray's. But this was something different. She thought Jeppe was a freak. She slipped on some shoes that weren't hers—they were too big, but she didn't care. She tried the front door, but it was locked. She went to the kitchen and found the back door locked also. She wandered around the first floor, looking for windows that might be open, but she found no way out.

She climbed the long stairway, curious to see what was in the other upstairs bedrooms. One had a treadmill and some free weights, all covered in dust. There were unopened boxes, a stockpile of toilet paper, dish towels, other household items. The next room appeared to be Jeppe's; it held a king-size bed, and in the closet, men's clothing hung neatly. She recognized a pair of his shoes from the day he picked her up by Pla-Boy Liquor.

There was a small room at the end of the hall that held a twin bed with a dresser and a bookcase. Princess pulled a book from the shelf and saw that it had been checked out of the Los Feliz Branch Library. There was a piece of paper stuck between the pages with handwriting that she recognized as Layla's. She opened the dresser drawers and saw clothes of hers as well, folded with a scented sachet tucked among them. Everything in the room confirmed what Evie had told her about Layla coming to live with Little Leo.

Princess snapped a few more photos, hoping she would run into Layla, who might be able to help her get out of Jeppe's weird house. If not, she'd have to wait for him to come home and tell him she wanted to go back. Back in the pink bedroom, she found her charger and plugged her phone in. If she couldn't get out soon, she'd call Aiden. She fell asleep, her head pounding like a sledgehammer.

Cassidy and Riley were back out on patrol, checking the list they'd divided with Postiff and Barrera. As they drove east on Franklin, they passed restaurants with tables on the narrow sidewalk, crowded with pedestrians. Across the street, the Scientology Celebrity Centre loomed in a 1920s building that had been built to resemble a seventeenth-century French Normandy chateau.

"Wait, I think that billiard place is over here. The one called Dray's. Have you ever been there?" Cassidy asked.

"No, I only shoot pool at places that call it that, not billiards. I did go to dinner at one of those restaurants back there once, the ones with the tables in the sidewalk," Riley replied. "And it wasn't like a French café; it was like eating in the gutter. Where's the pool place?"

"I think it's on the side street. Hang a U," Cassidy said.

Riley pulled into the Gelson's supermarket and turned around, heading west on Franklin. Cassidy signaled him to make a right turn at Cheremoya Elementary School. Dray's Billiards and Brews was across the street, next to a coffee bar and a newsstand. The door was painted in a Gothic purple-and-black design, and when Cassidy and Riley stepped inside, they found a modern mirror-backed bar and several pool tables, one occupied by two young guys.

"What did the kids do here? This is an over-twenty-one place with the bar," Riley said as a tall, striking man came to meet them, dressed like a mannequin from the *Pirates of the Caribbean* in a brocade topcoat. He had black, slicked-down hair and a handlebar mustache that reminded Cassidy of a silent movie villain.

"How can I help you, officers? I'm Gregory Villalobos, the manager here at Dray's. Are you interested in a game of billiards?" he asked with a sweeping gesture.

"No pool today, Mr. Villalobos. We're wondering about some teenagers who said they come here from time to time. Street kids from the area. Do you recognize any of them?" Cassidy asked, showing him the photos on her phone.

Villalobos blanched briefly, then said, "No, we are a drinking establishment, so we do not allow minors."

Riley gestured to a series of black-framed charcoal drawings of men and women hanging behind the bar. "Who're they?"

"Those are drawings of some of our patrons. We have a sketch artist here from time to time as a kind of amusement," Villalobos said.

Riley stepped in closer to the bar and pointed to one drawing. "Could you get that one down for me, please?"

Villalobos stood on a chair and climbed up to grab the drawing. It was of a black-haired girl with big dark eyes, wearing a rhinestone tiara in her hair.

"Who does that look like to you?" Riley asked Cassidy.

"It looks a lot like Princess," she replied, pulling up her photo again and setting it in front of Villalobos. "Charmaine Mendoza, seventeen, homeless here in Hollywood. Why do you have a drawing of her on your wall?"

"I really can't say . . . perhaps our sketch artist brought that with her. I don't recall that . . . the young lady was ever here on the premises . . ." Villalobos stumbled over his words.

"Is this the whole establishment? Are there other rooms?" Riley asked.

"We have a private back room, for guests who wish to play poker or other card games."

"Why don't you show it to us?" Cassidy asked.

Villalobos eyed them, warily. "Do you have a warrant?"

"Do we need one? Because we can certainly pull one and come back with the detectives working this case," Cassidy said.

"And maybe a whole team of officers to aid in a search of the entire establishment? I'm sure the local news stations would love a story like that about a popular joint like this. Very good visuals," Riley added.

Villalobos nodded tersely and turned to lead them down a corridor to a private room with a round table and wooden captain's chairs upholstered in bloodred Naugahyde. Through a doorway covered with iridescent beads, there was a lounge with several couches and a daybed, a large flat-screen television mounted on the wall.

"And this room is for what? When your guests get tired and need to lie down?" Riley asked.

Villalobos blinked rapidly and said, "Sometimes we have high-profile clients who require . . . more privacy and discretion."

Cassidy fixed him with a hard stare and said, "Thank you, Mr. Villalobos. We'll double-check with the minors who told us they had been here, and you'll be getting a visit from two detectives, Judson Postiff and Peter Barrera. Perhaps your memory will serve you better by the time they arrive."

"Of course. We'll be expecting them. Thank you again, officers, for visiting Dray's. If you ever want to play billiards, it will be on us," Villalobos said, leading them back to the front door. The two young guys playing pool had disappeared. Villalobos watched as Cassidy and Riley got into their squad car and left.

There were a number of people he knew he should call, to alert them to the sudden police interest in Dray's. The owners in Beverly Hills, a couple of talent agents at the big three agencies, whose famous clients had a particular fetish for the street kids he'd denied knowing. A prominent member of the city council, among others. But he didn't feel like making anything easier for those assholes. They treated him like dirt when they came in, like he was the help meant to give them whatever they wanted. He took a bottle of the most expensive whiskey from the bar and poured himself a double shot. He knew who those kids in the photos were. He knew a lot of things.

Sophia Rangel was working up a sweat; this was the third mile of her morning walk, and she'd just begun the hike up Fire Road Thirty-Two in Griffith Park. She'd already been up to the observatory and done the loop, but now she decided to add a little extra push to her workout. The ten-pound weighted vest she'd bought on Temu made it that much harder, but her agent had told her she should lose a few pounds if she wanted to be considered for ingenue roles in television.

Her dog, a ridgeback mix named Biggie, walked beside her, and she saw no sign of anyone else on the trail, so she unhooked his leash. He stayed with her for a few minutes, then took off after a squirrel that darted across the trail, leading him down a brush-covered hillside.

"Biggie! Get back here!" she shouted, wishing she had invested in off-leash training. She heard his crashing around in the bush, yipping and barking. She knew she'd have to pull ticks off him, and he could even get bitten by a rattlesnake. She called him again and waited, but he did not return.

"You better not make me go down there and get you, Big Boy! If I have to come down there, you're going to have consequences!" she called, hearing him bark excitedly.

"Screw this . . ." she muttered angrily as she pushed the prickly bushes aside to head down the hillside to retrieve him. The branches scratched her legs, and she felt her sneakers sinking into the soft dirt as it seeped in and made her socks feel gritty.

"You are in so much trouble, Biggie!" she shouted as he came into view, and she slid the last few feet down the hill. Her foot came to a stop against a black plastic bag that had been torn open by coyotes and raccoons. It was seeping liquid and smelled foul; she covered her nose as she grabbed Biggie's collar and pulled him to her. He jumped over the bag, raking his legs across it, and a human forearm fell out. Sophia Rangel screamed and vomited her overnight oats onto her new Skechers.

CHAPTER SIXTEEN

Cassidy and Riley answered the call for a 419 shortly after they left Dray's Billiards and Brews. It was for a dead body found on a fire trail in Griffith Park. When they arrived another patrol team had already called the coroner's office, and they were speaking to the young woman who discovered the body. Riley approached Officer Ted Crawley, who had been at the academy with him.

"So, what is it?" Riley asked.

"Young woman, maybe early twenties, dark hair. She'd been in a freezer, but at some point she must've been taken out, because the decomposition is setting in. She's been cut up, split into two trash bags. Her face is in bad shape. It's gruesome."

"Could it be this girl? We're looking into some missing street kids, she's one of them," Riley said, showing him Layla's photo.

"No way to tell with the condition of the body. We'd need DNA to match or dental records at this point. We didn't move her, so we have to wait until the coroner comes to take her and see what the medical examiner says."

"She was dumped here? No ID of any kind?" Riley asked.

"Nothing. It was probably last night, 'cause there were crews here working yesterday during the day. The girl who was walking her dog found her. She's pretty freaked out," Crawley said.

Riley joined Cassidy, who was helping to direct traffic that had slowed as park visitors lingered to see what the commotion was. Another officer was stringing yellow crime scene tape to block the street, a third one was photographing license plates of the cars that were jammed up.

"What did Crawley say?" she asked.

"It's a young woman, she was dismembered, and the decomposition is enough that they'll need DNA or dental records," he explained.

"Jesus Christ! We should let Postiff and Barrera know. This might be part of their investigation," she said.

"I'll text them now."

Cassidy stopped a line of cars from approaching and directed them to turn around. Some of the drivers honked in annoyance, others gawked and tried to see what was going on, but she turned them back, taking photos with her phone of each license plate and the driver of each car.

One of them, a pudgy boomer with a frizzy, gray ponytail, shouted "Fascist!" at her as he backed his car away, flipping her off.

She hoped the body would not be Layla Waters. She wanted to find a weirdo who lured kids to commit petty crime and home robberies. She wanted all of them to return to the Kidz Clubhouse safely. She didn't want to find a murderer who dismembered young girls.

Bill drove the 210 freeway toward San Bernardino, where they'd catch the 15 and head to Victorville. They had just passed through Fontana and stopped at McDonald's, where Bill ordered a senior coffee and Evie got a two-cheeseburger meal. Now she sat in the passenger seat, happily eating her burgers and slurping a large Coke.

"I like these cheeseburgers. My dad and I used to get them," she said.

"I like them too. But I can't eat them very often anymore," Bill said. "If you don't mind my asking, when your dad was alive, did you have a house or an apartment?"

"A house. It was kind of like a cabin, but it had to be sold to pay his medical bills. Once he wasn't able to work, he lost his insurance."

"And no other family?" Bill prodded, having decided not to tell her he spoke to her uncle Arthur.

"I have an uncle, but he's an asshole. His wife's no better. He was the only one, and that was never going to work. But my dad did ask him to take me."

"How do you know that?"

"I listened in on the phone call. My uncle sounded like a little bitch!" she said with a laugh, but Bill could only imagine how hard it had to be to hear that conversation.

"And no word on your mom? No idea where she might be?" Bill asked.

"I think she's in Europe somewhere. She's an artist, that's where I get it from."

"You like to draw?"

"Paint, draw, whatever. I like all of it. I was going to be an art teacher when I was still in school, but that's never going to happen," she said, popping a french fry into her mouth as she looked out the window.

"Maybe we could find your mom? Would that be okay with you?" Bill asked tentatively.

Evie shrugged again. "I guess. I don't remember her at all. She is my mother, but I don't think she has any interest in me. She never came looking for me, right?"

"How about finishing school? Did you like it before you dropped out?"

"Yeah, I had good grades too. I had a group of girls I hung out with. But once I went into foster care, it was like I was totally sus. Like I was a bad influence, and their moms didn't want them hanging out with me."

Bill was silent, stunned at the banal cruelty of some adults. He tried to imagine Evie's life back then: orphaned, abandoned by her uncle and her friends, and pushed into CPS. He knew the statistics of abuse in foster homes; he'd met plenty of people who got into it for the money and nothing more. He thought of Cassidy at that age, going to her soccer games and ballet classes, safe with two parents who adored her. He and Cathy had shown up at every parent-teacher conference since kindergarten. He'd gone to doctor's appointments, he knew her friends' names and what their parents did for a living, who else was in their home if Cassidy went over to play.

His phone rang; it was Cassidy. He took the call on his car's Bluetooth system.

"Hey, Binkie! What's up? I'm here with my client, Evie Peacock, driving to do some background digging on Layla Waters. We're heading up to Victorville, to the Black Bear Diner."

There was a pause on the line. "You're with Evie in the car? On speaker?" Cassidy asked.

"Yeah, what's up?"

"I'll try you later. I've got to go," Cassidy said, abruptly hanging up.

Forty-five minutes later, Bill pulled into the parking lot for the Black Bear Diner, hoping for good news about Layla. If he could locate her out here, safely with friends, he would be able to fix at least one broken thing in Evie's life. Inside they found a restaurant crowded with truckers and other people stopping on the highway between California and Las Vegas. The hostess was a middle-aged woman with a Loretta Lynn–style bouffant hairdo. As she seated them, Bill asked, "Do you by any chance remember a young woman who worked here several years ago? Dark hair, named Layla Waters?"

The hostess smiled. "Oh sure! I remember Layla! She used to live with Audrey's family when she worked here. Audrey is here today, I'll send her over. How is Layla? She just stopped coming to work one day."

Bill hid his disappointment that she hadn't returned to the area.

"She's in Los Angeles now," Evie offered.

"Los Angeles? What on earth is she doing there? Things are crazy out there," the hostess said.

"Lots of things. She was getting ready to go to community college," Evie said.

"Audrey will be happy to hear that," the hostess said as she walked off to speak with a blond woman in her fifties. A moment later the blond approached their table, wiping her hands on a kitchen towel.

"I'm Audrey Pardee. Jeannette said you know Layla. We worry about her. She stayed with us for almost a year. She's in Los Angeles now?"

"Yes, we thought that maybe she'd come back here to visit with friends," Bill said.

"We're looking for her. She's missing," Evie blurted out.

"Missing? How?" Audrey asked, clearly upset at the news.

"I'm sure we're going to find her. We're just retracing her steps in a way," Bill explained.

"Well, she came here after she left Nevada. She was doing real good too. She stayed with us when I figured out she didn't have no place of her own. A good kid. One day we had a bunch of bikers come in, they were at some gathering out in the desert and they were giving her a hard time, you know? Flirting, making rude remarks. One of them said he'd be back the next day to see her, and she left that night, after we were all asleep. Just gone, like poof!" Audrey said.

"She didn't leave a message or a note to say where she was going?" Evie asked.

"No, nothing like that. I knew those bikers scared her. They were rude and macho, you know? And she'd been through some stuff back in Nevada . . ." Audrey said, choosing not to elaborate in front of Evie but giving Bill a pointed look. His phone rang again; it was Cassidy.

"Evie, order anything you want. I've got to take this call," he said, stepping outside as Evie chatted with Audrey.

"Hey, Binkie, what's up?"

"Are you alone?"

"Yeah, I stepped outside to talk, Evie's ordering food in the diner."

"There was a young woman found dead today in Griffith Park. We're waiting for the coroner to come and take the body. It could be Layla Waters. Twenties, dark hair, but they'll need DNA to confirm. The decomposition is too far along for a physical ID. I didn't want to say anything when Evie could hear me," Cassidy said.

Bill's shoulders slumped; the heat from the highway seemed to rise off the asphalt, mixing with the ever-present dust, burning his eyes and nostrils.

"How soon will you know?" he asked.

"Postiff and Pete are on their way. They were interviewing the Banana Van guy when we called them. We picked it up as a 419. The coroner should be here within the hour, and we'll find out where we're at. Did you speak to Layla's mother earlier?"

"Yeah. A familiar story. She had a boyfriend who was bothering Layla, and she blamed the kid."

"You might have to ask her for DNA."

Bill nodded somberly. It was a call he'd hoped to never make again when he retired.

"I know. Keep me posted, and I'll call the mother if we need a sample. Maybe something else will come through, maybe another young woman's been reported missing in the area," he said, hanging up. He considered texting Melinda at the Clubhouse to let her know but decided against it. There was no need to cause her any more anxiety than she already felt.

Bill pocketed the phone and went back into the restaurant to find Evie with a large piece of pie in front of her.

"That's two pie places in two days for us!" Bill joked, trying to put on a happy face for Evie. She grinned at him as she took a forkful of lemon meringue.

He felt like he was walking on a tightrope with Evie Peacock. She had affected a tough, couldn't-care-less attitude, but he knew it was a defense mechanism. He saw how she'd teared up, recounting not being able to go live with Layla in Atwater. He worried that anything he said might trigger a bad memory or cause her some pain that he couldn't predict. She reminded him of the blown glass statues he used to buy Cassidy on every visit to Disneyland. She had a collection of them: Snow White, Cinderella, Tinker Bell, and the other Disney heroines. So fragile that the glass shop had to be the last stop of the day on the way out for fear they'd break.

Evie grabbed a second fork and stuck it into her piece of pie, holding it out to Bill.

"Have a bite. It's fire!" she said.

He took the piece of pie and ate it, waving Audrey over to their table.

"I was just wondering, since Layla left so suddenly, did she leave any of her belongings behind? We could take them to her when we locate her," Bill said, hoping there might be a hairbrush or toothbrush she left that would contain her DNA.

"Oh, that'd be nice! She left a bunch of stuff. Books from online classes she was taking and some real pretty dresses. I can go get them, my house is right next door," Audrey said.

As she walked away, Evie nodded at Bill. "That was a good idea. Layla will be so surprised to get her stuff back."

"I think so too," he agreed, praying silently that the body in the park wasn't Layla Waters.

Captain Landon Dykstra was at his desk in the Hollywood station, wondering how long he would have to wait before taking his next break. He'd left a box of Krispy Kreme donuts in the station kitchen fridge, and he wanted to make sure to get one more before anyone else snagged them all.

Postiff and Barrera had left mid-interview with a fat pedophile they'd picked up in Hollywood, now that there was an investigation into the missing street kids. Ramsey and Carbone had chewed him out over that, for not passing on the information from the Clubhouse director who'd called. There were cops doing extra patrols in the area, and they'd put Postiff and Barrera on it, when everyone knew it was a waste of time. Those kids came and went on their own schedule. Most of them didn't want help anyway, as far as he was concerned. They were kind of omnipresent, like cockroaches in an old apartment building.

His cellphone buzzed in his pocket; it was an unlisted number, which always made him nervous. He knew who it might be.

He tucked his head down and answered, "Hello?"

"Hello, cap-i-tan!"

Dykstra tensed at the sound of Acevedo's voice on the other end of the line. "What can I do for you?" he asked.

"Any updates on the Balcomb case? Anyone new in the mix?"

"No, the same suspect is still the main focus of the investigation," Dykstra replied, sounding officious.

"And what is my little friend Postiff up to these days? Where's he hanging out?"

Dykstra heard the threat in Acevedo's voice. They all knew that Diana Montoya had been in a serious car accident.

"He's working a missing kids case with backup from Cassidy and Riley. Extra patrols, all of that," Dykstra said, his voice sounding like air escaping a balloon. "I don't have much else to say."

"Really? Because I'm sure your wife and the lieutenant would like to hear about your relationship with that tranny hooker over by the army surplus store. You know the one I mean."

Dykstra almost bit his tongue at the mention of his girlfriend, Ja-won. He wished he'd never asked for Acevedo's help in hiding evidence from her drug bust several years earlier.

Acevedo continued with his threat. "I bet Ramsey and Carbone would love to know where that meth went. I'd be happy to tell your wife how you like them half done, girls on top, still boys down below, right?"

"What do you want to know?" Dykstra asked stiffly.

"Postiff's address, his hangouts, where he goes. And Cassidy Clarke's schedule."

"I'll text you the information. Postiff's dating that girl from the Hit Men case, the one who survived," Dykstra whispered before hanging up.

Acevedo lay on his futon in the cool basement, eating a bag of Doritos. Postiff had a girlfriend who survived a Hit Men attack. He smiled. There were a lot of ways to get retribution that wouldn't touch a well-styled hair on Judson Postiff's head.

CHAPTER SEVENTEEN

Postiff and Barrera arrived at Fire Trail Thirty-Two in Griffith Park to find the coroner's van and support vehicles parked on the blocked-off road. Cassidy and Riley were there with a handful of patrol officers to control the area. Several local television station vans had arrived, with reporters at the ready. Postiff peered over the edge of the trailhead to see the white canopy set up on the hillside.

"Any news yet?" Barrera asked.

"Not yet. They're down there with the body now," Riley replied.

"Are you still thinking it could be Layla Waters?" Postiff asked.

"Could be," Riley said grimly.

Postiff peered over the edge of the trail. "It's clearly a dumping ground. We should cordon off the surrounding area and search it." He noticed Pete sweating in the heat. His face was pale.

"Barrera, go back and sit in the car with the air blasting for a little while."

"I'll make some calls, see if we can figure out who she is. And I'll let Ramsey know," Barrera said, happy to get into an air-conditioned car. He sauntered back to the comfort of the sedan.

"How'd it go with the Banana Van guy?" Cassidy asked, turning back to Postiff.

"He's a weird, maladjusted pedo, but I don't know if he has the savvy to get a bunch of kids to work for him. We're waiting on a warrant for his house."

"I told my dad this victim could be Layla. He spoke to her mother earlier, and he'll ask for DNA if we need it," Cassidy said. The heaviness of her words hung like a mourning cloak over all of them.

Marjorie Mellencamp hung up the phone, annoyed that neither of the detectives had called her back. She'd left them so many messages about important things. People they needed to investigate: secret groups like the Freemasons, who control the judges and had Bobby Kennedy killed. Now that she had met actual detectives, she felt it was her civic duty to keep them informed about all the goings-on in the city. There was no way that they could stay on top of everything. But no one was returning her calls.

She'd left messages about what she'd seen in the park, the car on the fire road and the men dumping black bags. The disturbing face of the young man illuminated by her headlights. They couldn't have been up to anything good at that hour. The police always said if you see something, say something, and here she was, trying to report something suspicious, and no one would call her back. But she was used to being ignored and invisible to most people. It happened all the time at her age.

Once beautiful, once the focus of so much attention, she had learned the steep price to pay for shining too brightly. And then came age, and with it, the slow fade, like a movie screen going dark at the end of the picture. No one looked at you, no one listened. What could you possibly have to say of any value at seventy-five? Irrelevance was a mantle that was never worn with ease, but she tried to carry it with grace.

She hoped some of the Clubhouse youngsters would come by today. She needed help getting tablecloths down from the attic, and she wanted to organize her silver flatware. She also had to go to the store, and she would need help bringing her groceries inside. The last time she'd used Instacart, the shopper brought her all the wrong things. Who would bring whipped cream in a can instead of L'Oréal Whipped

Crème Facial Cleanser? Even though she hated going out during the daylight hours, she would have to make an exception and do it today. She put on her wide-brimmed sun hat and her long sun gloves, and searched for her keys to the Thunderbird, locating them under a pile of unread *Parade* magazines, and headed out.

Jeppe took Chris Russo's Corolla again, but this time he didn't ask permission. He just used the key he'd been given and drove away with it. Knowing that Russo had complained to his landlord, Jeppe didn't feel he owed the old man any further courtesy. In fact, he had already chosen the three of his lost angels that he would use to deal with Russo: ever-loyal Anya, Autumn, and Zeno. He was curious to see if he could make them cross the line, to go beyond petty thievery and car break-ins. He felt they were ready.

He drove toward Hollywood and Griffith Park, anxious to see if there was any activity where he'd dropped Layla's body with Rick and Jed. He figured it would be some time before she'd be discovered; the trash bags had rolled down the hill into the ravine. He also wanted to see if there were any new kids who caught his eye. He hoped to build a following of at least fifteen to twenty disciples within the next month or so. He needed fresh blood, new faces. With a small army of young people who would blindly carry out his will, he would be powerful in ways he had not ever been. The voices that rang in his ears sounded happy, like choir singers saying his name.

Jeppe, Jeppe . . .

stralende Jeppe . . .

genial Jeppe . . .

He turned on Vermont Avenue above Los Feliz Boulevard to head up into the park. As he came around the turn leading to the observatory, he saw that the police had blocked the road with yellow tape. A cluster of police cars were stationed, officers moving among them. A white coroner's van was parked at the entrance to the trail. Jeppe's heart began to beat wildly in fear. They had found Layla too quickly.

He counted back over the hours that had passed since they had dumped the trash bags. He was betting on her body decomposing completely by the time anyone stumbled upon her remains. They might be able to identify her, and how many people had seen him with her? Old Chris Russo had brought her back to the Raven's Nest. The kids had seen her, that busybody Melinda Drake had probably seen them together as well. And the clerks at the Los Feliz Branch Library.

He kicked himself for not waiting longer to dump her, but the fucking freezer in the shed broke, and if he hadn't gotten rid of her when he did, everyone would've smelled her, and that could've led to a rebellion among his lost angels. They loved Layla. He'd told them that she had gone back to Nevada to see her mother. If they'd found her rotting in the well, he didn't even want to imagine what might have happened.

He got caught in a line of cars that were forced to turn around. The officers were looking at every driver, checking license plates, snapping photos. He was trapped. There was no way to escape them without being noticed. He had to drive up to them and turn his car around, knowing that they were taking note of everyone. In his head, he heard the voice, the old man this time. The judgment, the hate.

Idiot, you didn't know what you were doing, did you? Thought you were the mastermind. You're a stupid, reckless fool . . . and they're going to catch you . . .

Jeppe turned his car around and drove as quickly as he could back to the streets below the park without attracting attention. He didn't think he could ever drive up there again. He told himself that they would not have any way of connecting him to the body; he made Rick and Jed handle the bags and do the dumping. They were too drugged up to remember what they had done or not done. He would be fine.

He followed Vermont to Hollywood Boulevard, planning to go to JONS Fresh Marketplace for the Turkish delight the lost angels loved so much. He pulled into the parking lot, and then he saw it. The vintage white Thunderbird he had seen in the park. It was backing out of a space, and Jeppe turned his car around to follow it. He had to see the woman who drove it and where she lived. She had seen things that were very dangerous to him. When the story broke in the news about Layla's body, she might contact the police, might give them a description of him, standing in the high-beam lights in full view.

Seeing the car was a sign, a beacon leading him to the right place, to protect himself and his lost angels who depended on him. He followed the white car through traffic, his body relaxing. Everything was going to be fine. He had no reason to worry.

The car was definitely a sign. The whispering voices in his head agreed.

Princess searched the refrigerator at Jeppe's house for something to eat. It was filled with leftovers from the party, but none of it looked appealing to her. Her stomach still felt queasy, and her head still hurt. She grabbed an open bag of Doritos and went to the living room, where she found Autumn, Zeno, and Anya acting out some kind of game. Princess pushed a pile of clothes off a chair and sat back in it, crunching chips.

"What the hell are you guys doing? You look like crazy people," she said.

Anya glared at her. "Jeppe has given us a special mission to carry out, and we're practicing how we're going to do it."

"What? You're like *PAW Patrol* or something?" Princess laughed.

Anya angrily scooped up the clothing Princess had tossed to the floor. "No, it's something serious that he'd only give to angels he trusted, which doesn't mean you!"

"Oh fuck, did you just call yourself 'angels'? He's just manipulating you, and you're too dumb to know it," Princess said.

"And you're not supposed to toss things on the floor like that! Those are clothes that need to go into the laundry!" Zeno shouted at her.

Princess sprang up and put her face close to Zeno's.

"Don't yell at me, you little punk! He has you acting like his slaves, cleaning the house, snorting drugs and all kinds of shit. He locks the door so you can't get out. There's not even a good Wi-Fi signal here! This whole thing is messed up, and you can't see it 'cause you think he cares about you. You're his lost angels, isn't that what he says?" Princess shouted.

Anya shoved her, and Autumn picked up a heavy bookend, moving toward her.

"Stop talking shit about him! He's saving us, he's the only one who's ever cared about what happens to us!" Anya screamed.

Princess grabbed a glass paperweight and threw it toward Autumn, intentionally missing her. It smashed into the wall, leaving the plaster cracked. Autumn backed off, frightened.

"See what you did? He's going to be mad now!" Autumn cried out.

Princess looked at them and backed out of the room. "You're all nuts. Stay here, do whatever he wants. But I'm gonna get out of here . . ." she said, hurrying back to the bedroom.

She didn't want to show it, but she was scared of what Anya and the others had become since living with Jeppe. She tried again to send the postparty photos to Evie and a text to let her know that she was at Jeppe's house. She wished she'd taken note of the address the day she arrived. She didn't have the Wi-Fi network or password, so she never knew if the messages went through or not. But she tried anyway.

She shoved a dresser in front of the door to block it and gathered her few belongings into her Hello Kitty bag. She had to find a way out when there was a chance and Jeppe was distracted. She hadn't seen any sign of Layla since finding her stuff in the small bedroom. She began to wonder if she'd had to escape also. Or maybe she'd never left at all.

Bill was about half an hour from Los Angeles, barely beating the soul-crushing traffic that would be trapping drivers by midafternoon. In the trunk they had a bag of Layla's belongings. Evie was thumbing through one of her books while sipping a Coke. Bill knew he couldn't tell Evie anything about the body in the park until they had an identification, but news like that traveled fast on the streets; he was afraid of what she might do if someone told her.

"So, what're your plans for the rest of the day?" he asked.

"Same as always. I'm gonna try to make some cash, try to get a spot for the night at the Clubhouse or Cesar's. I want to work on some drawings, too, from photos I have of Layla. I used to draw portraits of a bunch of us from the Clubhouse. I did it in the park once for money, but a cop ran me off since I didn't have a permit," she said.

"What kind of jerk would do that?" Bill scoffed.

"One of your buddies, in a uniform. Feeling all important with his shiny badge," Evie said sarcastically.

They hit a snag of traffic where someone had smashed into the divider, and everyone had to slow down and rubberneck. Bill looked over at Evie, so petite in the passenger seat, her raggedy tennis shoes and well-worn blue jeans that had been washed too many times. He knew he would never sleep, wondering where she was when night fell.

"Hey, you want to come stay at our house for a few days?" he asked suddenly.

Evie eyed him warily. "You're not getting weird, are you?"

"My god, no! Of course not! I live with my daughter, out in the valley. It's a good-sized house; we have a pool and all. We've got a guest room we rarely use, and you could stay there, just to chill out and relax. I'm a very good cook also, I'll have you know. I'm making those fancy meal kits now, stuff you've never heard of," he said with a hopeful grin.

"Does your daughter agree about your cooking skills, or is it a boomer delusion?" Evie asked with a small smile.

"I'm taking that as a 'yes' from you, Miss Peacock. Case closed," he said as the traffic began to move again. "You can stay with us until . . . whenever."

He didn't want to say anything about the body in the park until they knew if it was Layla or not. He was going to enlist Cassidy to help him find Evie's mother or a relative or some situation that would get her off the street for good. He was not leaving her alone and on her own, ever again.

Cassidy and Riley sat with Postiff and Barrera in Carbone's office, waiting for Joyce Ramsey to arrive. They were silent; the dead body of a young woman was not what they had expected.

"Sorry about this, Pete. I thought this would be a nice low-key investigation for you in the twilight months of your career," Carbone said.

Barrera shrugged. "Can't be helped."

"I've checked all the missing persons reports up and down the state in the past two weeks. There are a couple who could be a match, age and size wise," Postiff said.

"But what if it is Layla?" Cassidy asked.

"Then we have a more complicated situation on our hands," Carbone said as Ramsey arrived, her frustration palpable.

"It's a homicide, she didn't cut herself up and climb into trash bags. Postiff, you and Pete take it, and let's hope there's no overlap with the missing kids and that we don't find any more bodies dumped in the park, of all places. It's going to be all over the evening news!" she said as if it were an inconvenience that had ruined her Fourth of July barbeque.

"I'd like to get a warrant for Darrin Meecham's house. We know he's been trying to hang out with these kids. He's solicited sex from a minor, who no one has seen in the past twenty-four hours, at least," Postiff said.

"Which one is that?" Ramsey asked.

"The one they call Princess, she's an underage sex worker, a runaway. Real name is Charmaine Mendoza," Riley said.

"Jesus! It's almost ten teenagers missing! How did this spiral so quickly? Get on the warrant now, I'll put in a call to Judge Randall. We can have it by this evening. Maybe we'll get lucky and Meecham is our guy," Ramsey said. "It's going to be a long night, everyone."

Barrera stood up and moved to refill his coffee cup. Cassidy and Riley exchanged a weary look, and Postiff dialed Millie Grace to cancel their date for the evening. Now he'd be checking out alleyways and freeway underpasses for dead bodies and searching the house of the Banana Van pedophile.

Millie Grace was rinsing out the dishes, casting a glance to her roommate Rosalie McTeer, who stood at the window, subtly pulling the blinds back to look at a car that had been parked on their quiet street for the past hour. A lone man sat inside with a bucket hat pulled low over his eyes and sunglasses.

"Is he still there?" Millie asked.

"Yes. He might be waiting for someone, but I feel like he has a direct sight line to our front door," Rosalie said nervously.

They had both been on edge since Millie was attacked by Ron Whitty and Vithu Pham in the Hollywood Hit Men murders. Millie had barely survived the attack and still had vision problems in her left eye. They feared that Rosalie had been the intended victim, and both would testify in the trial that was coming up in the next few months. Since then, they'd been hypervigilant about keeping an eye out for unfamiliar faces in the neighborhood. Their landlord had installed extra security cameras, as had their direct neighbors.

Millie had noticed the man in the Jeep Wrangler earlier in the day, assuming he was picking someone up or making a delivery, but neither of those scenarios had played out, and he remained sitting in his car.

He wasn't a known person in their neighborhood, and the car wasn't familiar either. She was drying her hands when her phone rang.

"Hi, Jud, what's up?" she said brightly, happy to get his call.

"We've had a new development in the case I'm on. It's a homicide now, you may see it on the news. A girl was found murdered in the park. I'm going to have to work later than I planned, and we'll be executing a search warrant. I'm sorry to cancel," he said.

"That's okay. But do you think you could swing by on your way home, no matter how late it is? Rosie and I are kind of freaked out. There's been a guy sitting in his car up the street from our house for the past few hours. We're probably just paranoid, but could you come by?" she asked.

"Sure. Get a photo of his car. Walk right out on the front lawn and take it. If he sees that you've noticed him, he may take off," Postiff advised. "Creeps like that want to intimidate you. Show him you're onto him."

"Okay. See you later."

Millie hung up and opened the front door; Rosalie grabbed her arm to pull her back.

"What're you doing? He'll see you!" she warned.

"Judson said to go out and get his photo and let him see me do it."

Millie walked out onto the lawn with Rosalie behind her, both of them facing the Jeep as Millie began taking photos of the car. The driver immediately started the engine and drove away. Rosalie watched him go, impressed.

"Having a detective boyfriend pays off," she said.

"Judson said they found a dead girl's body in the park today," Millie said, anxiously.

"In the park? That's so close. It's just a mile away," Rosalie said.

"I know. It seems like there's always stuff like that going on," Millie agreed.

"Or we know more about it now that you're dating Judson. Maybe we should move?" Rosalie suggested, locking the door behind them as they stepped inside.

Millie didn't respond. It was a thought that had been on her mind a lot in recent weeks, and the day's events didn't make her feel any better. Her big-city dream was shifting into something more like a nightmare.

Ethan Acevedo turned onto one of the winding streets below the Bronson Caves recreation area. He couldn't believe that the little blond that Postiff was fucking had walked right out and taken a photo of his car. Good thing it wasn't really his car. He'd hot-wired it near the donut shop on Melrose and Vine and used it to make the ten-minute drive to her house and conduct some reconnaissance.

He wanted to get the layout of her street and how her house lined up, what type of access he would have if he decided to go in. Dykstra said her name was Millie Grace. He laughed softly. It sounded like a name from a different century, like someone in those English movies that Marilise liked so much. He could never understand them. Everyone talked too much, and nothing ever happened that held his interest.

Postiff's girl looked feisty, which he rather liked, but with two of them in the house, he might have to come up with a different plan. He noticed that they had a fancy camera system, and since she was a witness in the Hit Men case, he knew she was being protected to some degree. They were probably giving her extra drive-by patrols, especially if she was dating a detective.

Maybe Sandra Moody would be the best one to hit next. She had probably forgotten all about him, thinking he was in Mexico. The Clarkes lived way out in Chatsworth and that was a whole production number of effort and planning. He ditched the car near the Hollywood Forever Cemetery. He'd heard they put Eden in the mausoleum there and hoped he'd get the chance to visit her one day. Just to pay his respects.

CHAPTER EIGHTEEN

By the time Bill reached home, Evie was asleep. She was slumped in the passenger seat, and Bill went into the house alone to prepare the guest room for her. He grabbed blankets from the linen closet and folded them on top of the bedspread. In the rarely used extra bathroom, he grabbed a handful of Lysol wipes to freshen it up. He hung two clean towels and made sure there was shampoo, toothpaste, bodywash, and an unopened toothbrush for her on the counter.

He turned on several lights in the living room before he went outside to retrieve her from the car. She was out cold, and when he opened the door, she startled awake. She looked around, confused.

"Where are we?" she asked.

"You're at our house. I've got the guest room fixed up for you. The door locks, and you'll have your own bathroom. We've got food, snacks, drinks, whatever you need, if you get hungry. You can stay here as long as you want."

Evie looked up at him in mute gratitude, shaking off slumber. She got out of the car and grabbed her cross body and backpack and followed Bill inside.

"Are you sure this is okay?" she asked.

"Yeah, it's my house. I don't have to ask permission." He laughed. "C'mon, I'll show you to your room."

He led her down the hallway to the guest room, where she set her bags down and sat on the bed, taking it in.

"You said the door locks?" she asked.

"Yeah. You can lock it when you go to sleep, and the bathroom is connected, so you don't have to come to the hallway. You want to do any laundry?"

She handed him her two bags. "Yeah, everything. Thanks. We have to remember to bring Layla's things inside also. I don't want to forget them."

"I'll get them now, you can just chill for a while," he said, closing her door behind him as he left. He went outside to retrieve the bag of Layla's items from the car. He found a toothbrush and a hairbrush that still had strands of her hair tangled in the bristles. He put those in a separate bag, just in case the ME was unable to identify the body in the park and they needed DNA. He didn't want to call Denise Scobie in Elko with the disturbing request.

Back in the house, he tossed Evie's items into the washer and started the cycle. She hadn't eaten since the stop at the Black Bear Diner, so he opened a jar of spaghetti sauce and put some pasta to boil. He remembered that Cassidy always slept well after a big plate of spaghetti.

He heard the shower running and dialed Melinda Drake at the Kidz Clubhouse.

"Hello, Mr. Clarke! Are you the guardian angel who gave us the new washer and dryer?" Melinda asked warmly.

"Yeah, I thought new ones would be better than trying to fix the old ones. I'm glad they showed up. I just wanted to give you a heads-up that Evie asked me to help her find Layla, and we drove out to Victorville earlier, where she used to live."

"Did you find any sign of her?" Melinda asked.

"The people there knew her, but she hasn't been back. I just wanted to check to see if it's okay for Evie to stay with my daughter and me at our house for a few days?"

"Sure. We have no jurisdiction over the kids, they are basically on the loose on their own. But with everything going on, I feel better knowing that Evie is safe with the two of you."

"I'm hoping we can find Layla and the others and get everyone on a better path soon," Bill said.

"From your mouth to God's ear, Mr. Clarke," she said.

"You can call me Bill," he said.

"And you can call me Melinda. I'll let you and the detectives know if I hear anything about any of the kids."

Bill hung up. The water was still running in the guest shower; he figured Evie was enjoying a real shower with unlimited hot water for a change. He opened his laptop and began searching for any information he could find on Evie's mother and the Oregon CPS case. He was on a mission to find a permanent, safe place for Evie, even if it meant her joining their family in Chatsworth. Years ago, Cassidy used to ask endlessly for a younger sibling. Maybe she would be getting her wish.

Cassidy and Riley left work at the same time with a plan to meet up at Huntington Hospital in Pasadena to check on Montoya. Postiff and Barrera would execute the search warrant with other officers backing them up. Cassidy considered going to Meecham's to help, even if she was off the clock, hopeful that they would find the missing kids and everything would be over. She pulled into the hospital parking lot and then sprinted to the lobby to wait for Riley, who arrived a few minutes later. They rode the elevator to the third floor.

"I hope she's awake," Cassidy said nervously.

"Me too."

They found Diana's room and stepped in to find her family gathered. Diana's mother, Leonor, knew Riley and embraced him.

"Thank you for coming, Sean," she said.

"This is Cassidy, she and Diana worked together on a murder case a few months ago," Riley explained as Cassidy shook everyone's hands.

"Oh yes, you were the trash diggers," Leonor said with a weak smile. "She just woke up a couple of hours ago. An officer from Pasadena was here to talk to her."

Montoya gave them a smile and a thumbs-up as they pulled up chairs next to her hospital bed. She looked dreadful. Her head was wrapped, and both eyes were swollen and bruised. Her arm was in a sling, and she had a body cast on her torso. But at least she was awake and recognized them, which was a huge relief.

"What happened?" Cassidy asked, in disbelief at her friend's condition.

"Some asshole ran me off the road intentionally. He came up behind me and slammed into my car," she said.

"Did you get a look at him?" Riley asked.

"No, it was dark, and I couldn't see the driver at all. The high beams were on," Montoya replied.

"Was it road rage?" Cassidy asked.

"No, it was unprovoked. She said he was just crazy and came out of nowhere," her sister said.

"Was he following you?" Cassidy asked.

"I didn't notice. I left the gym like I always do. Took the same route I always take. It was messed up," Montoya said. Cassidy could see that the energy it took for Montoya to speak was draining her.

"We'll find whoever did this, Diana. Be sure of that. I'll chase that fucker down no matter how long it takes," Riley said in quiet fury as he squeezed her hand.

"That's Sean Riley, loyal like a golden retriever!" Montoya said, coughing suddenly.

Leonor gave Riley an appraising look and took his arm. "You're such a good man, Sean. She's lucky to have you as a friend. Are you free for a carne asada this Saturday?"

"Mama! This is not the time for matchmaking!" Montoya said. "Don't make me laugh, it hurts my ribs!"

Cassidy was relieved that Montoya was in good spirits and surrounded by family. She looked like she had a long road to recovery ahead, but at least she wasn't facing it alone. She and Riley left with a promise to return soon. Out in the hallway, they were clearly shaken by the condition she was in.

"It seems too weird, that a guy would just come up on her like that," Riley said.

"And that type of thing doesn't happen much in Pasadena," Cassidy agreed.

"I know that route, it's not a deserted highway in a remote area. It's a residential neighborhood that runs right next to the freeway. It's quiet but not like some stretch of road where there's no one around. It seems opportunistic, like someone was waiting for the right moment," Riley suggested.

A young female patrol cop from the Pasadena PD approached them in the hallway.

"Excuse me, officers. Are you friends of Diana Montoya?" she asked.

"Yeah, we work with her at the Hollywood station," Riley explained.

"After Montoya was discovered and brought to the hospital, we thought at first that she lost control of her vehicle, but the car had serious dents in the back bumper and on both sides. It had been struck intentionally," the Pasadena officer said.

"Yeah, that's what she said happened," Cassidy said.

"It was a hit-and-run, so we started keeping an eye out for any car that might show damage that would correspond to Montoya's vehicle. And we found one, left out by Hahamongna Watershed Park, near Altadena. It had paint that matched Montoya's car and was dented in exactly the places where impact occurred. It was reported stolen earlier in the evening, and then someone dumped it."

"So, someone stole a car, intentionally ran her off the road with it, and dumped it afterward? Like it was planned?" Riley asked.

"Looks like it. Does Officer Montoya have any enemies or stalkers or anything?"

"No, not that I know of," Cassidy replied.

"She doesn't date much, too busy with work. No dating apps or anything like that," Riley added.

The Pasadena cop left to meet her partner at the nurse's station. On the way down in the elevator, Cassidy and Riley considered what she had said.

Does Officer Montoya have any enemies or stalkers?

Cassidy grabbed Riley's arm suddenly. "Did Diana ever tell you how Acevedo used to wait for her at the gym? And ask her out?"

Riley nodded. "Yeah. She had to tell him she was engaged. Her cousin went along with it."

"She told me that he used to follow her home from the gym, that he was like a stalker," Cassidy said.

"But Acevedo's in Mexico," Riley said, doubtful.

Cassidy stared at him, her mind racing over the possibilities. "What if he's not?"

Jeppe sat at the big dining table with his lost angels; Chinese take-out cartons were spread out with big liters of soda. They ate and drank from paper plates and cups. They had cleaned up the house and put everything back in order. There was music playing on the old-fashioned turntable, LPs from the seventies that came with the furnished house. The kids had smoked some excellent weed an hour earlier, so they were deep into the munchies and eating hefty servings of *kung pao* chicken, their appreciation of him clear on their faces.

Except for Princess, who pouted and picked at her food, sitting apart in a chair by the fireplace. Jeppe smiled, but he was annoyed with her. Anya and the others told him how she'd fought with them earlier. She'd been complaining about going back to Hollywood, to the streets she knew and her familiar places. She didn't appreciate his generosity and hospitality like the others did. She looked at him with suspicion and distrust, which he hated. It made him feel dirty and dangerous, and he hated that even more. He was their savior, their guide; he was not a predator.

"So, my angels, do you know about the spiritual beings that walk among us? They are from other galaxies next to our own, and they are here to show us how to raise our vibrations, take our consciousness to a higher plane," he said, scooping a forkful of white rice into his mouth.

Zeno nodded, his chubby, freckled face rapt with adoration. "Yes, I can feel them sometimes. They have a different vibe to them, a different aura."

Princess rolled her eyes but said nothing. Jeppe pretended not to notice, but he did. He was keeping track of how many times she showed him disrespect, and at a certain point, she would go too far.

"And you know that next month, the extraterrestrials will be coming to the desert, to Joshua Tree, to show us their vessels? The ships that carry them through the galaxies. Shall we drive out there and see them? Sleep in tents under the stars?" he asked.

They nodded in excitement and began to chatter away about seeing aliens up close. But Princess was unmoved. He couldn't let her go; he might not find her again, and she had been a major attraction at his party. He'd have to find a way to keep her like his special pet, but she wasn't going to be easy. Layla hadn't been easy either.

He'd been checking the news since the afternoon, but there hadn't been any mention of Layla's body yet. He'd also followed the white Thunderbird to a big house in the Hollywood Dell, next to the DWP power station. He'd watched as the car pulled into the garage and the woman in a big sun hat carrying a small bag of groceries stepped out and went up the steps to the front door, disappearing inside. She was the driver who had seen him in the park, who made the surprise turn into the trailhead at the wrong moment.

"I have a question, my darlings. Do any of you know an elderly lady who drives a fancy, vintage white car? It's called a Thunderbird, it has little porthole windows in the back, like a ship?" he asked.

The kids looked at each other and then to Princess.

"Yeah, we know who she is. Princess knows her the best," Anya said.

"Is this true, Princess?" he asked.

She shrugged. "Yeah. That's Marjorie. She lives up by the dam. Why?"

"No reason. I ran into her today at the market, she was very charming," Jeppe said. "She's quite pretty, and I'm sure her husband is nice looking as well."

"She's not married. She lives all by herself in that big house below the dam. She has tons of dogs and stuff," Anya said.

Jeppe nodded, ruffling Anya's white-blond hair. He'd found the right house, with its big windows and the overgrown yard. The woman named Marjorie lived there all alone, at the end of the road, in the shadow of the looming Mulholland Dam.

Several patrol cars were pulled up outside Darrin Meecham's house on Wilton Avenue. They blocked the driveway; neighbors stood on their porches and lawns, curious about the law enforcement activity. Darrin Meecham stood handcuffed on the lawn, sweat pouring down his face. Inside, Postiff and Barrera moved through the house, stuffed with antiques; large oil paintings hung on the walls as if someone had grabbed a nail and put each one up haphazardly.

Meecham's invalid mother, Constance, sat in a wheelchair, cursing at them, a bag of Circus Animal Cookies open on her lap. As Postiff passed her, she hurled an insult at him, and he saw that her teeth were hot pink from the cookie frosting.

"You filthy son of a bitch! You have no right to come in here, no right!" she yelled.

He looked at her calmly and said, "You know, those were my favorite cookies when I was a kid, Mrs. Meecham."

"Motherfucker! You're not getting any!" she screeched.

He turned away with a small laugh. They combed through the rooms of the big house, but there was no sign there had ever been any teenagers there. They found Meecham's cache of child pornography, which would get him locked up for a long time, but he was obviously not involved with the missing teens.

It was 10:15 when the medical examiner called.

"Hi, Judson, I've got the results on the body in the park. The skull showed blunt-force trauma, that's what killed her. The decomposition had started, but she had a lip piercing, part of it was still attached. And I can see ink from a tattoo on her left forearm. Since the ink is injected into the dermis and there's been some skin slippage, the colors are more visible. It looks like a snake, but I don't think we can use it as a definitive ID marker. We'll need DNA or dental records," he said.

Postiff ended the call and hung his head, letting out a deep sigh. Cassidy had told him that Layla had a snake tattoo on her left forearm. He texted her that they would need the contact information for Layla's mother from Bill. He found Barrera directing some officers to remove boxes of pornography and a laptop computer.

"Victim in the park died of blunt-force trauma to the head. They need DNA. I'm asking Cassidy to get us Layla Waters's family contact information. Maybe we'll be able to rule her out," he said.

Barrera looked at him dejectedly. "You think so?"

Postiff shook his head. "No, my gut says it's her."

"Mine too. Let's wrap this up and throw the book at this sick fuck, Meecham. Let him see what happens to pedophiles in prison," Barrera said, his exhaustion obvious.

"Head home, Pete. You've got a long drive. I'll handle this."

"Thanks, young pup," Barrera said, turning to leave.

Postiff told the officers to finish up and texted Ramsey that they didn't find anything related to the missing kids. He included the cause of death on the body in the park. He didn't mind bothering her at that late hour. On the contrary, he rather enjoyed it.

CHAPTER NINETEEN

Detective Sandra Moody checked the wireless security camera feed on her phone as she scrolled through the offerings on Netflix. Her husband was asleep already; her son was out with friends. She was waiting for a callback from Lieutenant Ledezma down in Baja California, for updates on Acevedo or any missing American men who fit his description. Ledezma was working a demanding case, and she knew he'd have to call her at the end of his day, but she was restless, unable to settle. She'd heard earlier that Officer Montoya had suffered a bizarre automobile accident, losing control of her car. Since Acevedo disappeared, she'd kept tabs on the others who worked on his investigation.

She'd had new state-of-the-art security cameras installed around her home in Eagle Rock. The cameras were positioned inside the house, where they could not be tampered with; they were integrated into what appeared to be furniture, but they had the capacity to see clear images from as far as across the street and halfway up the block. She'd been considering how to handle the Acevedo situation if he did return and had any plans of revenge against the officers who had investigated him for Eden Balcomb's murder.

The higher-ups like Carbone and Ramsey were supposed to be in charge of things like this, but she didn't have much confidence in them. Ramsey always had so many political machinations clicking away in her brain, she could easily miss an important detail that would put them at risk. Moody was weighing the possibilities of making her own plans when the phone rang. It was Rubén Ledezma, from the Rosarito police department.

"Hello, detective, sorry for the delay. There's nothing new on Acevedo, but we do have a report of a missing American. His name is Roberto Lopez from Borrego Springs, California. His family reported him missing yesterday. He went on a solo trip and then visited a strip club in Ensenada and never came back to his hotel. We spoke to the owner today, and she said there was another American staying there, but he left. The name he gave was Armando Mendez, but when I showed her Acevedo's photo, she recognized him. The Lopez family say there's been no credit card usage, no bank activity from Roberto. But the weird thing is that we checked with CPB, and his passport and his car came through the checkpoint at San Ysidro two days ago."

Moody felt her stomach drop. Two days ago.

"So, either he came back and he's hiding from his family, or someone else used his car and his passport?" Moody asked.

"Yeah. He's got a decent job, two small kids. I don't think he came back. Someone is using his documents and his car. We have no idea what happened to Lopez," Ledezma replied. "I'll send over his passport and car information."

When Moody looked at Roberto Lopez's passport photo, she saw that he was a slender, olive-skinned Latino with close-cropped hair and big eyes. Acevedo could easily have passed for him, especially with a tired border patrol agent who'd been looking at faces all day. Next, she ran an online police check on Lopez's vehicle. It had been ticketed and impounded from the Pico-Union area the previous day. The Pico-Union neighborhood was ten minutes from where Acevedo's parents lived in Windsor Square. It wasn't hard proof that he was back, but there were too many coincidences linking him to Roberto Lopez's disappearance. She'd been a detective for fifteen years. She didn't believe in coincidences.

When Postiff arrived at Millie Grace's house, he found her waiting outside with an overnight bag packed. Rosalie's car was gone, and Millie approached his as he pulled into the driveway.

"What's up? Why're you out here?" he asked, opening the passenger door for her.

"I only came out when you called a few minutes ago, but Rosalie left to stay at her boyfriend's house, and I got freaked out, being inside all alone. Can I stay at your place tonight?" she asked, her eyes wide with anxiety.

"Sure, no problem. I didn't want to be too forward and suggest that you stay over," he said with a smile.

"I feel better with you there. Did you find out more about the girl in the park? It wasn't on the news," she said.

"I guess they asked them to hold off until they have an ID, probably because it could be a minor."

"A minor? You mean a kid?" she asked, horrified.

"We've been looking into some missing homeless teenagers, and the body we found could be one of them. We have to wait for a DNA analysis," he replied, his voice ragged with exhaustion. His head hurt, his eyes hurt. This was not how he wanted to spend the first night together with Millie.

"This is really scary . . ." Millie murmured, half to herself.

He reached out and took her hand, giving it a squeeze. "Yes, it is," he said quietly.

Twenty minutes later they arrived at his house in the sleepy, small-town Ranchito section of Burbank. As Postiff helped Millie out of the car and carried her bag, Cassidy suddenly stepped out of the shadows on his front porch.

"Postiff! My phone is dead, and I want to talk to you . . ." She stopped short when she saw Millie and the questioning look on her face.

Postiff looked awkwardly from one to the other. "What do you want, Clarke?"

"I went to see Montoya, and I had an idea. I can't find my phone charger, so I just came by on my way home." She turned to Millie. "I'm Cassidy, by the way. We work together, we're just friends," she explained, realizing she had interrupted a date.

"That's enough, Clarke. This is Millie Grace," he said.

"You're Millie Grace? From the Hit Men case? Thank you for your willingness to testify," Cassidy said. "I'm just a patrol cop, I'm not a detective."

"Nice to meet you," Millie said.

"Why don't you go inside, sweetie? I'll be there in a minute," he said, handing Millie his keys. He turned to Cassidy and muttered, "Good timing, Clarke."

"Sorry. So, I went to see Montoya . . ." She explained the accident and what the Pasadena officer had told her about the abandoned car used to push Montoya off the road.

"On the DNA stakeout she told me that Acevedo had a thing for her, used to wait outside her gym and show up at her house. He knew her route, her schedule."

"You think it could be him? He's back?" Postiff asked.

"Does it make any sense that someone would steal a car just to attack a random person on the road and then dump that car? Or is it more realistic that someone targeted Montoya and wanted to use an untraceable car so we wouldn't be able to identify him?"

"We're supposed to get an alert if he reenters the country with his passport."

"He could be using a stolen passport, right? He's a criminal, and he knows the system."

Postiff considered for a moment, then said, "Millie told me that there was a guy parked outside her house today for a couple of hours. She got a photo of the car. I'm going to run the plate. I'll check with Moody as well. You haven't seen anything odd around your place, have you?"

She shook her head and checked the surroundings nervously. Suddenly, the quiet street with big trees, thick Indian hawthorn, and tall hedges seemed like the perfect place to hide.

"What if it's him?" Cassidy asked.

"If it is him, we have to catch him. He's Metro. The guy can scale the side of a building, and he's an expert with multiple firearms. He's lethal."

He turned to go back inside, where Millie was watching nervously from the window.

"I think I've managed to scare the daylights out of Millie," he said.

"You two look cute together. She's really pretty—" Cassidy began, but Postiff cut her off.

"Go home, Clarke. And good work, by the way."

When Cassidy arrived at home half an hour later, she found Bill at his laptop, a cup of steaming coffee next to him.

He waved her over and whispered, "I don't want to wake Evie. I've been looking for her mom. There's a Geraldine Araluce who lives in Spain, and it looks like she was previously married to John Peacock. It is probably her, but the phone number didn't work when I tried it, and I can't find an email."

"Wait, what do you mean, you don't want to wake Evie? Where is she?" Cassidy asked.

"In the guest room. I just can't let her stay out on the street, it's too dangerous."

"Dad, we can't take a minor into our home. We have to get legal permission from—"

"From whom? She's almost eighteen, out of foster care, avoiding the system. I checked with Melinda, and she said it was fine."

"She did? So, she knows?"

"Yes, I didn't just go all rogue, Binkie."

"Yeah, but you've done that so many times before," she said.

"This is the new me, right? The new Bill Clarke. Have you eaten yet?"

"Yeah, Riley and I grabbed a bite after visiting Montoya. She was run off the road. We think Acevedo might be back in town."

Bill froze. "Acevedo? You think he did it?"

"Maybe. I checked with Postiff, he's looking into it. We have to be extra careful, which is not a good situation with Evie being here," Cassidy said.

"You're right. Did you hear back from the ME about the body in the park?"

Cassidy moved to the kitchen and grabbed a bottle of sparkling water, then flopped down next to her dad on the couch. Her limbs felt as if they were made of lead; she was so tired from the stress of the day.

"We're going to need DNA. Her face is gone. But she was killed by blunt-force head trauma. Postiff said there is ink from a tattoo where Layla had a similar one, on her forearm. And a piercing on her lip."

"Shit," Bill said quietly. "I have her toothbrush and a hairbrush from the folks she stayed with in Victorville."

Cassidy looked at him, impressed. "You got forensic evidence? While eating pie in Victorville?"

"How'd you know we ate pie?"

"You went to the Black Bear Diner, right? The best pie between California and Nevada. I'll let Postiff know about the brushes."

Bill shrugged. "Any updates on that Little Leo character?"

"We're looking into that. No one knows the guy's real name. Postiff said someone saw Princess with him yesterday or the day before, and he had an argument with that kid named Aiden, who's some kind of pimp."

"Have you met the one named Princess?" Bill asked.

Cassidy shook her head. "None of us have talked to her."

"You need to talk to the librarian at the Los Feliz Branch Library. I think she may have met Little Leo there. The clerk told me they used to hang out there. The clerk is a temp, doesn't know much."

"What's the librarian's name?" Cassidy asked.

"Don't know. She's on maternity leave. I can help you track her down if you want."

"Maybe. But right now, I'm going to go to bed," Cassidy said, avoiding any further conversation. "Did you set the appointments for the follow-up tests?"

"Not yet. They need more information from the doctor," Bill said.

"No, they need a call from me," she muttered, heading down the hall to her room.

She'd been weighing whether she should share the information about Tyler Derby's phone call with her dad, who was doing much better than the last time he fell under that monster's sway. She didn't want him to get pulled off course by a malignant psychopath, but if the information on Min Sun-Hee's murder was accurate, it could hold the key to the case that had haunted Bill for decades.

She knew her dad was not like Barrera; he wasn't a guy who could switch everything off once he got home and had a beer. Bill felt certain unsolved cases in his heart. He carried them on his back. Solving Min Sun-Hee's murder could release him from that weight, and she didn't want the responsibility of deciding what was best for him. But Derby had placed it squarely in her hands.

Jeppe had sneaked once again onto Chris Russo's driveway and used his spare key to get into the old man's car. He put it in neutral and backed it down the driveway without starting the engine, and once on the street, he drove off toward Hollywood. He didn't like using Russo's car again, but he couldn't risk using his own car for tonight's errand. He quickly covered the distance to the Hollywood Dell from Mount Washington; the streets were quiet at that late hour. He drove toward the dam, through the Holly Drive tunnel, until the street ended at the power station. The nearest homes were several lots away, and the cul-de-sac was thick with foliage.

He left the car under a crepe myrtle tree and slipped around the side of the run-down house he had seen the woman go into. He tried several doors and windows, but they were securely locked, and he heard the barking of small dogs inside the house, which complicated his plan. He pulled a rusted machete he had taken from the shed at the Raven's Nest from his jacket—with one swift blow he could neutralize any small animal that got in his way.

At the back of the house, he found a basement window that had a piece of heavy cardboard in place of a broken window. He climbed through it and found himself in a crowded, dusty space beneath the house. It was filled with old clothing racks, antiques, and shelves of cut-crystal serving bowls and dishes. He crept up the stairs and pushed a door that led into the kitchen. It was dark; he heard the dogs barking, confined to a room upstairs. He made his way through the crowded house to the ornate stairway. He was halfway up when a figure appeared at the top.

It was the woman he had seen in the Thunderbird; she was wearing an old-fashioned peignoir nightgown, mumbling to herself. He gripped the machete and bolted toward her in one sudden move. She never saw him coming.

In a living room closet, Pebble Smith hid, her body pressed between plastic-covered coats and furs. She'd been going through a box of old photographs that Marjorie wanted to put into albums, when she heard the man in the kitchen. As he crossed into the living room, she darted into the closet and waited, holding her breath, praying he hadn't seen her. She heard Marjorie's sharp scream and the thudding sound of her body falling down the stairway. Then silence, except for the dogs barking and yipping wildly upstairs in her bedroom.

Pebble closed her eyes, willing the man to leave without finding her. She heard his footsteps retreating, and he began walking around the rooms, picking up random items. From the sliver of a crack in the closet door, she could see his gloved hands. Finally, he left, and she heard the front door opening. She didn't move. She wished she had never seen him before, that he was just an unknown, malevolent shadow that had arrived like a *Harry Potter* dementor. But she'd seen his face, and she did know him. It was Little Leo.

CHAPTER TWENTY

Postiff sat in front of his computer screen, freshly showered, for the early morning Zoom meeting with Lieutenant Carbone, Ramsey, Cassidy, and Detective Moody. The mood of the group was somber; Moody and Cassidy had shared their information and suspicions that Acevedo was back and had been behind the attack on Montoya.

"If it's him, we have to move quickly but discreetly. We can't have this blow up in the press. It will be a nightmare for the department," Ramsey cautioned.

"He could kill any one of us, commander. He's Metro. He might also have people in the department who would help him," Moody said bluntly.

"I doubt that," Carbone interjected.

"I don't," said Postiff. "You know how those guys are. I'm sure a lot of them are sympathetic to him."

"Let's stay on track here," Ramsey said. "We have to reach out within the department to people we feel can be trusted, to begin tracking him down. We need people stationed outside his parents' house to see if he comes and goes. We need to keep an eye out for his vehicle and any bank or phone activity."

"He's way too smart for that. If he's back, he's a ghost. We're not going to catch him at an ATM branch of his bank, getting cash," Moody said, not bothering to hide her frustration.

"Let me and Lieutenant Carbone come up with a plan today, and we'll get back with you this afternoon. In the meantime, take extra precautions out there," Ramsey said, trying to take control of the situation.

Postiff left the meeting and opened his search on the license plate of the car that Millie had seen the previous day outside her house. It was reported as stolen, just like the car used to attack Montoya. By early morning, it had been found near Gower and Santa Monica. The license plate was listed as impounded at the LAPD lot on Melrose.

Next, he opened his notes on Layla Waters and the missing teens. They'd followed Bill's suggestion and spoken to the Los Feliz Branch Library clerk who didn't have a real name for Little Leo. None of the kids from the Clubhouse knew his real name, nor did Melinda Drake. He knew this was a strategic step; predators take pains to keep their real identities hidden. No one had heard from or seen Princess since she drove away with a guy matching Little Leo's description. He got up to refill his coffee cup and found Millie standing in the doorway, watching him.

"Morning," she said simply. He moved to her and gave her a kiss.

"Do you want coffee?" he asked. "I have different types of creamer. Hazelnut, mocha, Italian Sweet Crème—"

She took his arm to stop him. "I don't think I can do this, Jud," she said.

"Do what?"

"All of this. Live in Los Angeles, date a detective, all of it. I'm going to go back home."

Postiff gripped his coffee cup tighter. "But what about the job at the Getty? And all your plans?"

She looked at the floor, still holding his arm, as if for moral support.

"They were built on this idea I had about LA. That it was glamorous and exciting, that I could carve out a place here. But in the past month and a half, I've been attacked by two serial killers, and there was a guy outside our house yesterday who's probably a murderer who's after you. Every day you tell me about some new, horrible crime that's happened right in my neighborhood," she said, her voice shaking.

"Maybe I've shared too much about my work with you. I can dial that back, lots of detectives do," he suggested.

"But you shouldn't have to. You need to be able to talk about the stuff you go through. When I met the officer last night, the one who was waiting for you, it hit me. You need to be with someone who isn't terrified of your world . . . and I am. I'm from a small town where everyone knows everyone else. This is all too much for me."

"It sounds like you've made up your mind," he said.

"I have. I'm booking a flight today. You can drop me off at home when you go to work."

He nodded. "I'm leaving in five minutes," he said, walking into the bedroom and closing the door behind him.

He didn't want her to see him get emotional first thing in the morning. He hated guys like Ron Whitty and Vithu Pham. Like Ethan Acevedo and Little Leo. The creeps like Darrin Meecham. The ones who terrorized the city and the people just trying to live normal lives, go to work, raise families. He hated that he couldn't wipe all of them out and make it safe for everyone.

For the first time, he felt the overwhelming powerlessness that came with his work. There were always new, malevolent criminals lurking out there, waiting to explode into violence, to prey upon the most vulnerable. They were standing in line next to you at the market, or the gas station. They were installing your internet or watching you cross the intersection.

They were everywhere.

Cassidy prepared breakfast for Evie and her dad; she was on the evening shift with Riley and didn't have to go in until four p.m. After the Zoom to discuss Acevedo, she had checked all the security cameras and left a

Post-it Note on the front door to remind them to double-lock all doors and windows.

Her dad came in from the laundry room with Evie's freshly folded clothes and set them on the kitchen table.

"I can't believe how little her shirts are! It's been years since you were that tiny," he said, pouring himself a cup of coffee.

"Dad, I was never that tiny. At eighteen, I was already pretty athletic."

"I may take her to Target or some place today to get her some new threads."

Cassidy winced. "Threads? Did you just say that? Is it nineteen-sixty-eight? How about some groovy scrambled eggs?"

"Look, I know all the Gen Z lingo . . ." he protested.

"*Lingo*! Oh my god!" Cassidy said.

"I know what it is to rizz someone up, if a guy has drip, has a cool fit. I even know what a menty b is," he said proudly.

"No one says that, Dad."

"Really? I looked it up last night before bed. Menty b, bet, no cap, glaze, skibidi—"

"Stop, you're going to give me a heart attack," she warned.

He chuckled and grabbed a sausage from the skillet, popping it into his mouth.

"Postiff is sending a messenger over from the ME's office to pick up Layla's hairbrush and toothbrush. They want to run a rapid DNA test right away. The press agreed to hold the story for twenty-four hours," Cassidy said.

"I have them in a bag, in my closet. We can't let Evie see it, she'll ask questions," Bill cautioned, serving himself a plate of eggs.

Cassidy regarded him for a beat, then said, "And there's something I need to tell you. I spoke to Tyler Derby."

Bill froze, his fork in midair. "I haven't taken his calls. He's called a few times, but I haven't responded."

"I know. I saw the call and answered. I wasn't going to tell you, but he said he has information related to Min Sun-Hee."

She saw the look of surprise and sudden elation cross his face. Then he downshifted into doubt.

"How? He's probably making it up," Bill said.

"You should speak to him. Be careful, but I think you should talk to him," she said.

Bill nodded. She could see he was fighting the urge to pick up the phone immediately.

"I'll call him when I'm done with breakfast. Thank you for telling me," he said calmly.

"You're welcome. As much as I want to protect you, you're a grown man, and I can't hold that information from you. Even if you use embarrassing Gen Z slang."

He gave her a hug and whispered, "You're a very chill daughter."

"You're trying to kill me now!" Cassidy said, laughing as she left the room.

Jeppe stood at the back door of the Raven's Nest with Anya, Zeno, and Autumn. They all wore baggy sweats and ball caps pulled down low. It was midmorning; the street was quiet. If they crossed his property and climbed the low wall that separated it from Chris Russo's house, they would not be seen from the street. He knew that Russo was a late riser and usually came out to work in his garden around eleven a.m. The outdoor light was still on. Anya carried a heavy towel, Zeno a piece of lead pipe, and Autumn the revolver they had taken from Jason Weizman's house. Jeppe took the towel and wrapped it around the short barrel of the gun.

"This is how you do it. It will muffle the sound. You know the sign when it's done, right?" he asked.

Zeno answered dutifully, "We'll turn the outside light on and off three times!"

Anya nodded, and Autumn squeezed Zeno's arm in excitement. "I can't believe we're really going to do it!" she said breathlessly.

Jeppe stroked her hair and ran his hand along her pale cheek.

"You three are my most special angels. You are doing it for the family, to keep us safe." He loved using the same language that Manson had used, referring to his group as "the family." In a way, he and his lost angels were the keepers of the flame that Manson had ignited decades ago. He opened the door and led them outside.

They walked silently across the big yard and easily climbed over the low wall to Russo's property. Jeppe went back inside and stood at the window, watching them. He had done it. He had pushed them to cross the line. His power over them was total. He lost sight of them, knowing they must have gotten into the house. It wouldn't be long now.

From the upstairs bedroom, Princess saw Anya, Autumn, and Zeno walking across the yard toward the house of the old man next door. Jeppe had taken to locking her in at night, afraid that she would bolt. She had already tried the door several times, but it would not give. She had to gain his trust enough to get out of the room and look for the moment to escape.

She could hear Jeppe moving about downstairs as the other kids had gotten up and would be preparing breakfast. She decided that she would play along and hide her discontent. She'd act as if she had been taken in by Jeppe's bullshit about aliens and vibrations and all the rest. She was good at pretending to believe things that she knew were lies. She could see that Jeppe wanted control over everyone more than anything else, so she would let him think he had won. And when his guard was down, she would get away.

She imagined how it would be back at the Clubhouse, with Evie and Melinda. She missed Marjorie and her crazy dogs. She even missed Aiden a little bit. She went back to the window and saw that the outside light of Russo's house was blinking on and off. She had no idea what that meant; maybe there was a short in the wiring next door. She heard

Jeppe's footsteps in the hallway and the key in the door. She sat cross-legged on the bed and prepared her sweetest smile to greet him.

Postiff pulled up to Millie's house and saw Rosalie's car in the driveway.

"Rosie's home, so you should feel a bit safer," he said.

"Yeah. I'll call you later and let you know when I'm leaving for home," Millie said.

She stared at him with her big pale eyes, and he could tell that she was wavering. He didn't want a big discussion or tears and doubts. She was right to go home, and there was only so much he could do to protect her from his world. She nodded and got out, hurrying inside. He watched her go in and checked his phone messages. There was a new one from Marjorie Mellencamp. He felt bad that he'd ignored her calls, and as he backed out, he played her voicemails before erasing them.

"Detective Postiff, I've called numerous times about this, and I'm just at my wit's end. I want to alert you to a situation I saw unfolding in the park late last night. I went on my late-night drive as I am wont to do, and I came upon several young men tossing their dirty trash bags over the hillside. No respect for the landscape or the wildlife, just dumping garbage! I saw one very clearly, he was like they say—a deer caught in my headlights. He had a round, boyish face with dirty-blond hair . . ."

Postiff sat up as if a firecracker had exploded beneath him. Marjorie Mellencamp had seen the people dumping Layla Waters's body. And he'd ignored her calls. He called her back, but there was no answer. He swung his car into the street and gunned his engine, heading toward the Hollywood Hills. She didn't live far, just over the Cahuenga Pass, on the other side of the park. He could be there in ten minutes. He felt the sting of self-reproach rising in his gut. He'd dismissed Marjorie as a crazy old woman, a nuisance who wanted attention, but she had been trying to give him the information he desperately needed.

Postiff arrived at Marjorie's house to find it dark and silent. The Jimmy sat in the driveway, and when he opened the garage door, her white Thunderbird was parked neatly inside. He could hear the dogs barking in the house as he rang the bell repeatedly. He walked around to the side windows, but he could not see past the heavy draperies. Barrera was on his way, and Postiff had called for backup in case they needed to break the door down to get inside. He was concerned about Marjorie's silence after her repeated messages over the last two days.

"Ms. Mellencamp? This is Detective Postiff from the LAPD. Can you hear me?" he called out.

He was about to knock again when the front door was suddenly opened by a young girl. She looked like a middle schooler, her hair cut in a short bob. Her hands were covered in blood. She was going into shock. He recognized her from the Clubhouse.

"He killed her . . ." she whispered.

Postiff pulled his gun, guided her outside, and called 911.

"Is he still in the house?" he asked her gently.

She shook her head, holding her hands out for him to see.

"He's gone. I tried to stop the bleeding, but it was too much . . ." she said. "He came in while I was in the living room and Marjorie was upstairs . . . then there was a big noise . . ." She suddenly turned away from him and vomited on the concrete, her body shivering. Postiff took off his coat and wrapped her in it.

"Will you be okay here while I go in and check? The police and an ambulance are coming. You hear those sirens? They're on their way here. You're safe now. Promise to stay here, okay?"

She nodded, and he stepped inside with his gun drawn. He heard the dogs' agitated yipping upstairs, but the house felt still. At the foot of the stairway, he saw Marjorie with a huge gash at her neck, lying in a pool of blood. There was no need to check her pulse. Her eyes were lifeless, raised toward the ceiling as if in prayer. Postiff felt the air go out of him and steadied himself on the banister. It was his fault. He was too late.

Cassidy received the text from Postiff about Marjorie's death as she was serving a plate of pancakes to Evie, who was well rested and cleaned up in freshly laundered clothes. She was drinking a steaming cup of hot chocolate mixed with coffee with whipped cream on top. Cassidy had no idea how to tell her about Marjorie, so she said nothing. She'd never had to deliver news like that to someone, and she needed her dad's advice. The tech from the ME's office had picked up Layla's items before Evie woke, and the knowledge that they would be testing it against the body from the park had Cassidy on edge.

"You cook really well," Evie said, swallowing down a gulp of food.

"No, I don't. My dad is becoming quite the chef, though. He'll probably make some masterpiece for you tonight."

"He said I can stay here as long as I want. Is that for real?"

Cassidy nodded. "Yeah. We have the room, and you need a place to stay. It's cool."

"Have you found out any new information about Layla? Or the other kids?" Evie asked.

"Not yet. But they will. I think it has to do with Little Leo or whatever his real name is. Some people saw Princess with him the other day. Have you heard from her?"

"No, it's kind of sus. I'll keep calling her. I wish Layla would pick up her phone," Evie said, draining her cup. "Your dad is really cool. He reminds me of my dad, but Bill is tougher."

"You just think he is. He cries at commercials with dogs," Cassidy said.

"Maybe that's why he's great. He's not just a macho jerk, like most cops. He cares," Evie said simply.

"You're exactly right. He cares," Cassidy agreed.

They were washing up the dishes when Bill emerged from his room with his overnight bag packed. Cassidy knew he'd made the call to Tyler Derby, and now her heart sunk to see him preparing to leave. She could guess where he was going.

"I'll be back tomorrow. I have an appointment up in Coalinga," he said, excitement clear in his voice.

"Dad, you said you were going to keep everything under control," Cassidy admonished him, but he waved her concern off.

"I'm not getting out of hand with this, I promise. But I'm afraid Derby might die before I can talk to him, so I'm going now." He pulled a wad of cash from his wallet and gave it to Cassidy.

"Take this kid shopping for some new clothes. I'll let you know when I get there!" he said, hurrying out the door before Cassidy could even reply.

"Who's Derby?" Evie asked.

"A psychopath and a serial killer," Cassidy replied, subdued with worry.

Evie looked stricken. "He's not going to his house, is he?"

"No, he's in prison, honey."

Cassidy wondered if she'd done the right thing in telling Bill about Derby and if he would return in the same state of mental agitation he had worked so hard to control. She watched in dismay as he backed his car out of the driveway and drove away.

By the time Barrera arrived at Marjorie Mellencamp's home, an ambulance was there and several patrol cars. The street was cordoned off with yellow tape, which he ducked under to find Postiff talking with a young girl who sat in the back of a patrol car.

"This is my partner, Detective Barrera. This is Pebble Smith," Postiff said as the girl nodded silently at Barrera.

"Cute name," Barrera said, smiling at her as he crouched down next to her.

"She said she was helping Marjorie organize photos when she heard someone come up from the basement into the kitchen. We checked. A window was open, and there are footprints in the dirt outside and the dust inside," Postiff said.

"Then he started coming into the living room, and that's when I saw him, but he didn't see me. He was holding something against his side, like a big knife, and I got in the closet to hide," Pebble said anxiously, twisting her skinny fingers together.

"And then what happened?" Barrera asked gently.

"I don't know, but I heard Marjorie scream and like something falling down, a lot of thumping. And then he left . . . It was Little Leo," she said haltingly.

"You're sure of that?" Postiff asked.

"Yeah. It was him."

They walked out of earshot while an EMT gave Pebble a bottle of water and a granola bar.

"Marjorie called to tell us she saw them dumping the body. In the park. We fucked up," Postiff said.

"You think that's why he killed her? She saw him?" Barrera asked, guilt creeping into his voice.

"If we had answered her calls, we might've found him. We could've caught him before this. It's on us, Barrera," Postiff said with quiet ferocity.

A baby-faced young cop came up to them, holding a framed magazine cover of Marjorie as a young starlet.

"Can you guys believe that this hottie is the victim? That's what they told me. I mean, she was a babe! What happened to her?" he said.

Barrera swatted him across the head with his open palm.

"Life is what happened to her. Report me if you want, but get your dumbass out of here!" he shouted, his frustration and remorse erupting.

Postiff watched as the coroner's team wheeled the closed body bag out on a stretcher. He saw the horror on the faces of neighbors who hovered nearby. Animal Control had arrived to take the dogs, who were carried out in crates, their big, frightened eyes peering out at him as they were put into the truck. It was a scene where everything had gone wrong.

His phone rang. It was the ME's office. He took the call, and Barrera saw him falter, almost stumbling against the curb. He hurried over and grabbed Postiff by the arm to steady him.

"What's up, man?" he asked. "You okay?"

"They identified the body in the park. It's Layla Waters."

CHAPTER TWENTY-ONE

Jason Weizman watched in horror as the KCAL News reporter stood in Griffith Park, covering a story about a dead body found on a hiking trail. The screen flashed with the victim's photo and name, Layla Waters. He had seen that girl at Jeppe's house several weeks earlier. Just like the little blond who broke into his place and took the gun. He had no idea who Jeppe was; he just seemed like a cool guy who had good drugs and liked young girls like he did. They'd met at Dray's Billiards and Brews in the back room, where they had the girls for special events.

When he'd seen Anya at the last party, it had freaked him out and made him think that Jeppe wasn't so cool after all. That maybe Jeppe had made him a target, and they'd planned to hit his house. He'd sensed that the young cop and her partner didn't like him when they took the initial report, and he knew the two detectives had suspicions about him, like he had secrets to hide.

And he had a lot. He'd managed to keep his penchant for young girls under the radar, and it was easy in the industry. He could make tons of promises he didn't have to keep, tell them he had a role for them on a hit show. He could pawn it off and say the network didn't approve them, when they had no chance of ever landing any role at all. He had a couple of headshot photographers who were good connections for him. They'd meet the girls when they were taking photos, and they knew all the signs to look for, which ones were gullible and easy to manipulate.

The easiest ones were the girls from the Midwest, far from home, with no real support network. They'd been the prettiest girl in their town and then arrived in LA to discover that small-town pretty didn't cut it. Or the ones with grasping stage mothers, living through their kids. He knew one who would arrange overnight dates for her teenage daughter with middle-aged directors and executives in hopes of getting ahead.

He had a good crop of girls, but the Jeppe parties added an extra rush of risk and excitement. But now it had gone too far. He wanted to know about his gun, and he was sure that Jeppe knew where it was. He wanted it back before there was any trouble. He was set to direct seven episodes of a new Apple TV show, and he couldn't risk that getting ruined over criminal allegations against him. He would go to the Raven's Nest that day.

In the SAE house on USC's fraternity row, Rick and Jed sat in the living room, watching the news on the giant-screen television as their fraternity brothers milled around in various states of undress. The local news anchor was covering the story of a woman's body found in Griffith Park.

"The young woman's dismembered body was found in trash bags, down a steep ravine. The police have identified her as nineteen-year-old Layla Waters from Elko, Nevada . . ."

Rick felt his bowels loosen and ran to the bathroom just before they exploded in the worst diarrhea he had ever experienced. When he returned, pale and unsteady, he found Jed with his head buried in his hand and the television muted.

"What the fuck is this, man?" Rick whispered. "I thought we were tossing trash!"

"You're the one who knows that guy, you invited us. He's a freak. That was a fucking dead body!" Jed said, retching involuntarily.

"What're we gonna do? We touched everything, those bags have our fingerprints on them!"

"Have you ever been arrested for anything? Do they have your prints in the system?" Jed asked.

"Fuck yeah! I had a DUI last summer in Balboa. Do they come up in a background check?"

"I don't know. Google it. But I'm saying I wasn't there when the cops come looking, man. You're the one who knows that nut. You're on your own," Jed said, bolting from the couch and up the stairs to his room.

Rick sat alone on the couch, his gut rumbling. If they found him, there would be no sorority wife, no country club membership, no boat in the Newport harbor. He'd be someone's bitch in prison for the rest of his life. A spasm hit his belly, and he raced to the bathroom again.

Jeppe had the news on in his bedroom, watching the story about Layla while he pretended to listen to his mother droning on about their anniversary party and how they planned to make a trip out to California in the next few weeks. He wished she would shut up. He needed to see what they had discovered about Layla, but his mother was now recounting a story about a kid he knew in middle school who fell off a ski lift. He heard the doorbell ringing downstairs.

"There's someone at my door, *mumme*. I have to go. *Kyss!*" he said, hanging up.

He smoothed his hair and checked on his lost angels, who were upstairs watching television. Princess was seated among them, content and taking a long hit from a bong. She smiled at him, and he winked at her; the whole vibe was much smoother now that she had adapted. He hurried downstairs and looked through the peephole to see the frightened eyes of Jason Weizman. He took a deep breath and opened the door.

"Hi, Jason! What's up?" he said casually.

"Hi, Jeppe. Can I come in for a minute?" Weizman asked, fidgety and scanning the street below.

"Sure, man. You want something? I have some excellent weed!" Jeppe offered.

"No, thanks. I want to know about that little blond, the one I saw at your party. I think she's one of the kids who broke into my house," Weizman said.

"One of the kids at my party? I don't think so. How would she know where you lived?" Jeppe said. He had cased Weizman's house himself after meeting him at Dray's, and followed him to learn his schedule. He'd shown Anya and Autumn the best way in and had waited for them up the street.

"I don't know, but I'm sure it was her," Weizman insisted. "She was at Dray's also, right?"

"Might have been. They have a lot of girls there. But no, she couldn't have broken into your house. She's a good kid, never been in any trouble."

Weizman looked at him skeptically. "A good kid? A good kid wouldn't be at your parties, man. Doing the stuff she was doing."

"Look, Jason. There's no way she was involved in a robbery at your place. She was probably in school!" Jeppe said, forcing out a laugh.

"They took a gun. And I need it back," Weizman demanded.

Jeppe's eyes shifted, raw hostility and rage falling like a curtain over his countenance.

"I don't know what you're talking about. I think you're crazy," Jeppe said, standing up.

Weizman stood, blocking his way to the door. "I want the gun back, Jeppe. And I saw the news about that girl that used to stay here with you."

Jeppe blinked several times, then said, "How about if I ask them about your gun? They're upstairs, hanging out. I'll go get them and bring them down so you can talk to them about it yourself."

Jeppe went to his bedroom, where he pulled out a stash of drugs from his closet and prepared a syringe with an NMBD drug that could be injected to cause temporary paralysis. He'd gotten it from the manager of Dray's, who had a physician patron. The doctor employed it recreationally.

Jeppe came down the stairway and led Weizman toward the dining room.

"They're coming down in a minute, we can hang in here . . ." he said, turning suddenly and deftly jabbing Weizman in the chest with the syringe. He looked on as Weizman began to lose control of his muscles and stumble.

"What the fuck . . . ?" he said before passing out on the floor.

Jeppe dragged him into the den and bound him with rope, sticking a heavy rag into his mouth and taping it with duct tape. He shoved him behind the couch. The news about Layla had ruined everything. He felt as if his world was spinning so fast that he might slip off and find himself flung into a dark, bottomless void. He heard the old man whispering in his ear.

A stupid fool as always . . . a waste of human energy . . . you can't get anything right, can you? Everything you touch turns to shit . . . useless cretin . . . they found the girl in the well . . . they will find you . . . find you . . .

Jeppe sank into the corner of his room, pressing his hands over his ears to block the growing intensity of the old man's voice, but it kept getting louder and louder until his head felt as if it would explode.

Cassidy was at a loss for what to do with Evie, now that Bill had abruptly taken off for Coalinga. They had driven through McDonald's for big, frothy frappés.

"I have to go in to work late today, so you'll have to go to the Clubhouse if my dad isn't back yet. I can pick you up when I'm off," Cassidy said.

"Why can't I stay in the house?" Evie asked.

"Because there is a guy, a bad cop, who is trying to cause trouble for me and some other cops who investigated him. So, you can't be alone until we catch him."

"He's like *Dirty Harry*? My dad loved those movies," Evie said.

"Worse than *Dirty Harry*, but yeah."

They were heading toward the mall, and they passed the exit for the New Life Rehabilitation facility where Kylie lived. Cassidy pulled over and sent a text to her caregiver, Jaretta.

I'm in the area with a young teenage friend. Thought it might be fun for Kylie to have a visitor besides me. Is that okay?

Jaretta replied immediately.

That would be good for her. Also, heads up, she knows that we spoke about her situation.

Cassidy was stunned but covered it for Evie's sake.

"I have a friend who lives near here, in a rehab facility," she said.

"Is she an addict?" Evie asked.

"No, she had a bad accident years ago. She's in a wheelchair. I visit her all the time, and I think she'd like to see a kid like you."

Evie snorted. "Almost eighteen is not a kid. And I knew you wouldn't have a friend who was an addict, I was just fucking with you."

Cassidy nodded and took the off-ramp toward New Life. Ten minutes later, they were walking into Kylie's room, where she sat watching a show on Netflix. She smiled her lopsided smile when they arrived.

"Hi . . . I'm Kylie . . . you're a . . . friend . . . of Cassidy's?" she asked with difficulty.

Evie was shocked to see how Kylie struggled to do the most basic movements, but she extended her hand and said, "Yeah. I'm Evie. I'm staying with Cassidy and Bill for a while."

Kylie shifted her gaze to Cassidy, her eyes soft with compassion. Cassidy smiled, fighting the tears that threatened to expose her struggle.

"What are . . . you . . . two . . . doing today?" Kylie asked.

"We're going shopping for some new clothes for Evie, and I have to go into work late, but we'll be hanging out at home after that."

"Do you . . . like . . . to swim? Cassie . . . has . . . a big . . . pool," Kylie said.

"I haven't gone in it yet, but I'm hoping to," Evie said.

Cassidy's phone rang. She saw it was Barrera calling and excused herself to step out into the hallway.

"What's up, Pete?"

There was a pause on the other end of the line, then Barrera said, "They identified the body in the park. It's Layla Waters. And there's a witness for Marjorie Mellencamp. She saw Little Leo. He probably did Layla too. Postiff is falling apart. It's a bad day for him."

Cassidy slumped against the wall, closing her eyes at the news. In the past forty-eight hours, two people had been killed by the elusive Little Leo, who they could not identify. She didn't know how she would break the news to Evie.

"I'm coming in later today. Could you text my dad? I'm with Evie Peacock right now."

"Will do," Barrera said, hanging up.

She went back into Kylie's room, trying to keep her face composed and calm. Kylie was showing Evie how she had rigged the TV remote to use it. Suddenly, the room felt too small and close for Cassidy. Her face flushed, and she felt sweat rising in between her shoulder blades.

"Sorry for the short visit, but we should probably get going if we're hitting the mall," she said. "I'll be back later this week."

Kylie nodded. "That's . . . good . . . lots . . . to . . . talk about."

As Cassidy and Evie walked to the car, Evie shuddered.

"God! I could never live like that!" she exclaimed.

"What do you mean?"

"What kind of life is that for someone so young? She's your age, and she has nothing to look forward to. Just trapped in that chair, in that room. I'd take myself out, if it were me," Evie said, settling into the passenger seat.

Cassidy was quiet, brought up short by Evie's astute assessment of Kylie's situation. Maybe she had been blinded by her own emotion. Maybe she'd been selfish. Maybe the old phrase from the Bible was true: *Out of the mouths of babes.*

Princess carried a pile of plates from the dining room to the sink in the kitchen. Jeppe was somewhere upstairs. No one had seen him since someone came to the door earlier. He had been much easier to get around than she imagined. All she had to do was act sweet and as if she had given in to his power plays, and he folded like a flimsy deck chair.

Men were all the same . . .

All you had to do was flatter their egos and make them believe that they were who they thought they were and not pathetic losers or nutjobs. She knew Jeppe liked her. He loved to run his hands over her thick, black hair and his thumbs across her closed eyelids. He couldn't stop saying how exotic she was, which meant he was another creep with an Asian fetish, but she didn't care. He was letting her move freely through the house, and she had already unlatched one of the big windows in the den, setting it so it appeared locked. She would climb out when everyone else was distracted.

She ran the hot water over the dishes, watching the food debris swirl into the garbage disposal and disappear. She took her phone from the pocket of her sweatpants and sent texts to Melinda and Evie, hoping they would make it through.

She would get out. Soon.

CHAPTER TWENTY-TWO

Evie and Cassidy roamed the aisles of Target in Northridge, pushing a basket that had a pile of cargo pants and T-shirts in it. Cassidy tossed some packages of underwear and socks, and a new backpack into the cart. She added a cute box purse with a gold chain. The news of Layla's death hung over her, putting her nerves on edge.

"That's cool but I can't fit much in it," Evie said doubtfully, picking up the purse.

"If you're staying with us, you won't need to fit much in it, will you? Just your keys and ID and wallet, right?"

Evie's face lit up in a surprised smile. "I'm going to get keys?"

Cassidy felt her heart contract. She could see why her dad had been taken in by Evie's plight. There was something about her that was so raw and innocent, despite how hard her life had been. She could switch from wary, jaded suspicion to childlike optimism in a split second, and it caught Cassidy off guard.

"Yes, you'll get keys, and we'll get the snacks you like and the food you like. Let's go to the grocery section," Cassidy said.

"Do you think we should get some of the stuff that Layla likes? For when we find her?" Evie asked.

Cassidy paused, then said, "Sure. That's a good idea."

"Maybe I could pick up some drawing supplies? I only have a few left," Evie said.

"Sure. You like to draw?"

Evie opened her backpack and pulled out her pad. "Yeah, these are some of the faces I've drawn."

She proudly showed the pad to Cassidy, who stopped short when she saw the drawings. They were the exact style and medium as the drawings she and Riley saw at Dray's Billiards.

"Some of these are up at the pool place, right? Dray's?" Cassidy asked.

"Yeah. I was there to draw the guests, and they paid me ten dollars for each, so I made some cash," Evie replied.

"What did you and your friends do at Dray's Billiard Club?" Cassidy asked carefully.

"I used to sit in the main room, where they played pool, and do drawings of people for money. But most of the other kids would go into the back room, where they played poker . . . and stuff," Evie said uncomfortably. Cassidy could see that she knew what type of entertainment the other kids provided to Dray's patrons. She dialed Riley.

"What's up?" he asked.

"We need to go back to Dray's Billiards today. I'm with Evie, and she did the drawings we saw on the wall there. She said the kids hang out there, completely different story than the one that Villalobos gave us," she said.

"We'll go there first thing," he said.

She considered calling Postiff, but she knew he was dealing with the aftermath of two murders and wouldn't have time to go to Dray's. Evie flipped through the pages of her drawing pad and found a series of portraits of Layla. She handed the pad to Cassidy.

"Aren't these cool? Maybe I could frame them for her. She'd be so surprised. What do you think?" she asked.

Cassidy felt the weight of withholding the truth from her like a boulder on her chest. She looked at the drawings, at Evie's hopeful, innocent face, and something inside her broke.

She took Evie's hands in hers and said, "I have some news, Evie. It's not good. Layla's body was found in Griffith Park. She was killed.

We think it was Little Leo who did it. And he also attacked Marjorie at her house."

Evie stared at her, unmoving. Her hands were limp in Cassidy's grasp.

"That's not true! I would have heard from someone. Melinda would have called me. I would have heard!" she said.

"We just found out. The body was found yesterday, and they just confirmed it was Layla this morning. While we were at Kylie's, I got the call. I'm really sorry."

Now Evie began to scan the store aisles like a trapped animal.

"Why didn't you tell me you found a body? You've known for a day!" she shouted. Several customers looked at them, concerned.

"I didn't want to tell you in case it wasn't her. I didn't want to frighten you," Cassidy explained.

"Does Bill know?" Evie asked, her eyes dark with accusation.

"About the body, yes. But he doesn't know it's Layla."

Now Evie backed away from her, pushing the cart between them.

"You lied! You should've told me! And why haven't you caught him yet? Why can't you find him?" she screamed.

Cassidy moved toward her to calm her down, but Evie shoved her away and bolted from the store.

A clerk approached and asked, "Is there a problem? Should I call security?"

"No, no problem. I have to go!" Cassidy said, running after Evie. When she got outside the store, the parking lot was busy with shoppers coming and going. A delivery truck was unloading boxes of merchandise. Her eyes swept the parking lot, searching for her. But she was gone.

Bill sat in the visitor's room at Pleasant Valley State Prison across from Tyler Derby, who was almost unrecognizable. His body was so thin, he seemed translucent. His hair that had once been thick and dark was wispy, like dried straw. He sat with his arms crossed over his torso, as if he were trying to become invisible. He saw Bill's shock at how quickly he had deteriorated.

"I look like shit, don't I?" he said.

"No, you just look . . . thin."

Derby's laugh sounded like the rasping of a barn owl.

"I look like an evil son of a bitch paying the hard price for what he's done," Derby said with resignation. "I believe in all that, you know, about where you go and how you get stuck there."

"Where do you think you're going?" Bill asked.

Derby shook his head. It looked like a dried apple on a stick.

"I only know it's gonna be hot and I might be sitting next to Hitler," he said with a bitter grin. "I have some information for you. There's a guy in here, he came over from San Quentin. He brags all the time on his brother, how he's killed several people and never been caught. He's a stupid ass if it's true, talking like that to everyone."

"What's his name?"

"Sonny Harris. He's one of those Black dudes that wears pink foam rollers in his hair. I don't know the brother's name. But this Sonny was bragging one day how his brother killed a little slanty-eyed girl in LA. He laughed at her name, called her Min Sun-Hee."

Bill's stomach dropped. "You sure about that? The name?"

"Yeah, I heard him say it a few times. He never shuts up. If you can track that brother down, you might get the answer you've been looking for all these years."

Bill wrote Sonny's name down.

"Why didn't you just tell me this over the phone?" he asked.

Derby smiled weakly. "I wanted to have a final visitor before my time comes. The phone ain't the same as seeing a friend face-to-face."

Bill nodded in silent agreement. He was moved that Derby thought of him as his friend. For all of his malicious bravado, Derby was now just a frightened, lonely man disappearing a little bit more each day.

And he had no legacy beyond the pain and violence he'd visited upon so many innocent people.

"Thanks, Tyler. I appreciate it," Bill said.

Derby passed his hand over his eyes, as if the light hurt them.

"Sometimes bad people try to do good things," he said quietly.

Melinda Drake paced in her office, watching the news coverage about Layla's body being found in the park. She felt numb. She hated to imagine how she died, what type of injury had caused the blunt-force trauma to her head. She wondered how long her body had been in trash bags, laying in the dirt of the park, as if she were garbage to be tossed out. She would have to break the news to the kids if they hadn't heard it already. She needed to call in some extra social workers from Health and Human Services to help them process their grief. Her kids would all be scared now, as if their daily life wasn't difficult enough.

To make matters worse, she'd received a call from Detective Barrera that Marjorie Mellencamp had been murdered in her home and Pebble Smith was a witness. He asked Melinda to come down to the station to be with her while they tried to sort out a foster care situation for her.

Pebble Smith was the last one who would be able to handle being the witness to a murder. She was afraid of so many things: thunder, stray dogs, spiders. She'd seen some of the worst domestic violence imaginable and fled for her life from Utah two years ago. Pebble was the most introverted of all the Clubhouse kids. She cried easily. She had nightmares, which was why Melinda always tried to make sure she had a bed in the dormitory room.

Over the years, several larger organizations had wanted to take over the Kidz Clubhouse and fold it into their service model. It might mean more money, more corporate sponsorships. She'd resisted doing it because she felt that her kids at the Clubhouse didn't just need county services, they needed people who knew them, who saw them and heard them. They needed community and connection on a personal level, a sense of family that they had lost so profoundly when they needed it the most.

But now, perhaps it was time. She didn't think she could survive any more losses. She didn't have the strength, she didn't have the will, and the heart that she needed to keep going was broken beyond repair. Her phone buzzed with a new text message. It was from Princess. It showed several photos of the missing kids, sprawled out on furniture in a house that she didn't recognize. Melinda's heart jumped with a combination of surprise and fear. The message was short, just eight words.

Getting out, coming to you from little leos

Melinda called Detective Barrera to give him the good news, but it went to voicemail. Next, she dialed Officer Clarke. They would know what to do with the text, how to trace the IP address to where it came from.

She cried in relief. Evie was safe with the Clarkes. Princess and the other kids were still alive. Maybe there was still some hope left in her.

Ethan Acevedo hung up a phone call to Captain Dykstra, who hadn't been able to tell him anything. Dykstra hadn't heard a word about the car outside of Millie Grace's place or that it was stolen. Maybe it hadn't been reported at all. There was no gossip or rumbling about Acevedo being back or suspicions about Montoya's accident.

According to Dykstra, everything was quiet. Acevedo had decided it was better to hit Postiff directly rather than use his girlfriend. She was too cute, and he didn't want to do anything that would ruin her pretty face. She hadn't done anything to him. It would be much better to take Postiff out when he was alone.

But first, he would deal with Sandra Moody. He hated that bitch. Metro had been called in on one of her investigations, and he could sense that she was unimpressed by his skills. He'd been suited up like a ninja, ready to scale a building, and he caught her giving him the side-eye. He'd heard that she said Metro looked like a bunch of guys playing video games that day. Fuck her.

Acevedo liked to work off his list. He didn't like being impulsive. That was what had happened with Eden Balcomb, and what a mess he had gotten into with that. He had taken care of Montoya, next would be Moody, then Postiff. He could save Bill and Cassidy Clarke for last; he was patient. He pulled his dad's car out of the driveway of the family home and headed to the freeway that would take him to Eagle Rock. He wanted to get more familiar with the landscape of Moody's life. He wanted to be prepared.

CHAPTER TWENTY-THREE

Bill was on the freeway coming back to LA, his mind doing somersaults over Derby's news. As soon as he got home, he'd do a deep dive into Sonny Harris and find his brother, Lamar. He'd run his own private investigation, and if it turned out to be true, he would be able to put Min Sun-Hee's photo away and let her memory rest in peace.

He saw a call from Cassidy coming through and answered it happily.

"Hey, Binkie! Your old man is just fine. I'm totally chill and in control, just leaving the prison," he said.

"Dad, Evie's gone! I took her shopping, and we got the word that the body in the park is Layla, and that other lady, Marjorie, was also found dead. And I just couldn't keep it from Evie, so I told her, and she flipped out! She ran out of the store, and I lost her!" Cassidy cried.

"What do you mean, she's gone? She just ran off, into the street?" Bill asked, panic rising.

"We were at the Target in Burbank, the big one. And she just ran off. I looked everywhere for her. I've called her a bunch of times, but she won't answer. I have to go into work soon. When will you be back to look for her?"

"I'm a few hours away. Call Melinda at the Clubhouse, and let Postiff and Barrera know. Ask Kriss to put the word out at roll call for everyone to keep an eye out for her!" he said.

"I'm sorry, Dad."

"You didn't do anything wrong, Binkie. We'll find her, don't worry," he said, hanging up.

He dialed Evie's phone, and after two rings she answered, to his relief.

"Evie, its Bill. Cassidy told me what happened—"

"Forget it. You both lied! Little Leo did this, and you can't find him, can you? None of you can find him, so I will!" she shouted before she hung up.

He called her back, and it went straight to voicemail. He pushed the gas pedal to the floor, feeling his car lurch forward, the engine working hard. With Layla and Marjorie dead, he had to get home and find Evie before anything happened to her.

"So, Melinda said she got a message from Princess? Earlier today?" Riley asked Cassidy as he pulled their patrol car into traffic outside the Hollywood station.

"Yeah. She left me a message just as I was dealing with Evie, and when I called her back, she said she got a strange text from Princess. It just said that she was getting out and coming to the Clubhouse. And it had photos of the other missing kids, said she was at Little Leo's place."

"'Getting out' sounds like she's escaping or something. Like she can't just come and go as she wants," Riley said. "I'm just glad she's still alive."

Cassidy banged her palm against the dashboard. "How is it that we can't find this asshole? How is it no one knows his real name or where he lives?" she said.

"Let's hit Dray's. They might know him. I want to see what that Jack Sparrow guy has to say about the drawings," Riley replied.

Cassidy laughed despite her frustration. "Jack Sparrow . . ." she said to herself.

They arrived at Dray's a few minutes later and found Greg Villalobos wiping down the bar.

"Hello, officers. I was expecting another visit from you," he said.

Cassidy opened Evie's drawing pad and set it on the bar.

"I spoke to the seventeen-year-old who did these drawings here, for money. She told me how you have a lot of kids here for entertainment purposes. Most of them minors, street kids. In the back room," she said pointedly.

Villalobos nodded and looked at the drawings.

"She's very talented, isn't she? I believe her name is Evie. And the black-haired one is Princess, as you pointed out last time. I recognize most of these kids."

"Why'd you lie about underage kids being here?" Riley asked.

"I've taken the days since our last visit to reconsider a lot of things. I've spoken to an attorney, and I'm prepared to give you a lot of important information in return for immunity from prosecution. After all, I'm just an employee here. But I know a lot about the people who come here and what they're looking for. You'd be surprised by some of the names," Villalobos said.

Cassidy eyed him suspiciously. "I think you're talking about the trafficking of minors? Illegal alcohol and drug use?"

"I might be," Villalobos replied cryptically.

"Do you know a guy, early twenties, probably European. Looks like Leonardo DiCaprio. The street kids call him Little Leo?" Cassidy asked.

"Yes, he comes in frequently. I don't know his real name. He always pays cash for his drinks. But I know the kids call him Little Leo."

"You never carded him?" Cassidy asked. Villalobos gave her a dry, withering look.

"Do you think the people at this place are concerned about anyone being underage, officer? This is Hollywood."

Evie boarded a bus on Victory Boulevard, heading south. The map on her phone showed that the Kidz Clubhouse was on the other side of Griffith Park, but there was no direct route. She'd have to catch three buses to get back to the area. She sat in the back of the bus, her face pressed against the window, trying hard to maintain her composure. Layla was dead. They'd found a body, and no one had told her anything. They let her hope and hang on to something that they knew was never going to happen. Her tears fogged up the window, making it difficult to see, but she didn't care.

Bill and Cassidy were no different than all the other people who had let her down. She'd found out, since her dad died, how many people acted like they cared but they never did. She remembered the times she'd seen Little Leo out and about in the neighborhood. At Dray's. At the library. She knew he must've been planning to get to Layla from the beginning. That was how he convinced her to go live with him, to move far away from everyone she knew and trusted, away from where she was safe.

Evie was done having people take things from her. She wasn't waiting for anyone's help any longer. Maybe the police couldn't find him, but she knew the streets he liked to prowl, the corners he cruised. She would put herself in his path, and she would do what Bill and Cassidy hadn't been able to.

Back at the station, Villalobos waited for his lawyer to arrive while Cassidy and Riley met with Carbone in her office.

"You're saying this is some kind of trafficking situation?" she asked.

"It appears to be. They use Dray's as a connecting point. The guy we're looking for, the one they call Little Leo, is a regular," Riley said.

"We'll have to speak to the DA about any deal. Just let him cool off in a cell for a while. Postiff and Barrera can question him when the time comes. We'll meet later today with Commander Ramsey," Carbone said.

Riley and Cassidy left and headed to the detective division, where they found Postiff and Barrera poring over the videos taken in the park the day they found Layla's body.

"We picked up the manager at Dray's. He says he has a lot of information about underage kids being trafficked, but he's lawyered up. Carbone said we'll meet with Ramsey later," Riley said.

"Does he know who Little Leo is? A name? An address?" Postiff asked bluntly.

"No, he said the guy always pays cash for his drinks," Cassidy replied cautiously.

Postiff looked like hell. His eyes were red, and his demeanor was brusque and impatient.

Barrera shot her a warning look and said, "We'll get to him in a little while. We're deep into these videos from the park the day of the body dump."

"Any sign of Evie yet?" Postiff asked.

"No. But Melinda Drake heard from Princess. She sent a text with photos from his place, showing the missing kids. She said she was leaving Little Leo's place."

Postiff shook his head. "We have to find this guy. We have a witness who saw him in Marjorie's house with a weapon and heard the attack. Layla went to live with him and wound up dead. We have someone who saw Princess with a guy matching his description in a white compact car, and now she's sent a photo with the other missing kids? Who the fuck is he?"

"We'll keep going through these videos. He might've come by to check on the dump site, and we'll see him or the car. You two follow up with the Clubhouse, see if Melinda has any updates. We'll get to the Dray's guy after we talk with Ramsey. If it's trafficking, it's going to blow up," Barrera said.

After they left, he turned to Postiff, who was glued to his laptop, reviewing the photos and videos taken in Griffith Park.

"The guy who saw him with Princess said it's a compact car, white. Maybe a Fiesta or a Corolla . . ." Postiff muttered to himself. Barrera grabbed his arm to get his attention.

"Listen to me, Jud. You've got to stop doing this."

"We missed it, we dropped the ball, Pete. We could've stopped him before—"

Barrera interrupted him. "Before what? This guy is a psycho. He's got the drive to kill people, to hurt them. He goes after kids and old ladies, so he's a fucking coward. And we miss things. We're human, we make mistakes. You'll be a great detective, Jud. You've got all the instincts. But you're not the one who killed them. This crazy motherfucker did it, okay? You're not to blame!"

Postiff rubbed his eyes, and Barrera could see that his hands were shaking.

"The Hit Men was my first case as a detective, right? I was so thrilled when we caught Vithu Pham and had them both behind bars. I thought it was over, and then Eden was killed and we all thought Pham had done it before we got him. That feeling, that moment, was like someone reached in and pulled my guts out. I feel the same today, about Layla and Marjorie. I was too late . . . for both of them," Postiff said quietly.

"Let's keep looking. It'll be some small detail. We're going to get him, Jud. We're going to stop him."

Jeppe pulled himself up off the floor and stood, his legs wobbling. He'd been curled up for the past hour, after seeing the news about Layla. But he had to keep moving forward, keep his momentum. His angels had come back from Chris Russo's house and completed their task. It was a huge hurdle that had been cleared. He was not going to let a news story that might never lead to him derail his plans.

He went downstairs to the den to check on Jason Weizman, who he hoped had calmed down. He would simply explain to Weizman that there was nothing to be gained by making trouble. Jeppe knew too many incriminating things about him, and he had videos and photos of the type of things that would end Weizman's career and land him in jail. Jeppe knew he'd see reason once he explained it to him.

But when he pulled the couch away, he saw Weizman at an odd angle, with a puddle around his body. He tapped him to rouse him, but Weizman was strangely immobile. Jeppe leaned down and found that his skin was cold to the touch. He had no pulse. He was dead.

Jeppe's eyes darted around the room. He'd have to dispose of Weizman somehow. He could have his angels do it. He could have them dig a nice big hole in the yard in preparation for planting a vegetable garden. Or they could do what he did to Layla. A faint whisper started in his ears.

Ding dong bell, Jason's in the well . . . Jason's in the well . . .

Who put him in? Little Jeppe Lind . . . Jeppe Lind . . .

He shook his head, wanting the voice to stop, but it didn't. He couldn't deal with Weizman until after dark. He shoved him back against the wall and pushed the couch in front of him. The voice in his ear grew louder. He found his angels in the living room, watching television. They had gotten into his marijuana brownies and clearly eaten too many, as they were completely spaced out.

He wanted to check on Russo, to make sure the job had been done correctly. There were so many threads he had to keep track of now, and the task was more than he could handle. He felt his control slipping away. He stepped outside and began the trek across the property to Russo's. Maybe there were some vegetables ripe for picking in the old man's garden. That would be a special twist.

While Jeppe walked with purpose across the big yard, Princess was pushing the unlocked window open and lowering herself to the ground outside. The other kids were loaded on weed; they didn't even notice her. She hurried away from the house and down the steep driveway without looking back. She knew there was a big boulevard nearby, and she followed the narrow, winding streets until she found it: Division Street. It ran right through the Mount Washington neighborhood where Jeppe lived.

She saw an MTA bus approaching and boarded it; she didn't even care what direction it was going in. She opened her bag to call Melinda and Evie, but her phone was gone. She knew she'd had it when she opened the window to escape. Had it fallen in the grass? Or did she leave it on the windowsill? She didn't care; she could get a new phone. She was just happy to have left Jeppe and his lost angels far behind.

Postiff poured himself another cup of coffee. He didn't bother with creamer or sugar; he wanted the bitterness and acidity. It matched how he felt inside. He'd decided he wasn't going back home until he found a link to Little Leo. He would sleep at his desk if he had to. He slumped back into his chair and resumed reviewing and running the license plates of the cars that got caught in the traffic jam at Layla's dump site. He hoped the coffee would kick in quickly. The task was monotonous, and his eyelids felt heavy.

He pulled up another vehicle, a blue Hyundai Sonata, license plate 8MJE 741. Registered to Maria Godoy in Van Nuys. A red Lincoln Navigator, license plate 9EAL 621, registered to David Jensen in Santa Monica. A white Toyota Corolla, license plate 7TSU 639, registered to Christopher Russo of Los Angeles.

He almost missed it. But he didn't.

"Pete, look at this!"

Barrera leaned over his shoulder as Postiff checked the car registration again. It matched the style and color of the car they were looking for. He ran a background check on Christopher Russo. He was a balding man in his fifties.

"That guy doesn't look like Little Leo. Maybe his dad, the guy's way too old," Barrera said.

"That's what the registration says. But look at the driver!" Postiff said.

The image of the driver, captured by the cop who was taking photos at the scene, was of a young man with sandy-blond hair and a round baby face.

"Fucking hell! I'm watching *Titanic* here!" Barrera shouted.

They had a car; they had a driver who could be Little Leo. Postiff pulled the address: 7614 Cypress Lane in Mount Washington, right next to Atwater, where Layla said he lived.

He texted the information to Cassidy and Riley.

We may have found him! Meet us there, on our way!

CHAPTER TWENTY-FOUR

Sandra Moody had taken the afternoon off from work to help her husband and son prepare for a last-minute road trip to Vegas. She had suggested they go. She'd seen an unknown car with a driver that looked too much like Acevedo to ignore parked outside her house the day before. Her new cameras had captured his image, and she knew she should have reported it to Carbone and Ramsey, but he left before they would've had time to get any patrol cars out to her street. He was smart. He wouldn't linger too long, especially if he had been seen outside Millie Grace's home.

Moody knew that it didn't matter what steps the department took. They would not be able to neutralize the threat that Acevedo posed to all the people on the Balcomb investigation. They would follow protocol, the same kind that allowed too many women to be killed by domestic partners every year.

Is he in your home, threatening you?

We can't do anything until your ex-husband commits a criminal act and/or a physical attack.

Sorry, ma'am, even if he said he has a gun and is coming to your house, we cannot do anything until he trespasses and breaks the law.

If they succeeded in arresting Acevedo, he would not come easily. He would fight back, most likely with firepower. He was a firearms expert. People would be hurt, some might die. Given how he had evaded any consequences for his criminal actions for so long, his family's contacts and money might secure him an acquittal. Stranger things had happened. Or a misguided judge could give him a dangerously light sentence.

She was close to retirement. She and her husband had already bought a cute home in Mexico. She stood on her front lawn and waved at her family as they drove away. As the afternoon wore on, she stayed home and puttered around her house, working in her front yard, cooking and putting up food in the freezer. She kept her windows open to let in the breeze. She left her front door unlocked. Anyone could see that she didn't have a care in the world or anything to be afraid of, if they were watching.

Jeppe returned from Chris Russo's house, invigorated. It had been an emotional rush to step inside and find the house so deathly quiet. He walked into the dining room and saw him, just where Anya had said he would be. Laid out under the big wooden table. A smear of blood was on the floor, like a Jasper Johns painting.

From the looks of things, Russo had been preparing his morning coffee. The lid of the sugar bowl was off, the half-and-half left out. Jeppe grinned. What a shock it must have been. The old fool probably thought Jeppe's angels were coming on a simple errand. He had no idea that retribution would strike so swiftly and with such precision.

Jeppe looked around the room for the gun, the green-handled revolver they had stolen from Jason Weizman, but he did not see it. He checked the cupboards and the cabinets. The angels had not returned with it. He retraced his steps, hoping to find it discarded during their retreat, but he did not. Perhaps they dropped it on the way home, in their excitement. He went outside, grabbed two fat tomatoes from a vine, and headed back.

Inside the Raven's Nest, he did not find the gun. He began checking every room, and when he got to the den, he saw the open window. He hurried to check on his angels. They were all present, except for Princess. His heart raced as he ran upstairs and pushed open the door to the bedroom where he had placed her like a cake topper, but it was empty as well. He knew before he scoured every room in the house that she was gone. From the open window he peered down the driveway, but it was deserted. The street was quiet. His head hurt. His breathing was labored. She had escaped.

Then he saw a phone lying in the grass. He went outside and picked it up. He expected it to be locked, but it was not. He scrolled through the photos and found many of his angels in differing states of intoxication. He looked at the texts and felt a surge of fury shoot up from his gut. Princess had sent photos with a message to Melinda Drake, the director of the Clubhouse. Layla had pointed her out several times. Melinda would see the angels. She would see his house. She would find him.

He pinched the bridge of his nose hard enough to cause his eyes to water. He went to the couch and reached behind it, into Jason Weizman's pockets for his car keys. Weizman's green Audi was still in the driveway.

Jeppe had to hurry. He had to find Princess.

Cassidy and Riley were with Melinda when they received Postiff's text with the address of Chris Russo's house in Mount Washington. Melinda had shown them the text from Princess.

"I'll be here all day. I'm not going to go anywhere, just in case. I want to be here when she shows up so I can take her over to speak to the detectives right away," Melinda said.

"Let us know when she arrives. We may have found the address for Little Leo," Riley said as they left.

Twenty minutes later, they pulled up to the house on Cypress Lane to find Barrera and Postiff walking the exterior of the property. In the driveway, they saw Russo's white Corolla.

"Is he home?" Cassidy asked.

"We knocked a moment ago, but there's no answer. I figure he'll see us. The car is here," Postiff said.

They tried windows and doors, but they were tightly shut. Then, as Cassidy walked past the dining room windows, she saw a figure lying on the floor.

She shouted to Riley, "Hey! I think there's a body in this room!"

Barrera and Postiff came running with him to look inside and saw the body of a large, middle-aged man visible under the dining room table, flat on his back.

"We have to get in, he needs help!" Riley said. He took a rock from the garden, smashed the window, then hoisted himself in. He opened the door for Postiff, Barrera, and Cassidy, and they walked cautiously into the dining room, where the man lay. When they were close to him, they saw that he was clearly dead, a hole the size of a mixing bowl in the center of his chest. By the counter, there was blood splatter and large splashes of it on the floor.

"The kids might be in this house. Let's clear all the rooms!" Postiff said, drawing his gun.

They split up and searched all the rooms but found no sign of the missing teenagers ever having been there. All they had was a dead body on the dining room floor. Barrera signaled them to step outside.

"Let's wait out here. We've contaminated this crime scene enough. I don't know what the fuck this is. No sign of the kids, no Little Leo. Just this old guy, who sure as shit didn't shoot himself, since we have no weapon," he said, holstering his gun.

"We'll check the yard," Cassidy offered as Riley followed her. Postiff sat on a folding chair, his disappointment clear.

"So, this Little Leo guy has been driving Russo's car. It's probably deliberate so we can't tie it to him," Barrera said.

"Like everything else he's done to stay under the radar," Postiff agreed.

Cassidy and Riley returned with plastic gloves on, holding a green-handled .38 revolver.

"We found it tossed in the yard. Looked like it was dropped in haste," she said.

"I think this is the gun that was reported stolen by Jason Weizman when those kids robbed his house. It matches the description with the unique handle," Riley said.

Postiff slipped on a pair of gloves and placed the gun into a plastic evidence bag, turning it over in his palm.

He looked at the others and asked, "So, is Little Leo turning into Charles Manson now? Sending kids out to kill?"

Bill was still an hour and a half outside of LA, willing himself to cover more miles than was possible. He'd tried Evie several times but gotten no answer. The emotional equilibrium he had worked so hard to maintain was evaporating by the minute. All he could think of was Evie on the street, vulnerable to all kinds of danger. He wanted to move, to be active, but all he could do was keep his foot glued to the gas pedal and pray there wasn't traffic getting into the city.

He had his background files on Evie in his briefcase, the information he'd found about her mother, Geraldine Howser. He needed to do something that felt like progress as the flat farmland of the San Joaquin Valley spread out in front of him. He dialed the number for Oregon CPS.

"I'm a detective with the LAPD, out of the Hollywood station. I wanted to see if you had some information on a minor who was in CPS named Evie Peacock." Bill lied about his current work status.

The social worker, Kynesha Jenkins, asked, "Name and badge number, please, and is this related to an investigation?"

Bill gave his name and badge information, hoping it would pass, then said, "Yes, we're investigating a group of missing homeless minors from the Hollywood area. And putting together a timeline of their arrival in the city, where they came from, how they ended up here."

"I remember her name, it was unique. I've found her file in my database. She came from Corvallis, Oregon, was first picked up in November of 2022. She was placed in two different foster homes but ran away from both," Jenkins said.

"Do you have any information on her mother? I may have found her in Spain but can't find a way to get ahold of her," Bill said.

He heard Jenkins's nails typing quickly on the computer keyboard.

"We don't have it, but the social worker in Corvallis might. Her name is Kerry Beeston. Phone is 458-673-1214."

"Thank you," Bill said, hanging up before Jenkins could ask any more questions. He dialed Kerry Beeston's number, hoping they still had files on Evie. He was transferred to a series of assistants until he finally reached Beeston, who had a pinched, nasal voice that went perfectly with her name. Bill identified himself and asked after any information on Evie's mother.

"Oh, yes! We have spoken to her several times. She lives in Spain now, but she had no idea that her daughter was left orphaned when her ex-husband died. She didn't find out until last year, and she called us and came to Oregon to look for her, but the girl is no longer in state. We have no record of Evie Peacock in Oregon now."

"Evie is in California. She is safe and living with friends. She was homeless for some time, but she is now off the street in a secure living situation. Do social workers from different states speak to each other? I mean, when she was picked up by CPS in Los Angeles, did they call your office?" he asked.

"No, we did not speak, we exchanged voicemail messages. When we heard from Evie's mother, I contacted Ms. Jenkins, but she said they had lost track of Evie by that time since she had run away from her foster home."

"Did you give Kynesha Jenkins the information about Evie's mother?"

"According to my notes here, I left a voicemail to that effect. But I never heard back from her. You must understand, we have so many cases, and Los Angeles is completely overwhelmed. Once Evie was out of the system, she was not Ms. Jenkins's responsibility any longer."

"You're saying that a kid like Evie runs away from a foster home and is unsupervised in a city like Los Angeles, and no one can reach out to her mother to let her know?" Bill challenged her.

There was a pregnant pause on the other end of the line.

"As I said, she was no longer Ms. Jenkins's responsibility. Is there something else I can help you with?" Beeston asked.

"I'd like Geraldine's contact information. We are involved in an investigation involving Evie, and I need to speak to her," Bill said, biting back his anger at the dysfunctional and disordered system that was supposed to keep children safe.

He wondered how many other kids Kynesha Jenkins and Kerry Beeston had failed. He hung up once he had secured what he hoped was a current phone number for Geraldine, and he hoped she would be ready and willing to come back and claim Evie. But he had to find her first.

Jeppe drove Weizman's Audi through the self-serve car wash, his mind spinning. The soap sprayed over the windshield in a mix of foamy colors, and the enormous circulating brush descended on the hood, moving toward him like a giant insect. He hoped it was washing away any sign of a collision. The rumbling of the machines was deafening, but he felt safe in the car. Invisible.

He shouldn't have done it, but he had lost control. Everything was gaining speed that he couldn't keep up with. He had cruised the streets of Mount Washington and then Hollywood, drawing near to the neighborhood that had been Princess's territory. She would go back to the places she was comfortable with. She would go back to the Clubhouse and Melinda Drake.

He saw her, after searching for over an hour. She was a few blocks from a bus stop on Sunset Boulevard, near the Vista Theater. She was wearing her shiny tiara, her long, silky hair hanging down her back. He saw the little Hello Kitty bag, the platform sneakers she favored with tall knee socks. She had turned on a residential street and was walking toward a house with a big jacaranda tree in front. The street was quiet, with no pedestrians. No drivers. No postal truck.

He watched as she crossed from one side of the street to the other, and suddenly his foot felt like it would burst through the floorboards of the Audi, leaning on the gas pedal. The car jumped forward and accelerated to sixty miles an hour in moments. Then he hit her with a sickening thud, and her petite body was tossed high in the air before landing on the pavement like a broken doll.

Princess was erased; she would not be able to tell anyone about him. But he'd been reckless. There were home security cameras that saw the car and the moment he slammed into her. He smiled, wishing he could rewatch that scene. But it was Weizman's car they would see, and he wore his usual hoodie, obscuring his face. He had to return the car to Weizman's house and leave it there. But not before dealing with Melinda Drake.

Cassidy and Riley went back on patrol, keeping an eye out for both Princess and Evie. Postiff and Barrera stayed at Chris Russo's house, while a forensic team processed the scene and the car, and the coroner removed the body. After checking the premises, they discovered Russo's cell phone and his file folder directory of phone numbers for his physician, insurance agent, his gardener, and a social services worker. They also found footprints from a size five shoe in the dust of the living room floor and in the damp earth of the garden. There were other footprints that appeared to belong to smaller adults or possibly teenagers.

"Someone came in from outside and shot this guy. No sign of them in any other part of the house," Postiff said.

"You think this was supposed to be one of those robberies that went south?" Barrera suggested.

"But nothing looks disturbed, and there are valuable items here in the house. His cell is dead, I want to charge it and see what calls and texts he has," Postiff said.

"Maybe we'll get something from the car when they process it since we have video of Little Leo driving it," Barrera said.

"He's escalating. If we don't catch him soon, there will be more murders like this," Postiff said darkly.

"This bottom-feeder Villalobos thinks that the DA is going to cut him a deal?" Joyce Ramsey asked Cassidy and Riley, who were seated in Carbone's office. "For what? Procuring underage girls for a bunch of perverts?"

"He says he can give up a lot of names if he has immunity," Riley said.

"What do Postiff and Barrera say?" Carbone asked.

"They haven't talked to him. They're dealing with the Chris Russo murder," Cassidy said.

"Please tell me he was not killed by a bunch of homeless teenagers," she said.

"He probably was. We found a gun at the scene that matches one stolen on an earlier robbery in Los Feliz," Riley said.

"I'll speak to the DA before they interview Villalobos so we know what we can or can't offer him. Good work, you two."

When Cassidy and Riley left, Ramsey brooded. If the missing kids investigation turned into sex trafficking of minors, there would be a huge public uproar, and she would look like a hero. But there was another angle to consider. If the people involved in a sex trafficking case were high-profile figures in LA, there would be tremendous blowback.

Upending the career of a major movie star or executive would cost studios and networks millions of dollars, and they were part of the economic foundation of the city. If a member of city council or a staff member of any elected official was involved, it would ruin a number of careers that had been built over time with backdoor deals and arrangements that were not public knowledge. If any county sheriff or other person in law enforcement was implicated, the damage would be incalculable.

This was the type of situation that required very carefully plotted steps, like a high-stakes chess game. The harm done had to be weighed against the losses incurred and the intrinsic value of the people who were hurt. She needed to make sure she came out of it looking like a champion.

CHAPTER TWENTY-FIVE

It was late afternoon, and Evie had made it back to the streets of Hollywood. She had her fanny pack with her phone and cash, but she'd left her backpack when she fled from Cassidy. She crossed under the freeway overpass at Vine and Franklin, heading toward Cesar's Auto. She called Melinda, who answered in one ring.

"Hi, Evie. Are you okay?" Melinda asked.

"Yeah, I guess. Did you hear about Layla?"

"Yes. The police called me, and I saw it in the news. I'm so sorry, Evie. I know how upset you must be. We're all devastated."

"It sucks. And Bill knew about a body in the park, and he never told me!" Evie said, her voice shaking with anger.

"The police have certain rules about these things, dear. They have to wait until they are sure," Melinda explained.

"They should've told me. They can't do anything right, they can't even find Little Leo," Evie grumbled.

Melinda noted her agitation and asked, "Can I speak to Cassidy or Bill? I know you're staying with them, which is much safer in these circumstances—"

"No. I'm not. I left. I don't want anything to do with them. I can find Little Leo and deal with him on my own."

Melinda's heart leaped to her throat. "Where are you, Evie?"

"Don't worry about me. I'm fine."

"Tell me where you are, and I'll come and get you," Melinda said.

"No. I'm handling this on my own," Evie blurted out before hanging up.

Melinda felt a wave of despair wash over her. She had to get someone out on the street to find Evie right away, before she met up with trouble. She dialed Bill Clarke.

Cassidy and Riley were driving through the McDonald's on Sunset and Alvarado when they saw an ambulance roar by, lights flashing, followed by a patrol car. They had heard a call for a hit-and-run victim off an intersection near Los Feliz and Sunset, but another patrol car had picked it up. Now it looked like they might need backup, and Riley swung out of the parking lot to follow them.

At where a handful of streets converged, they saw two patrol cars blocking Sunset Drive and Virgil, a handful of onlookers peering over the yellow police tape. They got out and walked to the scene, where they found officers Jack Waltham and Henry Osorio.

"What's up? How bad an accident was it?" Riley asked.

Osorio shook his head, glancing over his shoulder, where the EMTs had covered a prone body in the street with a white sheet.

"A hit-and-run fatality. Neighbors said their cameras showed a car just run on this girl and hit her intentionally. Her body went fifteen feet in the air. It's bad," Osorio said.

"So, it wasn't an accident?" Cassidy asked.

"No, it's a homicide," Osorio said. "And just a little thing too. She doesn't even look like she's drinking age yet."

Riley felt a sick plunge in his stomach and looked to Cassidy. "I have a bad feeling about this," he said quietly.

"Me too," she agreed.

"I'll go and check. I don't want you to see it if it's Evie, okay?" he said, with a steadying hand on her shoulder. He could feel her body trembling. She nodded in mute fear.

Riley approached the body on the ground and spoke to the EMTs. They pulled back the sheet, and he saw the pool of blood and the thick black hair spread out on the pavement like a Japanese fan. Crushed and splintered, the Hello Kitty bag was half covered by the body. A few feet away lay a cracked plastic rhinestone tiara. Riley looked at her small, battered form lying helpless in the street, and he was unable to hold back his tears.

They had finally found Princess.

Bill didn't bother stopping at home. He drove straight to Hollywood, determined to find Evie. He'd gotten a message from Melinda, who felt she was in the area. He took the off-ramp on Cahuenga too fast and almost rear-ended a minivan, whose driver flipped him off. Bill drove toward Cesar's Auto and pulled in just as Cesar Sarellano was closing up the bays.

"Cesar! Have you seen Evie?" Bill shouted, jumping from his car.

Cesar nodded. "She passed by here about an hour ago, but she didn't stop in. I tried to flag her down, but she kept going. I heard on the news about Layla."

"Which way was she headed?" Bill asked frantically.

"Over toward El Centro and south. Maybe to Santa Monica. It's a rough area over there," Cesar said, worried.

"Thanks, man," Bill said, getting back into his car.

He knew the area of El Centro and Santa Monica Boulevard. It was dense and crowded, slowly gentrifying but still with a hefty drug trade, and prostitution was thriving after dark. It was no place for Evie to be. He drove too fast, unable to keep his anxiety in check. If something happened to her, he would never forgive himself. His thoughts ran over every single mistake he'd made since meeting her, the ways he should've done better, been more attentive to the trauma she'd been through. He wanted to be the big guy, the hero who saved her, but all he had done was drive her straight into the lion's mouth.

Jeppe had cruised the Kidz Clubhouse for the past hour, watching teenagers come and go. He noted that there was a small parking lot with three spaces behind the Clubhouse and a concrete area where the city trash cans were kept alongside the north wall of the building. He had seen Melinda Drake carrying several large trash bags out and setting them near the front door before carrying one of them to the city receptacles. He figured she must be doing some type of cleaning out of the facility as the pile of trash bags grew.

He parked Weizman's Audi several blocks away on a side street and walked back toward the Clubhouse. It would be dark soon. He wanted an iced coffee, but he couldn't risk going into any of the local convenience stores or restaurants and being seen on security cameras.

He felt the taut, thick cord in his pocket. It would do the job easily, and Melinda would never even see him coming if he positioned himself correctly. He would strike from behind, and she would never get a look at his face. Although part of him wanted her to see him, to be able to stare into his pale eyes and mark the visage of the one who would strangle the breath and life from her body. In the narrow concrete corridor where the trash bins were kept, no one would see them, and she would be unable to make any sound. He could leave her between the bins and would be long gone before she was discovered.

He smiled to himself; he had planned it all so perfectly. The accusatory voice of the old man was quiet now. The miserable son of a bitch had nothing to say, no more blame or ridicule, no more threats and intimidation, the gravelly voice in his ear, tormenting him. Amazing Jeppe. Brave Jeppe. Powerful Jeppe had won the day.

Postiff and Barrera had received the news about Princess, whose body had been taken to the coroner's office. They needed a formal identification by an adult over eighteen, and they were attempting to track down her family up in Bakersfield. Postiff wanted to ask Melinda Drake only if they had no other option; she had been through so much in recent days, he didn't want to make it worse. Now he and Barrera were waiting for Greg Villalobos's lawyer to arrive so they could interview him about the illegal activity at Dray's.

He saw a call from Cassidy come through and answered it.

"We picked up Aiden Howe, the pimp and ex-boyfriend of Princess Mendoza. He says he had nothing to do with the hit-and-run, and he has an alibi, but he says he has information about Little Leo," she said.

"Meet me in the interview room, now!" Postiff said. "Pete, I'm going to question Aiden Howe. Stay here and wait for the lawyer, okay?"

"Sure, when he gets here, I'll take the guy from Dray's," Barrera said.

In the conference room, Postiff found Aiden, whose eyes were swollen and red from crying. He leaned back and set his neck like a bull when Postiff came in, assuming a macho posture to cover his obvious distress.

"Don't play the tough guy with me, Mr. Howe. I know she was your girlfriend and also one of your sex workers. The officers said you have some information about the fellow that Ms. Mendoza went with the other day?" Postiff asked.

Aiden wiped his nose on the back of his hand and adjusted his chair and his posture. Cassidy and Riley watched from the observation room as he abandoned his defensive stance. He suddenly looked younger and more vulnerable, like any young man from a small town overwhelmed by his circumstances.

"I saw her in the parking lot of the CVS. We'd had a fight, and she'd left my place. She was in a car, a small white car with that guy they call Little Leo 'cause he looks like the *Titanic* guy." Aiden fidgeted nervously.

"Go on."

"We argued, I tried to pull her out of the car, and the guy got all up in my grill, calling me trash and bullshit like that. He had an accent, and he was dressed up, like he wore good clothes all the time. So, I followed them 'cause I wanted to get Princess back. They drove out near Mount Washington, where all the old houses are. And they went inside this big old place that looked like something from a horror movie."

"Do you remember the address?" Postiff asked.

"No, but I took a photo of it on my phone," Aiden said, scrolling through his photos.

Postiff's pulse quickened. He signaled for Riley and Cassidy to come in and join him. He wanted more eyes on the photo in case they recognized the house or the area.

Aiden slid the phone across the table to Postiff. "Here it is. Creepy as shit, right?"

Postiff, Riley, and Cassidy looked at the photo of a large, sprawling turn-of-the-century home covered in thick ivy with gabled windows. The long driveway was bordered by dense hedges and plants, giving the impression that this was inviolable space, not open to strangers. Aiden was right; it reminded them of a house imbued with malevolent evil from a movie.

"I've seen this place. I can't remember where," Cassidy said.

"We can do a Google property search, it'll pull up different options," Postiff said.

Suddenly Cassidy grabbed the phone. "It's next to Chris Russo's house! We saw it when we were over there!"

Postiff stared at the house. Next door to Chris Russo, whose car Little Leo drove regularly. Where the old man had been shot with a gun stolen by kids from the Clubhouse, running robberies for someone who was pulling the strings, setting it all in motion.

"We're setting this up within the next hour or so. We'll go in with backup. We don't know how many people are inside and if they're armed or not. I'll pull the property records to get a name on the occupant,"

Postiff said, suddenly energized. "Thank you, Mr. Howe. You've been a great help to this investigation."

Aiden nodded. "Can I see Princess one last time?"

Riley patted his arm and said, "You don't want to do that, son."

Aiden looked up at Riley, slowly understanding his meaning. He hung his head as tears overtook him and sobs shook his body.

Jeppe drove the dark streets of Hollywood, his blood pumping through his veins like lightning. His fingers tapped the steering wheel in excitement. He had done it. He had eliminated Melinda Drake in one swift move. She'd struggled against the coil, trying to wedge her hands to free her neck, but she was helpless against his superior strength. She wasn't even able to utter a sound as he twisted the life out of her. He felt her body go limp, and urine ran down her legs as she lost control of her limbs and collapsed. She was not heavy; he easily stuffed her body between the bins and sauntered away.

Now he was looking for something to reward himself with. He turned the corner near El Centro and saw a petite girl with a fanny pack standing in the yellow glow cast by the streetlamp. She wore her hair short like a boy, but her face was pretty, with delicate, feminine features. She saw his car drive past and looked at him squarely as his eyes met hers.

He pulled the car to the curb, rolled down the window, and asked, "Have you eaten?"

She shook her head with a shy smile. "No, sir. I'm pretty hungry."

"You want to go to Al Wazir Chicken with me? The Armenian place over on Gower?"

She nodded and approached his car as he swung the door open for her to get in.

"You ever been to Al Wazir? It's really good," he said.

"I have. It's one of my favorites," she said, staring at his face with a slight grin. "You know who you look like? That actor, the handsome one from *Titanic*."

Jeppe smiled self-consciously. "You mean Leonardo DiCaprio?"

"I guess that's his name. What's yours?"

"Jeppe. What's yours?"

"Nice to meet you. I'm Evie Peacock."

CHAPTER TWENTY-SIX

Bill continued his search, driving up and down the avenues of Los Feliz, through the back alleys of Thai Town, the side streets of K-Town, looking for Evie. He texted Cassidy.

Hey binkie any luck finding evie? I'm out driving in Hollywood looking for her

She responded quickly,

no we've had a lot go down. Princess was found, dead by a hit and run. We have a house and an address for little leo. Postiff is digging up his real name, heading over full force in about an hour or so!!

What's the address??!!

Dad you can't go there by yourself. You shouldn't go at all!

What if evie met up with him??

You're getting too wound up, I will keep you posted

Bill gripped the steering wheel in frustration. He needed that address. He could go right now and see if Evie was there. If Princess was dead, Evie was in mortal danger. He called Cassidy, and it went to voicemail. He was near the Kidz Clubhouse; perhaps they had given Melinda the information he needed. He pulled into the small parking lot and went to the front door to ring the bell. There was no sign of Melinda, and he knew that she wouldn't leave the kids alone at night. He waited for another staff member to respond.

Then he heard a soft moaning from the side of the building. He thought it was a feral cat for a moment, or perhaps two raccoons getting ready to have a trash fight, but the next time he heard it, it sounded human. He walked to the narrow concrete passage where the trash bins were kept. He saw two large bags open and garbage strewn about.

"Hello? Is anyone here?" he called out.

A low, weak cry rose up from the area behind the bins. Bill pulled them away to find Melinda on the ground, a large, deep welt on her neck. Her breathing was ragged, and her eyes opened and then rolled back in her sockets. Bill dialed 911.

"I'm at the Kidz Clubhouse over on Gower. A woman has been attacked, we need an ambulance now!" he shouted, settling next to Melinda and taking her head in his hands, laying it across his knees.

"Hang in there, Melinda. Help is coming, don't let go! Stay with me!" he said, looking directly into her eyes. She squeezed his hand lightly. Her touch felt like a feather brushing his fingers. She looked at him, then she went limp and lost consciousness.

Sandra Moody turned the porch light off as well as the outside lights that illuminated her side yard and backyard. She left the windows open; the weather was mild. She disarmed the security system. Usually, she kept several interior lights on, but tonight she left only a small table lamp on in the hallway. She locked her little dog in her bedroom with the television on, the blue light visible through the curtains. She loaded her GLOCK automatic pistol and sat against the wall in the corner of her living room with her high-powered mini flashlight. And she waited.

She knew it would be a quiet night in Eagle Rock. The residential neighborhood was primarily families with children and elderly couples. People were indoors early. Few, if any, were out on the street. Her husband and son were safely in Vegas at the Aria Hotel. She had been waiting over an hour when she heard a noise in her front yard. She listened as someone cut through the screen of the side window in the dining room. She didn't move. She didn't flinch. She waited.

She saw the window sash push up and a man climb silently through to land on the floor, like a cat. She knew who it was. But she waited. He took in the surroundings, his eyes adjusting to the low light. He paused to see if there was any movement in the house. Then he moved like water spilled on the floor, smooth and even, low to the ground.

She didn't move as he went up the hallway toward the bedroom. She knew he saw the blue light and heard the dog bark. She heard him try the knob, but it held fast. He came back toward the living room and locked the front door. He couldn't see her as he moved into the room.

He was almost where she wanted him, at the head of the hallway that led to the bedrooms. When he passed through the beam cast by the hallway lamp, she saw Ethan Acevedo clearly. She flipped her flashlight so the high beam hit his eyes as she fired the full round from her GLOCK. And then he fell. He died instantly, seventeen bullets in his chest. She turned on the overhead light and looked at his face, locked in a scowl of surprise and rage.

She picked up her phone and called 911. She'd been a cop a long time. She knew a good shooting from a bad one.

Lieutenant Carbone stood in her office, coordinating with Joyce Ramsey to extract the missing minors from the Mount Washington home they believed them to be in. Postiff and Barrera had pulled the property records and located the owner, a real estate investor named Mark Smolin. Mr.

Smolin was currently abroad on a family vacation in Portugal. The detectives had called numerous numbers for business associates and family members before tracking down the phone number of Smolin's hotel in Lisbon. Now, Postiff waited on the line as the concierge tried his hotel room.

Smolin answered. "Hello?"

"Mr. Smolin, I'm Judson Postiff, a homicide detective in Los Angeles. We are trying to verify the identity of the tenant at your property in Mount Washington. On Cyprus Lane."

"Homicide? What is this about?" Smolin said, clearly frightened.

"We're running an investigation into missing minors, and we have a reason to believe your tenant is involved."

"Oh my god! The neighbor, Chris Russo, called me about a week or so ago, complaining about the noise from the parties over there. I rented it to a nice kid, a grad student at USC. He's Norwegian or Swedish, I forget. His parents rented it for him. He seems pretty well-off," Smolin explained.

"What's his name?"

"Jeppe. Jeppe Lind."

"Can you give me his contact information?" Postiff asked.

"Sure. He seems like a nice kid. He hasn't done anything wrong, has he?" Smolin asked.

Postiff thanked him and hung up the call as Carbone and Ramsey went into overdrive to prepare the force necessary to enter the home of Jeppe Lind and detain him on suspicion of kidnapping, robbery, and a slew of other charges. They didn't know how many people were in the home or if they were armed. A tactical unit of ten special officers would accompany Postiff, Barrera, and four patrol units as backup.

Two ambulances would be at the ready in the event of injuries, and a number of social workers from Child Protective Services would be on hand to assist the minors and get them placed into temporary foster homes. It would take a couple of hours to coordinate, which would put them at the house around eleven p.m. It would cause a commotion in the neighborhood and generate a lot of interest from the community.

Ramsey had already contacted her media liaison to orchestrate the press coverage. She wanted good visuals of officers entering and evocative images of endangered minors being spirited away to safety.

Ramsey had calculated the pros and cons and decided it was better to be seen as a protector of vulnerable youth than aligned with corporate interests. The world was changing, social values were shifting, and it was no longer considered a positive to be seen as an establishment crony. Joyce Ramsey had to be seen as an ally, not a defender of the status quo. Every detail would be perfectly planned.

Evie rode with Jeppe toward his house, where he had invited her to stay. The dinner at Al Wazir Chicken was delicious, but Evie had been too nervous to eat. Her stomach was in knots as Jeppe chatted with her, laughing at her jokes and making her feel important in his eyes. She saw how intoxicating that could be to the kids she knew from the Clubhouse. No one looked at them that way; many had never known what it was like to be important to anyone. People in the city saw them as a nuisance or a threat. Or perhaps as the objects of pity to be driven past and forgotten about.

But all through the dinner, Evie had wanted nothing more than to grab the plastic fork and stick it into Jeppe's eye. She wanted to bang his head against the table and scream at him, demand an explanation as to why he killed Layla. Now she sat nervously as he drove to the house he called the Raven's Nest. He told her she would have friends there, other kids she knew from the Clubhouse. The house was heated and warm in the winter, and cool in the summer. Everyone had their own bed, and the showers came with clean towels. The kitchen always had food stocked up. It was going to be paradise after living on the street, he told her with a little wink.

Knowing what he was, her resolve began to fade as they climbed the winding streets near Mount Washington. She didn't think she would ever find her way back, and the higher they went, the more frightened she became. She regretted not telling Cassidy or Bill where she was or what she was doing. She wondered if Melinda was looking for her. Even though Jeppe acted as if they were buddies, he was a grown man, and she was no real match for him. If Layla hadn't been able to handle him, how did she think she could?

She pretended to watch TikTok videos on her phone and saw that there was no signal in the area. The car pulled up to the Raven's Nest, which loomed like a haunted house from an amusement park. The porch was engulfed in deep shadows. The driveway seemed endless as Evie climbed out of Jeppe's car and followed him in.

Several hours later, Jeppe and his lost angels slept soundly while Evie struggled to stay awake. She had planned to be extra careful inside, especially when she saw Anya and Autumn looking nothing like the girls she had known. They wore dark makeup around their eyes, and with Zephyr, they seemed like a small coven of witches or spooky wraiths. Zeno and Kyle were zoned out and skinny, with dark hollows under their eyes. Jeppe had handed out brownies, and Evie had eaten half of one before she noticed the odd, woody flavor and realized they were laced with something.

Now she was slightly groggy, drinking water and hoping to explore the big house for any signs of Layla and how Jeppe had killed her. But she was scared to wander around and get caught where she wasn't supposed to be. She was sitting in a big velvet chair when she sensed something outside. She walked to the front door and found it locked. She looked out the paned sidelights to see what looked like an army of police cars and officers outside, their sirens and lights off. In the group she saw Cassidy, and her heart leaped.

She had found her. She had come for Evie to bring her safely home.

Jeppe and his lost angels slept the sleep of the dead, until the tactical unit broke down the front door and swarmed in.

Evie shouted when she saw them, "I'm here! He's upstairs! The rest are in the rooms on the second floor!"

Cassidy saw her and grabbed her by the collar, pulling her outside. The tactical unit charged the stairway as the teens emerged from their rooms in panic and began screaming. The officers found Jeppe half asleep, getting dressed, when they grabbed him and pushed him onto the bed, cuffing his hands behind him. Postiff stood beside him, reading him his rights as he was led down the stairs and out to the waiting police cars.

"You are mistaken, I have done nothing wrong! Call my parents in Oslo! I have done nothing!" he protested, on the verge of tears.

Inside the house, Barrera, Riley, and the other officers found Jason Weizman's body behind the couch.

"This Jeppe kid is a serial killer! We have five dead bodies in a few days. Who knew looking for some missing homeless kid would turn into this?" Barrera said in disbelief.

"So much for a nice easy case to close out your career, Pete," Riley said.

"I'm putting in for early retirement. I can't take this anymore . . ." Barrera said, walking off.

Evie and Cassidy watched as the teens were led out in confusion and into the waiting vans of the CPS social workers.

"Do I have to go with them?" Evie asked.

Cassidy nodded. "Yeah. My dad will have to go in and ask to have you released to us as your legal guardians, but that might take a few days and some paperwork."

"But you'll come back for me, won't you?"

"We'll come back for you. Definitely," Cassidy reassured her as a social worker took Evie by the arm, then walked with her to the van.

At the foot of the driveway, Joyce Ramsey stood with a news crew from KCAL, speaking with reporter Jenny Liu. In the flash of the lights, Cassidy watched Ramsey spin the whole operation into a public relations win for herself. She heard Ramsey talking about her commitment to the marginalized communities and the most vulnerable Angelenos.

Cassidy texted her dad. we have evie safe and sound sorry I couldn't let you in on it

He responded right away. I'm with Melinda at the hospital. She was attacked. And you were right. I had to let go and let you guys do your job. Say hi to evie for me. I think I found her mom but don't mention it yet.

Cassidy sent back a thumbs-up emoji. Of course Bill had saved Melinda and found Evie's mom on another continent. He was the Big Dog, after all. He was her dad.

As the tactical unit dispersed and the forensic teams settled in to work with the Jason Weizman crime scene and search for evidence of Jeppe's other victims, Cassidy, Riley, and Postiff stood together in the shadows of the porch, looking out at the quiet neighborhood, enveloped in darkness. The neighbors who had gathered to watch the police activity had returned to their homes. Chris Russo's house sat silent and empty. They didn't talk. They just stood in contemplative silence, remembering the victims of young Jeppe Lind and his malevolent drive to hurt others for his own pleasure, wondering how many others just like him were out there in the teeming, pulsing urban sprawl of the city of angels.

CHAPTER TWENTY-SEVEN

Fraternity Row at USC was still quiet. Classes hadn't started for the day, and the crush of students had not yet begun their trek to campus on foot and on bicycles. Two police cars from the Los Angeles Southwest Community Police Station pulled up in front of the SAE fraternity house. Two officers went around the back of the house and two knocked on the front door, which was opened by a baby-faced pledge named Jaden.

"Can I help you, officers?" he asked, clearly intimidated.

"We're here for Mr. Rick Brittenham," the female officer said.

"I don't know if he's here . . . I can go look . . ." Jaden said, hurrying up the stairs toward the bedrooms. A moment later he returned and said, "Uh . . . Rick's not here right now . . ."

Shouting broke out behind the house, and the two officers brought Rick Brittenham around the front of the building, in handcuffs.

"He tried to run," one officer said. "He jumped from a window, but we got him."

As they put him in the squad car, he shouted, "I didn't do anything. I thought they were just trash bags. And it wasn't just me! Jed was there also!"

From the windows of the nearby houses, frightened sorority girls peered out to see what was going on, then quickly retreated. Jed stayed in his room, the covers over his head with the door locked. He hoped Rick wouldn't talk, but he knew they'd be coming for him next. He called his mother to ask if she could book an immediate trip out of the country for him. He didn't care where he went as long as it was too far for them to find him.

Bill poured his coffee and took his medication with a piece of cinnamon toast. Now that Jeppe had been caught, Bill would commit to getting his doctor's appointments arranged. He had texted with Evie, and she seemed content staying at a group home for teenagers in Altadena. He dialed a number in Bilbao, Spain, hoping it was the right one for Evie's mother, Geraldine.

A woman's voice answered. "Bueno?"

"My name is Bill Clarke, I'm a retired detective in Los Angeles, and I'm trying to locate the mother of Evie Peacock—"

"I'm her mother! Is she okay?"

"Yes, she's fine. She was homeless for a while, but she's in a safe living situation now—"

Geraldine cut him off. "Homeless? Evie has been homeless?" The anguish was obvious in her voice.

"Yes, when she left Oregon, she came to LA and ended up living on the street."

"What? I can't believe this! How could this happen? What did Arthur do? Why didn't any of them reach out to me?"

"I don't know, ma'am. I'm just trying to find a family relation who might be interested in taking Evie in," Bill said.

"Of course I'll take her! John never wanted me to see Evie. He was so angry that I left him. He made it so difficult, and I finally moved abroad and got married here in Spain. But I had no idea he was so ill and had died. No one ever told me until Evie had been put into foster care," she explained.

"You knew she was in foster care?"

"Once I found out, I came to Oregon, but she had already run away from those foster homes, and they said they didn't know where she was. I came every few months to look for her, I walked up and down streets, I checked shelters. No one told me she had gone to LA."

"Well, she's been through some very rough stuff lately. How soon do you think you'd be able to come for her?"

"I'll be on a plane tomorrow. I have all of her documents in a folder. We'll go to the embassy and get her a passport to travel. But, do you think she wants to see me? I don't know what John told her, but I'm sure it's not good," Geraldine said with trepidation.

"Evie is a smart kid, and she's tough. I think you two will be able to work it out, but I'll let her know you're coming so it's not a shock," Bill said, relieved that he had found a permanent solution for Evie. Probably the best solution.

"Thank you, detective. I don't know how I would've found her if you hadn't called."

"I'll send you all of her information, and feel free to call me if you need any help when you get here, Ms. Howser."

Bill hung up and saw a FedEx truck arrive in his driveway. He walked out to receive a package from Pleasant Valley State Prison. He opened it and found a toothbrush in a plastic bag and a note from the warden, Quake Rennison.

Tyler Derby passed a couple of days ago. He wanted me to send this to you. It's a toothbrush he nabbed from Sonny Harris, if you need a family DNA match. He said you'll know what this means. Thx-QR.

Bill looked at the plastic bag. He hadn't had any time to search for Sonny Harris's brother, but now he fired up his laptop and ran a family tree background search on Sonny. He found his older brother, Lamar Harris, was an electrician in Perris, California. He was married with two grown kids. He had never been arrested, and his DNA was not in CODIS or any other database. Bill wondered if Derby had been mistaken. There was nothing about Lamar Harris that pointed to him being the murderer of Min Sun-Hee. Bill checked the previous addresses for Lamar. He'd lived at

1417 Dewey Avenue in Korea Town—in the same building, at the same time that Min Sun-Hee was killed.

There was still DNA evidence found at the scene of Min Sun-Hee's murder. It was archived with her case files. He called Barrera, who answered right away.

"Hey, brother! Good work on the missing teens case. You guys did a great job!" Bill said.

"I'm just too old for this, Bill. I'm home today with my feet in a bowl of warm water and Epsom salts. Got a headache that could kill a cow. What's up, man?"

"I got a serious lead on the Min Sun-Hee case, from Derby up in Pleasant Valley. I think it's real this time. I need to pull the cold-case DNA. Could you do it for me?"

Barrera shook his head with a laugh. "It used to bug me, man, the way you never give up. You never stop. You're worse than a dog with a bone. Sure, I'll pull it tomorrow so we can run it."

"Thanks, man."

Bill hung up, plotting how he would approach Lamar Harris. If he just came up on him and questioned him, the guy could bolt. He needed his DNA, and if he couldn't get it, Derby had given him a way to have a genealogist do a family search to determine the identity of the killer. Or he could wait and watch, keep Harris under surveillance, and pick up a public sample. He decided a drive out to Perris might be fun. He knew a great Mexican place out there that made killer *taquitos*. But first he had a stop to make.

Evie played Jenga with the other kids in the group home, and she had an appointment with a therapist to talk about everything that had happened. Bill told her that Jeppe Lind had tried to kill Melinda, but she survived, which was more than Princess did. She couldn't believe that she had lost so many friends in such a short time. It was as if life was telling her to get out, go away, and start over in a new place. She just had no idea where that might be.

The director of the group home came to the doorway and said, “Evie, you have a visitor.”

Evie saw Bill behind her with his goofy smile and a little teddy bear.

“This is for little kids, Bill!” she said, taking it and playing with its ears.

“I have some news. We might want to talk in private,” he said as the director led them to her office and closed the door for them.

“Am I going home with you soon?” Evie asked.

“Well, I contacted your mom, Geraldine. Turns out she’s been looking for you since your dad died. She went to Oregon a few times and had no idea you were in LA.”

Evie blinked several times in disbelief. “She came looking for me?”

“Yeah, she was really upset to hear you were in foster care and homeless.”

“But I thought she wasn’t interested in me!” Evie protested.

“She said that there were tensions with your dad when she left, and she didn’t get to see you. Things can be like that with people who get divorced, Evie. Feelings are hurt, and people do foolish things. And when he died, no one told her. No one looked for her to tell her.”

Evie paused, pulling on her knuckles nervously. Then she said, “Did she say anything else? Like is she coming to visit me?”

“She’s flying in tomorrow to get you and take you home with her. If that’s okay with you. She’s kind of nervous about how you might feel about that,” Bill said.

Evie crossed her arms tightly over her chest, as if she were trying to keep something inside. Then her face scrunched up as she started to cry, a mixture of relief and shock, releasing the heavy weight of feeling unloved, unclaimed, that she had carried for so long.

Through her tears she said, “Tell her I’ll be ready when she gets here.”

Postiff lay in bed, still exhausted. He had slept fitfully and did not feel ready for the day and the interrogation of Jeppe Lind. Lind's parents had hired a well-known criminal defense attorney for him, so the interview would probably be short and sweet, and the case would be built on forensic evidence, which they had a ton of. The lost angels were ready and willing to talk about what they had seen and done under orders from Jeppe.

Postiff's brain felt like oatmeal, his stomach was cramping, and his eyes were so scratchy and dry he could hardly see. He kicked off his sheets and turned on the shower. He stood under the hot water, closing his eyes and trying to forget all that he'd seen in the past few days. He lathered himself and scrubbed, as if he could wash away the images of Layla's body in trash bags, and Marjorie at the bottom of her stairs, slashed by a rusted machete, in a river of blood. He hadn't even seen Princess, but he could well imagine the impact on her small body.

At least he didn't have to worry about Ethan Acevedo any longer. They had all received word that Sandra Moody had shot him when he broke into her home. That was a huge relief, and they could finally close the Eden Balcomb murder based on blood DNA. He wondered when Millie Grace was going to fly home to Missouri. He would see her again at the Hollywood Hit Men trial and decided it would be better to have no contact at this point. It would just make them both sad. He was turning the water off when he heard a knock at his door. He slipped into his terry cloth bathrobe and looked outside to see Cassidy with two smoothies and breakfast sandwiches in a takeaway box.

He smiled as he opened the door. "What is this, Clarke?"

"Pete told me you had a hard time yesterday with everything. I figured a morning pick-me-up might help. Now that all the bad guys have been caught," she said.

"Until new ones show up," he said as she stepped inside. "I'm going to put on clothes, if you don't mind."

"Please do. Seeing you in a robe is a little strange," she said.

When he emerged a few minutes later, she had set the food out on plates and started the coffee in his French press.

"Sorry, I'm used to doing these things for my dad."

"How's Bill doing?" Postiff asked.

"Working a cold case. He found Evie's mom. The same as he always is. How's Millie?"

"Going back to Missouri. LA scared her off," he said.

"Sorry to hear that. She seemed nice. And good for you," Cassidy said.

"Well, you know what it's like. You went through a serious breakup recently."

Cassidy looked at him in surprise. "Do you mean Carter Sims?"

"Yeah, that was a heartbreak, wasn't it?"

"Please, Postiff. I didn't even like him that much," Cassidy said, taking a large bite of her sandwich.

Postiff chuckled. "You are brutal, Clarke."

Sean Riley stopped by the medical examiner's office to speak with the case information specialist working on Princess Mendoza's case.

When the specialist emerged from his office, Riley asked, "I wanted to know when Charmaine Mendoza's family will be claiming her body. I wanted to see if they're making funeral arrangements for her."

The case specialist looked up her file and said sadly, "No, they're not claiming her. The brother said she brought shame to the family, and they want nothing to do with her remains."

"So, what happens to her?" Riley asked, shocked.

"She'll be part of the Los Angeles County Burial of the Unclaimed Dead. It's a ceremony we have once a year in December at the LA County Cemetery. It's usually about two thousand people who aren't claimed. She'll be included in that."

Riley stood, unsure what to do but unable to leave. Then he asked, "Can I pay for her burial?"

"Yes, they've relinquished all rights to her remains, so you can do it, officer. I'll get you the paperwork," the case specialist said, printing the documents.

Riley took them and said, "I'll return them later today."

"Fine. Where are you going to inter her?"

Riley considered for a moment and replied, "I don't know. Maybe Glendale Forest Lawn or Rose Hills. Someplace pretty."

Bill sat outside the DJ Coffee Shop in a strip mall in Perris, California. He had followed Lamar Harris when he left his home and stopped by the Home Depot for work supplies. He'd followed him to a job site at an assisted living facility. And now, he waited while Harris ate lunch at DJ, hoping he'd toss a cigarette butt or some other personal item with his DNA on it.

Half an hour later, Lamar left, holding a Styrofoam drink cup. He opened his truck door and then turned to toss the cup into a trash bin before driving away. Bill waited until he was gone and retrieved the cup, slipping it into an evidence bag. Then he got on the freeway and drove as fast as he could to meet Pete at the ME's office to run the DNA from Min Sun-Hee's case against the cup, hoping he would finally be able to close her case.

Cassidy braced herself and walked through the doors of the New Life Rehabilitation facility, ready to face whatever Kylie presented her with. She knocked on the doorjamb, seeing Kylie seated upright in her bed, the television on. Kylie waved her in with a smile, and Cassidy sat at the edge of the bed.

"How're you?" Cassidy asked.

"Same as . . . always," Kylie replied. "How's . . . work?"

Cassidy did her best to recount the events of recent days and how Evie was finally reunited with her mother. Finally, Kylie turned the television off with the remote and took Cassidy's hands in hers, holding them the best she could with muscles that didn't respond the way she wanted them to.

"Jaretta told me . . . that . . . she spoke to . . . you. About . . . my plan," Kylie said.

Cassidy nodded, unable to find the right words to say.

"I . . . know you'll be . . . mad, but I . . . need . . . your help . . . to make this . . . decision," Kylie said.

"What do you want me to do?" Cassidy asked.

"I want . . . to be free, Cassie," Kylie said. "I'm . . . done . . . fighting my . . . body. I'm letting . . . it win. My doctor . . . said everything in . . . my body is breaking . . . down, that's why . . . I have so . . . much pain."

"But what about new treatments, new drugs or surgeries?"

"They aren't . . . going to be . . . viable for . . . me any . . . time soon, if at . . . all. What . . . if it's . . . like they . . . say? That on . . . other side we're . . . free of pain . . . and . . . infirmity?" Kylie asked. "Maybe . . . it's like . . . the rainbow . . . bridge?"

"That's not the same. That's for pets," Cassidy said.

"But . . . if you had a dog . . . or a cat . . . in my condition, what would . . . you . . . do? Make them . . . live another . . . thirty or . . . forty years this . . . way?" Kylie asked.

Cassidy dropped her eyes to the floor and considered, knowing what choice she would make.

"And what if it's nothing? What if you're just gone?" Cassidy replied, her voice shaking at the thought of it. "And what do I do without you?"

"You have . . . a life, a big . . . life ahead of . . . you. You have . . . things to look . . . forward to. I'm . . . trapped here . . . or someplace like . . . it, forever. Leaving you . . . behind is the . . . hardest . . . thing for me."

Kylie began to cry, and Cassidy leaned over to pull her into an embrace.

"Please . . . let me . . . go," Kylie whispered in her ear.

Cassidy gripped her tighter. Her first friend, her best friend. She couldn't ask her to stay and keep up the fight against impossible odds. She had to release her.

"What do you want me to do?" Cassidy said finally, pulling back.

"Help me . . . look . . . for the best . . . option. It won't . . . be right away . . . They make . . . you . . . jump though . . . a lot of . . . hoops, but I think . . . I will . . . qualify for some . . . of the programs . . . here and . . . maybe . . . in Oregon."

"Okay," Cassidy said, her voice thin and small, knowing this was going to be the most difficult thing she ever faced in her life. "We'll do it together. And I'll be with you until the very last moment."

EPILOGUE

Two weeks later, Pete Barrera stood with a group of police officials outside Los Angeles City Hall while Police Chief McCall spoke from a podium to a gathered crowd of reporters. The chief spoke about the dogged determination of the LAPD homicide detectives who worked to close long-standing cold cases like that of Min Sun-Hee, which was investigated by Pete Barrera and William Clarke almost two decades ago. Her murderer, Lamar Harris, had finally been brought to justice. McCall gave Barrera a plaque, and they posed with Commander Joyce Ramsey for photos that would look good in the next edition of the *Los Angeles Times*. Bill Clarke was noticeably absent from the public relations event, because he had a more pressing appointment.

Bill stepped off the plane in Winnipeg to find the weather warmer than he expected it to be. He bought a large bouquet of white chrysanthemums, the traditional mourning flower in Korean culture. He had kept an updated address for Min Sun-Hee's family for years, just in case he ever needed it. In his backpack, he carried a framed photo of Sun-Hee as a smiling, beautiful fifteen-year-old girl.

He took a cab from the airport to a well-maintained house in Fraser's Grove. He walked up through the small garden and knocked on the door. It was opened by Sun-Hee's father, Hyun-woo. He looked like a shadow of the man he had been. He did not recognize Bill.

"Can I help you, sir?" Hyun-woo asked.

"I know you don't remember me, Mr. Min. I'm the detective who worked on your daughter's case many years ago. Bill Clarke."

Hyun-woo's expression changed, and he nodded.

"I've come here to tell you that we've arrested the man responsible. His name is Lamar Harris, and he is in custody. He has confessed, and we have his DNA. He's been found, sir. Sun-Hee's case is officially closed. My deepest apologies that it took us so long," Bill said, bowing before Hyun-woo.

Now Hyun-woo grabbed Bill's hands and pulled him up before bowing low to him, overcome with emotion. He pulled Bill in for an embrace, and they stood there for a long time, united in their joy and the release of the long shadow cast over both their lives. Then Hyun-woo led him into the house, calling his wife's name to give her the good news brought by the miraculous visitor.

ACKNOWLEDGMENTS

I'd like to thank the amazing team at Thomas & Mercer / Amazon for their support of this book, especially Jessica Tribble, Alexandra Torrealba, and Megan McKeever. It has been a pleasure to work with all of them on every step of this journey. My agent, Jill Marsal, helped me tremendously, balancing two book deals with overlapping deadlines and delivery dates. I was given advice and input from past members of the LAPD who wish to remain anonymous, but I appreciate their candor and perspective. Many thanks, as always, to my son, José Daniel, for his encouragement and flexibility in the past year of my crazy writing schedule, and for being the brightest star in my universe.

ABOUT THE AUTHOR

Photo © 2024 Paul Gregory

Michele Domínguez Greene is a Southern California native with a long-standing career in the arts. As a working actress, she has appeared in numerous television, theater, and indie film productions, including *The Kill Floor*, a 2023 festival favorite. She received an Emmy nomination for her work on the groundbreaking NBC series *L.A. Law*.

Greene's YA novels include *Keep Sweet* and her American Library Association Award–nominated debut, *Chasing the Jaguar*. Special Agent Emily Ray was her first series aimed at adults, followed by *Hollywood Hit Men* and the Cassidy Clarke thrillers.

Greene lives in California with her family and serves as artistic director of the Adelante Arts Collective, a performing and language arts program for at-risk youth and underserved communities. She enjoys cooking, hiking, roller-skating, and art. She has too many rescue pets already but still stops for stray dogs, yard sales, and weird stuff by the side of the road.